continued . . .

Poison Pen

"Suicide or murder? Only the graphologist knows for sure in this dynamite debut, the first in a new series, from forensic handwriting expert Lowe. The author's large nonfiction fan base augurs well for the series." —*Publishers Weekly* (starred review)

"[A] fast-paced, crisp, and gritty novel that penetrates the world of celebrity and the dark appetites of those who live in that world." —Armchair Interviews

"Debut novelist Lowe wins readers over with her well-developed heroine and the wealth of fascinating detail on handwriting analysis." —*Booklist*

"The well-paced plot develops from uneasy suspicions to tightly wound action." —Front Street Reviews

"A perfectly paced mystery with an easy fluidity that propels the reader through the story at breakneck speed." —BookPleasures.com

Dead Write

A FORENSIC HANDWRITING MYSTERY

SHEILA LOWE

AN OBSIDIAN MYSTERY

OBSIDIAN
Published by New American Library, a division of
Penguin Group (USA) Inc., 375 Hudson Street,
New York, New York 10014, USA
Penguin Group (Canada), 90 Eglinton Avenue East, Suite 700, Toronto,
Ontario M4P 2Y3, Canada (a division of Pearson Penguin Canada Inc.)
Penguin Books Ltd., 80 Strand, London WC2R 0RL, England
Penguin Ireland, 25 St. Stephen's Green, Dublin 2,
Ireland (a division of Penguin Books Ltd.)
Penguin Group (Australia), 250 Camberwell Road, Camberwell, Victoria 3124,
Australia (a division of Pearson Australia Group Pty. Ltd.)
Penguin Books India Pvt. Ltd., 11 Community Centre, Panchsheel Park,
New Delhi - 110 017, India
Penguin Group (NZ), 67 Apollo Drive, Rosedale, North Shore 0632,
New Zealand (a division of Pearson New Zealand Ltd.)
Penguin Books (South Africa) (Pty.) Ltd., 24 Sturdee Avenue,
Rosebank, Johannesburg 2196, South Africa

Penguin Books Ltd., Registered Offices:
80 Strand, London WC2R 0RL, England

First published by Obsidian, an imprint of New American Library,
a division of Penguin Group (USA) Inc.

First Printing, August 2009
10   9   8   7   6   5   4   3   2

Copyright © Sheila Lowe, 2009
All rights reserved

OBSIDIAN and logo are trademarks of Penguin Group (USA) Inc.

Printed in the United States of America

Dedicated to Erik and Benjamin,
the best sons in the Universe

Acknowledgments

There are special challenges to writing about an unfamiliar neighborhood. After all, Google goes only so far. With that in mind, I want to give a big thanks to Detective Steve Giaco of the NYPD for filling me in on procedure and terminology in the 18th Precinct, and for the LAPD side, Bob Brounsten (no clichés here, BabBob!). Thanks to Doug Lyle, MD, who always makes himself available for medical questions. To Jane Myers, who reviewed and gave helpful comments on narcissistic rage. This is beginning to feel like an Oscar acceptance, but there are a few more. . . . Thank you, Suzanne Bank, for decorating Grusha's office. Thank you, indefatigable Bob Joseph, for listening to me read, even from afar. Thank you, Ellen Larson, for always reminding me of Claudia's strengths. And to a special friend, Roger Rubin, for loaning part of your persona for a minor but important series character, and for all the cyberhugs, sent as needed. And how cool it is to be able to say, "Thanks to my agent, Irene Webb," as well as Kristen Weber, my editor at Obsidian. Also, to Rita Frayer, who bid on and won a character name to benefit the Ventura County Professional Women's Network. And finally, it would have been much harder without my wonderful critique groups; you know who you are.

Chapter 1

The Olive Avenue off-ramp materialized out of the predawn fog like something from a dream. The exit sign, chalkboard green during daylight, looked almost black in the darkness. Claudia Rose steered the vintage XJ6 off the Golden State Freeway, melting smoothly into the light stream of street traffic.

The late-winter morning had started cold and early—three thirty. Chill bumps had rippled her skin as she slipped from under the covers and silently gathered her clothes. Jovanic had stirred and mumbled a promise to keep the bed warm. Working as a detective for the LAPD, he was accustomed to being roused in the middle of the night. But though he had urged her to hurry back, Claudia had known he would be asleep again before she closed the front door behind her.

The GPS was telling her to turn left, then right on Front Street, not far from the Metrolink Station. Another left, another right. She followed the directions blindly, scanning the row of industrial buildings for the television studio. With any luck, she would get her *Hard Evidence* interview done and make it home to Playa de la Reina and Jovanic by six thirty.

A segment producer for the faux-news show had called the day before, needing a handwriting expert for the weekend's lead item: the latest celebrity mis-behaving. The producer, Peggy Yum, said that the early-morning show aired live on the East Coast at eight a.m. Given the three-hour time difference, Claudia would need to arrive at the Burbank studio before sunup.

She had almost turned it down. But Peggy Yum didn't easily take "no" for an answer. Her pretty face and misleading smile hid a personality tougher than a strip of rawhide. She'd been quick to point out that if Claudia refused the job, there were other handwrit-ing analysts, some perhaps less ethical, who would be more than happy to fill the breach. Besides, the free advertising Claudia would get in terms of TV time was worth more than she might earn in six months.

The handwriting Yum wanted examined stemmed from the DUI arrest of a young female singer who had taken over the headlines. Her third arrest. Worse, this time the disgraced diva's two-year-old son had been in the car with her, which added child endangerment charges. Yum had somehow obtained a copy of a note the singer had written to her boyfriend while in cus-tody at the Lynwood Jail, Los Angeles County's main lockup for women. Despite the singer's star status, the Beverly Hills judge who'd sent her there had run out of patience and was threatening to extend her stay to thirty days.

Claudia had agreed to analyze the handwriting, which Peggy Yum subsequently scanned and e-mailed to her, but as soon as Claudia opened it she could see that there was little she would be willing to publicly discuss. The first thing she noticed was the large size and extreme roundness of the letters, which reflected the singer's profound need to have the world revolve around her. The girl had already proven the truth of that assessment by her behavior. The lower loops were left open in a hook shape that pointed to the left. After studying the writing, Claudia formed the opinion that the young woman had probably been the victim of childhood sexual abuse. But she wouldn't say that on the air. Even misbehaving public figures deserved some privacy.

Greeting her in the studio's reception area, Peggy Yum led Claudia to a small room, explaining that the production company rented the remote space when they needed to interview someone far away from the in-studio hosts. She wouldn't be able to see the New York hosts as they questioned her about the handwriting, but they, and the audience, would see her on the monitor.

With the exception of a club chair, a television camera mounted on a tripod pointed at the chair, and a monitor, the makeshift studio was bare. A swath of black fabric had been draped behind the chair where Claudia would sit for the interview, providing a backdrop.

The videographer, a youth in a sweatshirt and jeans, was doing double duty as soundman. He hooked her up with an earpiece and a lapel microphone, snaking the wire up under her suit jacket and clipping it to her collar. When he was satisfied that both were as unobtrusive as he could get them, he stepped away and asked her to count to ten for a sound check. Yum said to sit tight; she would be on after the next commercial.

Waiting for the signal that they were going live, Claudia rehearsed in her head what she was going to say. Then Yum came to stand behind the monitor and held up three fingers . . . two . . . one . . . mouthing the countdown.

The host's voice came through her earpiece: "Next, internationally recognized handwriting expert Claudia Rose, who is going to give us her opinion on the handwriting of . . ."

Almost before she could blink, the segment was over and she was being de-miked, gathering her briefcase and jacket, getting ready to head out. It didn't feel as if the segment had been her finest five minutes.

Peggy Yum seemed to think otherwise. Hollywood excitement sparked through the hip black frames of her DKNY glasses. "Claudia, what you do is so awesome. I'm gonna use you in a *really big* segment. People need to hear more about handwriting analysis. This is gonna be huge—I can *feel* it!" She leaned into a pretend hug and air kisses. "Gotta run. I'll call you!"

Alone in the frigid Jag, waiting for the heater to kick in, Claudia watched the sun rise over the San Gabriel Mountains, glad the interview was over. She was looking forward to crawling back into bed with Jovanic. Working in the hours after midnight appealed to her in a way that getting up early didn't. It was as if the secrets hidden in handwriting were easier to access late at night when she was free of the distractions of phone calls and e-mail. *Maybe I'm part vampire. Note to self: Check the mirror for a reflection.*

Not bothering to cover her yawns, she retraced her drive and got back on the freeway, rerunning the interview and Yum's parting words through her head. She'd heard the hype before, and told herself not to take it too seriously. Maybe Yum would call; maybe not. *That's showbiz.*

Then her new cell phone rang and sent her heart into overdrive.

Only yesterday Jovanic had insisted upon the purchase of the phone, dragging her to the mall and standing over her for forty-five minutes, leading her through various models before she lost patience and told him to choose one. It didn't matter to her whether her cell phone could download music or allow her to Twitter the world. Why did she have to be in touch with the world at all?

For more than a month, she had resisted thinking about the reason why she needed a new phone: Her last one had been destroyed by a murderous psychopath who'd killed someone Claudia had known, and then had pursued her, too.

She'd been the one who had found the decomposing body of her friend. Over the intervening weeks, the memory of that horror refused to be erased or even softened. Yet she had also put off replacing the old phone, as if doing so would be an act of disloyalty to the psychopath's victim. As if the purchase of a new one would be a final step in closing that chapter of her life, allowing her to move on and leave her friend behind.

The phone continued to ring. She glanced at the LCD and read PRIVATE CALLER. Early-morning calls didn't usually bring good news. She felt a flicker of apprehension as she tapped the answer button on her earpiece. "Good morning, Claudia Rose speaking."

"Please hold for Baroness Grusha Olinetsky," a female voice said, not waiting for her to respond before the line went silent.

Claudia's attention sharpened. *Baroness?*

She heard a change of sound on the line and a throat being cleared.

"Claudia Rose?" The husky voice pronounced it *Cloudia.* "I need to meet vit you as soon as possible." The heavy accent curled around the words, transforming w into v. "I need you to analyze some handwriting. Is *oorgent* matter."

Claudia rolled her eyes. *Every* client thought their matter was urgent. "What kind of analysis is it that you need?" she asked. "Is this a forgery case, or . . ."

"No! No forgery. I am matchmaker—*vorld-class* matchmaker. You never hear of me?"

"I'm sorry, but I don't think so.".

"Is okay. You call me Grusha. Ve be friends. When you come to New York to see me?"

"New York?"

An old Camaro doing ninety raced past, closely followed by a motorcycle, its rider looking like Green Lantern in black leathers and a neon lime helmet. Even at dawn, L.A. traffic had its own special brand of insanity.

"You come right away to my office," Grusha Olinetsky said. "Look at some handwriting. Tell me about the people, what they are like."

She made it a demand, not a request. An image of what Grusha Olinetsky's own handwriting might look like crossed Claudia's mind. It was a game she played with herself when she met someone new and interesting. As pushy as the baroness sounded, she would probably crowd her words close together and press the pen deeply into the page, demonstrating emotional intensity. And with her imperious manner, long t-bars.

Claudia said, "If you need the analysis quickly, you can overnight the handwritings to me. I'll return the originals afterward. I don't need to come to New York for that."

"*Nyet!*" Just one word, but adamant. "Cannot take from here. Don't vorry—I pay you good. You come tomorrow. I make plane ticket for you. Is *oorgent.*"

She'd said that before. Still, Olinetsky's urgency did not have to become hers. And so far, the baroness hadn't said anything that made Claudia want to get on a plane on Monday and fly to the East Coast.

She interrupted as Grusha started to talk about flight arrangements. "Wait, please. I'll need you to give me more information than this. You're asking me to travel a long distance to see you, but you're not giving me any details. I need you to tell me something about the purpose of the analysis."

The silence on the other end of the line dragged out, the reply so long in coming that Claudia began to wonder whether she had hit a dead zone and lost the call. She was about to ask, *Can you hear me now?* when the baroness spoke again.

"So. I use graphology for long time. I know is good tool to learn about people and I have every member analyzed. Helps me know more about them and who is good match. But last graphologist make some mistakes. Bad mistakes. I see you on TV show this morning, I call them up and ask for your number. I vant to meet you face-to-face, and then I vill know if you are the one who should replace this bad person."

Claudia was beginning to get the feeling that there was a lot being left unsaid that might affect her decision as to whether she would accept the assignment. "What's the name of the graphologist?" she asked more sharply than she had intended. "Who have you been using?"

Grusha Olinetsky spat the words as if they tasted bad in her mouth. "His name is Andrew Nicholson. Incompetent! I do not trust this man to vork for me another time."

Claudia hesitated. She and Andy Nicholson might work in the same field, but she couldn't bring herself to think of him as a colleague. Throughout the years she had known him, Andrew Nicholson had made it a habit to inflate his credentials out of all proportion to the truth. It didn't seem to bother him that he was committing perjury. A few months back, he and Claudia had gone toe-to-toe on opposing sides of a major forgery case. Her client's attorney had exposed Nicholson's lies and was now threatening to file charges against him. Andy had been seeking revenge against Claudia ever since, concocting outrageous tales and telling them to anyone who would listen.

Maybe Andy's luck had run out. Maybe Grusha Olinetsky had found a chink in his armor.

"Tell me more," said Claudia at last.

She quickly stripped out of the business suit she'd worn for *Hard Evidence*. Jovanic rolled over and followed her with sleep-bleared eyes as she slid under the covers and backed up against his long, lean body. After a couple hundred nights of practice they fit together like pieces of a puzzle.

A couple of hours later, after they had steamed up the windows, then dozed for a while, Claudia told him about the phone call.

"You'll never guess who my new client is."

Jovanic got up and headed for the bathroom, his voice floating back to her. "Is it, ummmm, Michelle Pfeiffer?"

"You wish."

"Barack Obama?"

"Now you're just being silly." She heard the toilet flush and the faucet running; then he was back, diving under the covers and snuggling next to her. She gave his arms a vigorous rub. "You're freezing."

"So warm me up," he said, nuzzling his cold chin against her neck and making her squirm.

She slid a leg over his hip. "You plumb wore me out already, Columbo."

"You wimp," he teased. "So, tell me. Who's the new client?"

"Her name is *Baroness* Grusha Olinetsky. She runs a ritzy dating club."

The rude Bronx cheer he gave made his opinion of her new client more than clear. "I know exactly who you're talking about. She was on some trashy TV show a while back. What does she want with you?"

"To analyze handwriting, of course." She turned over to face him. "What's wrong?"

He gave her a skeptical look. "I don't know, babe. She looked like a sleazy character to me. You might want to think twice before you get involved with her."

Claudia arched up and gently caught his bottom lip between her teeth, then let go. "I've had other sleazy clients and you've never complained. Anyway, my job is to analyze handwriting for them, not judge their morals. And check this out—she wants me to come to her office in New York and meet with her. Tomorrow."

Jovanic's fingertips halted their lazy journey along her thigh. "New York? What about Annabelle?"

Annabelle Giordano was a troubled young teen who was staying in Claudia's home for a while. She had been another intended victim of the psychopath. Although she put up a front of fierce independence, the girl's vulnerability was apparent to Claudia, especially in sleep, when nightmares made her cry out in panic.

"You know I'll make arrangements to take good care of Annabelle," Claudia said. "I don't think that's gonna be a problem. Are *you* gonna be a problem?"

He frowned. "That kid clings to you like a life preserver. She's not going to like it."

"I know, but maybe it's about time she started loosening her grip on me a little bit."

"Now you're just rationalizing. I can see that you've already decided to go."

Claudia tickled the hair curling across his belly. "Listen, Columbo, in case you've forgotten, you're the cop; I'm the one with the psych degree. I'll take good care of Annabelle. Don't worry your pointy detective head about it."

Jovanic was silent for a long moment before his fingers started moving again, brushing her skin with the lightest of touches. "Why doesn't this woman just FedEx you the handwriting she wants analyzed?"

"I don't know, except it sounded like she didn't want to let the samples out of her sight. Maybe there's something valuable about them. I'll find out when I get there."

"How long?"

"She didn't know for sure, but at least three or four days, maybe a little longer." Claudia braced herself for a bigger objection, mildly surprised when he didn't offer further argument. She added, "Andy Nicholson's been working for her. Apparently he screwed up—no big surprise—and that's why she wants to hire me." The prospect of being called in to fix Andy's mistakes pleased her immensely. "How could I refuse an opportunity like that? It's one thing that I personally can't stand him, but he gives the whole field of handwriting analysis a black eye."

Jovanic continued to look unhappy. "I think you

ought to stay out of his face, babe. That asshole would just as soon put a hit out on you as look at you. He won't appreciate your scooping up his client."

"She's not his client anymore, and I didn't take her away from him; *she* called *me.* Hey, I'm not worried about Andy Nicholson; his only weapon is words." She began to recite in a singsong voice, "Sticks and stones may break my bones but names will never hurt me."

Jovanic removed his hand and sat up, throwing off the blankets. His scowl sent a clear signal that he didn't appreciate her lame attempt at humor. He stood up and reached for his shorts, pulled on a T-shirt. "Claudia, for god's sake, haven't you had enough shit in your life lately? Do you really need to do this right now?"

She knew he was talking about the discovery of her friend's body. His words were like a bucket of icy water, dousing her enthusiasm for the job.

What she had gone through had left her feeling that she'd lost any semblance of control over her life. It didn't matter how much she tried to push away the grotesque images of the bloated body she had stumbled across; they nipped endlessly at the periphery of her consciousness like a little yapping dog. She thought this must be what schizophrenia was like, battling voices that wouldn't be silenced.

Jovanic had been aware of her depression and anger since the murder, but she didn't want anyone, including him, to see how nakedly exposed she felt. She'd been there before.

A flash of memory: large hands pulling her where she didn't want to go; threatening—*I'll hurt you if you don't do what I say.*

As if she hadn't been hurt anyway. She pulled the

covers up around her neck and squeezed her eyes shut, as if doing so would protect her.

"Claudia?" Jovanic was leaning over her and he sounded concerned. He sat down on the edge of the bed, encircling her in his arms, holding her safe.

As if she could ever *really* be safe.

"Baby, you don't have to go to New York right now," he said, letting her know that despite her best efforts, he could see through her with his detective's eyes. His lover's eyes.

She wanted to answer that she would call Grusha Olinetsky and cancel the assignment; that she would stay here and let him take care of her. But she knew that if she gave in now, she would never be able to stand on her own again. So instead, she said in a tight voice, "Andy Nicholson isn't going to hurt me and there isn't any danger in this job; it's an exciting opportunity."

"Did Olinetsky tell you what kind of mistakes Nicholson made?" Jovanic prodded, refusing to let it go.

Claudia lifted a bare shoulder in an elaborately casual shrug. "It doesn't matter. I'll find out when I get there."

Chapter 2

"But why do you have to go?" Annabelle Giordano practically stamped her foot.

"I've already told you," Claudia said, keeping her voice level. "It's a job I can't afford to turn down right now."

Her young ward turned a sullen face away, arms crossed in a defiant pose that reminded Claudia of herself at fourteen.

"But what's going to happen to me? You know I can't go back to the Sorensen Academy after . . ." The girl's voice began to tremble and she shut her mouth tight, determined not to let anyone see her cry.

Claudia gave her shoulders a quick squeeze, knowing she wouldn't accept anything that might look like sentiment. "I'll be gone only a few days. You know I'm not going anywhere without making arrangements for you, kiddo. And we can talk on the phone every day."

Annabelle shrugged, feigning indifference. "I don't care. I'll just go stay with my friends."

Muzzling the temptation to argue that the gang-bangers Annabelle used to hang out with were not her friends, Claudia said, "I'm going to ask Pete if you can stay with him and Monica so you won't miss any school. I thought it might even be fun for you two."

Pete was Claudia's brother. His daughter Monica and Annabelle were best friends and classmates.

"Pete hates me."

"That's not true and you know it. He just doesn't understand some of the things you've been into in the past. But he let Monica go to Six Flags with us last week, didn't he? And it was cool, wasn't it?"

Annabelle smiled at the memory, but she quickly wiped away the smile. It wouldn't do to let on that she had enjoyed herself. They had spent the day at Magic Mountain in Santa Clarita at Jovanic's suggestion. He had expressed the view that after the all-too-real terrors that Annabelle and Claudia had experienced together, amusement park screams would be liberating. Watching Annabelle and Monica navigate the rides like other rambunctious fourteen-year-old girls in the park, posturing for young dudes who played it casual and pretended not to notice, Claudia had to admit that he was right.

"That was pretty fresh," Annabelle conceded. "But I know Pete won't let me stay at their house. I could stay here."

"Here? You want me to leave you here on your own? I don't think so."

"What about Joel?"

"As in, you stay here with Joel? Like that's gonna work. Not! For one thing, it would be totally inappropriate. For another, I wouldn't trust the two of you not to kill each other." The moment it was out of her mouth she wished she could take it back. Talk of killing could no longer be taken as a joke.

But Annabelle wasn't listening. A calculating look had stolen into her eyes. "I could watch him for you," she said. "I could make sure he's not hooking up with that girl—his partner, while you're gone."

"Alex. His partner's name is Alex. And no, you're not gonna keep an eye on him. You're gonna stay under the radar and out of his face. Got it? He doesn't need watching and I don't need you to spy for me."

The pout was back. "If he was *my* boyfriend, I wouldn't want him hanging out with someone who looked like her. Those tight T-shirts she wears, all stretched over her gigantic boobs . . ."

"Annabelle!"

The girl caught the warning tone and backed off with a smug look, satisfied that she'd gotten a rise.

"I'm going to call Pete now," Claudia said. She pointed a finger at the girl. "See if you can stay out of trouble for the next five minutes, okay?"

"Okay, but I know he won't let me stay. Pete fucking hates me."

It wasn't until she had boarded the flight to New York that Claudia was able to appreciate how much the responsibility of caring for Annabelle had been weighing on her. It was ironic that buckling herself into the seat belt gave her a sense of freedom—something that she recognized had been missing for weeks.

Since the murder and everything that had happened afterward, the constant vigilance she'd had to maintain over her emotions had taken a toll. Fighting tears that stung her eyelids without warning. Biting back angry words Jovanic hadn't earned. She needed some time away from the sidelong glances of appraisal that he thought she didn't see. The physical space would be therapeutic, she told herself. Some distance from Annabelle's problems would be a welcome break, too. The girl had a twisted history and she was as immersed in it as she could be.

They had met the previous fall when Claudia was invited to be a guest lecturer at the private school where Annabelle was a student. The headmistress had asked her to design a program of graphotherapy for the girl—handwriting exercises done to music, which were intended to help level out the shaky emotional ground that had taken Annabelle to the brink of suicide. As they'd worked together, the two of them had formed a close bond, made stronger by shared tragedy.

A wave of fatigue washed over her and she leaned her head back against the seat and closed her eyes. She loved Annabelle like a daughter, but there was no denying the girl was a handful. Watching the receding tarmac through the aircraft porthole, Claudia felt a surge of gratitude toward Pete, who had agreed to allow Annabelle to stay with him and Monica despite his misgivings. As a widower, he tended to be overprotective of his daughter, who was innocent for her age, which Annabelle wasn't.

As the plane climbed to altitude, Claudia's thoughts shifted to Grusha Olinetsky. The matchmaker had been as slippery as an oil slick, avoiding any direct questions about the mistakes Andy Nicholson was supposed to have made. *Why?*

She gave a mental shrug. What did it matter why? The new account promised to pay well, she would have some time to herself, and at the end of the assignment, she would enjoy a romantic reunion with Jovanic. And yet . . .

Their parting kiss when he had dropped her off at LAX had a distinctly perfunctory flavor. She wondered whether it was a reflection of his disagreement with her decision to accept the assignment. Or had there been something else on his mind?

*   *   *

Claudia arrived midafternoon at her hotel in Manhattan's Theater District under skies boiling with thunderheads. After a long day of travel, she was looking forward to a quick shower and a change of clothes before meeting with Grusha Olinetsky.

Opening the door to her tenth-floor hotel room, she was disappointed to find it only slightly larger than a jail cell. She had hoped for something a little nicer. The furniture was institutional and not particularly good quality. The bedspread was an unattractive orange and yellow polyester ribbing with matching drapes. In defiance of the NONSMOKING ROOM sign on the dresser, the lingering odor of cigarettes made it smell like an ashtray.

Maybe if she'd been a client rather than a consultant, she would have warranted nicer accommodations. Claudia plugged in the laptop and hooked into the hotel's wireless connection to check business e-mails that might have arrived while she was en route. Her friend Kelly, who was an attorney, had tried to talk her into a BlackBerry, but she'd held out. She didn't want to be *that* accessible.

While the computer was booting up, she switched on the air conditioner blower to freshen the stale air, and tugged open the drapes. The window gave on an uninspiring view of Forty-eighth Street: construction cranes raising steel I beams up the side of the office building opposite; down on street level, camera shops and pizzerias; a human tsunami flooding the sidewalks.

Unzipping her suitcase on the double bed, she gave herself a pep talk. *At least the Internet connection works. And the bathroom has a new-looking marble countertop. And it seems reasonably clean.*

Not quite trusting the dresser drawers, she left her

lingerie in the suitcase and hung up her clothes: black silk suit, gray knit turtleneck dress, a dressy outfit in case she went out to dinner, a few other items she could mix and match. Taking Annabelle and Monica with her on a hurried shopping trip to Nordstrom and Macy's, she'd spent some of the advance Grusha Olinetsky had paid through PayPal.

It's the big city. You have to dress the part.

After showering, Claudia touched up her makeup and got into the navy Anne Klein jacket and slacks with a cream-colored shell. She pinned a white enamel fountain-pen brooch onto her lapel, clasped around her neck the gold chain that Jovanic had given her for her birthday, stepped into imitation snakeskin pumps. A quick inspection in the mirrored closet door told her she looked good. She fetched her briefcase and rode the elevator back down to the lobby, ready for her meeting with Grusha Olinetsky.

The clouds had broken while she was inside and the air was damp with a steady drizzle. Her first visit to the Big Apple in years and she felt about as welcome as a case of measles. If Jovanic were with her, she knew she would be seeing the city through different eyes.

The taxi driver was on his cell phone as she climbed into the backseat, chatting to someone in a foreign language. Listening to his accent, Claudia guessed he was Eastern European. He rang off, asking over his shoulder where she was going as they joined the traffic on Forty-eighth Street.

She read him the address from the Post-it note she'd written it on. "About how far is that?"

"Distance? Mile and quarter maybe. How long? Ten, fifteen minutes."

She sat back in the seat. The taxi smelled like some

kind of meat—lamb, maybe, and onions. Strong, but not unpleasant. Savory enough to make her hungry for something more than the dry turkey sandwich she'd eaten on the flight across country.

The taxi wove through the traffic and turned onto Broadway where the lights were already bright in the gathering dusk. Times Square, the Coca-Cola sign, the endless advertisements, the theaters. It all made her wish again that Jovanic were with her.

"Where are you from?" she asked the driver, to distract herself from her thoughts.

"Belorussia," he said, flicking a glance at her in the rearview mirror. "You know where it is?"

"Yes, some of my boyfriend's family come from Minsk. The rest are Croatian."

The cabbie took a closer look at her in the rearview. His voice warmed up a few degrees. "Minsk is capital of Belorussia."

"How long have you lived over here?"

"Twenty years."

"A long time. I'm actually on my way to meet someone from your country."

"*Da*? Maybe I know him. I know lot of Russians in neighborhood."

"It's a her, not a him. She's a matchmaker—Grusha Olinetsky."

The sound the driver made in his throat was the guttural equivalent of an eye roll and reminded her of Jovanic's reaction when she'd told him about the matchmaker. "*Akh, Olinetsky. Noo kanetzna, da da, ya iyo znayoo.* That one! She call herself baroness. *Da,* I know Olinetsky."

"You know her personally?"

He shook his head. "People talk about her. She's friend of yours?"

"No, it's business."

"In Russia, last name would be Olinetskaya," the cabbie offered, warming to his subject. "Husband would be Olinetsky. When a woman come to United States, she keep her husband's name, drop -*aya*. So, Olinetskaya become Olinetsky. See?"

"I just learned something new," Claudia said. Had Grusha been married when she emigrated to the U.S.? She wondered where Mr. Olinetsky might be now.

"Grusha," the cabbie mused. "Comes from *old* Russia. You don't hear that name no more."

"Really? I didn't know that."

"Maybe her father read Dostoevsky."

"Why's that?"

"The name. From *Brothers Karamazov*. Grushenka was beautiful girl. Everyone is in love with her."

Claudia smiled. "What did you do back in Russia?"

The cabdriver snorted. "I was schoolteacher. Grow up under Communists. Came here to make better life. So now I drive cab." He hesitated for a beat. "This Olinetskaya, I hear something . . ." He broke off.

"What have you heard?" Claudia pressed. "Oh, come on, that's not fair. You can't not tell me after a start like that."

She met his eyes in the mirror. His slid away and he gave a quick shake of his head. "*Nyet*. Just stupid gossip. Look, here is address for you."

End of conversation.

Okay, so maybe he didn't believe Grusha was a baroness. Neither did Claudia. What else might he have been on the verge of saying?

The cab had stopped outside an attractive building with a redbrick exterior that dated from early in the twentieth century. She handed the driver a twenty and waited for her change, her curiosity unsatisfied, and got out into light rain. The coolness on her face was refreshing after the stuffiness of her room and the hodgepodge of odors in the taxi.

She took her time crossing to the arched doorway that bore the address of the building where Grusha Olinetsky ran her business—one of the many industrial lofts around the city that had been renovated into office buildings. On the ground floor was a storefront that faced the street. Manicured dwarf trees in clay pots were spaced a few feet apart in front of the plate glass windows. Claudia entered the modernized lobby and found *Elite Introductions* on the touch screen directory. The dating club was located on the building's top floor. Loft 14.

She got on the elevator with a couple of men with briefcases and two women who chatted loudly to each other as if they were alone. By the fourteenth floor, Claudia was glad to be the only one left on board. Exiting, she navigated the silent corridor, arriving at a door with *Elite Introductions* engraved on a brass nameplate.

A disembodied voice sounded over the intercom when she rang the bell. Claudia gave her name, heard a subtle click, and the door cracked open.

She entered, stopping for a moment at the wrought-iron entry table to admire a bouquet of three dozen perfect yellow roses artfully arranged in a silver champagne bucket. The soft glow of a Murano glass chandelier bathed them in a romantic light.

As she glanced around, the large space appeared empty, but a voice drifted across the room. *Someone* knew she was here; they'd given her entry. She moved around the table and called out a hello.

A young woman stuck her head out from what Claudia recognized as a glass-enclosed conference room. Petite, attractive, mid-twenties, dark hair that covered her shoulders, bangs low on her eyebrows and blunt cut. She gestured at a telephone headset hooked over her ear, holding up one finger, asking Claudia to wait.

So Claudia waited, taking advantage of the opportunity to absorb the understated grandeur of the place. It was easy to imagine wealthy clients feeling comfortable in these surroundings as they waited to discuss a prospective love match with Baroness Grusha Olinetsky. Whitewashed walls and eleven-foot ceilings in a rectangular open plan. Spectacular views of Madison Square Garden and the Empire State Building through windows that ran the length of the space. Beautifully embroidered Oriental screens that offered the illusion of privacy.

The young woman ended her call and left the conference room. Pencil-thin in a dove gray sweater and black ruffled miniskirt, she wore gray tights that matched the sweater and ended in suede ankle boots. "Sonya Marsi," she said, extending a hand with nails painted bloodred and decorated with tiny silver rings. Her nasal twang—which, despite her alabaster skin, dispelled any notion of delicacy—reminded Claudia of the actress Fran Drescher's whiny TV nanny. "I'm the baroness' executive assistant," Sonya Marsi said. "I'll be coordinating with you while you're here."

Claudia quickly released the limp fingers. "Claudia Rose. Is the baroness ready to see me?"

"She's finishing up with a VIP client. She'll be with you in a few minutes." Sonya started to walk back the way she'd come, beckoning Claudia to follow her to a sofa. "Have a seat, Ms. Rose. How was the flight over from L.A.? Everything okay at your hotel? How about coffee?" She tossed the questions over her shoulder one after the other, already walking away as she made the offer.

"Don't trouble yourself," Claudia said with a thin smile, recognizing that Sonya Marsi's attention had already drifted to something else. Her handwriting would be large in the middle zone, short in the upper and lower zones—short attention span.

It was nearly twenty minutes later that a pair of French doors at the rear of the loft swung open and a woman swept through, accompanied by a hunk in his mid-thirties.

Even if Claudia had not looked up Olinetsky's Web site or found a couple of videos about Elite Introductions on YouTube, she would have immediately recognized her new client. Tall at five-eleven and slender, the matchmaker's chic silk dress swayed as she walked. As tall as she was, she wore high-heeled pumps that put an emphasis on muscular calves. Sensual lips liberally daubed with a deep crimson gloss drew the eye upward. Hair the color of jet had been rolled into a tight French twist that made her resemble a darker Ivana Trump.

"You are Claudia Rose," the baroness said unnecessarily, her husky voice sounding like bourbon and cigarettes as she came toward Claudia. "I am Grusha."

Claudia stood and went forward to meet the pair, offering her hand. "I'm happy to meet you, Baroness Olinetsky."

The matchmaker dipped her head graciously. Her handshake was much firmer than her assistant's. "This is Avram Cohen," she said, indicating the hunk with a wave of her hand and a broad smile. "He is one of my favorite clients, but do not tell him I said so. Claudia, I vant you should show him how to make handwriting analysis sample for you before he leave. Then ve talk."

The abruptness of the demand came as something of a surprise. Claudia had expected that the matchmaker would want to sit down and have some conversation, get to know her a little before she was expected to start work. Apparently, she had other ideas.

"Of course," Claudia said, smiling at Avram Cohen. "I'll be happy to." Cohen smiled back, shrugging his splendid shoulders in acceptance.

"Sonya," Grusha called out. "Ve are ready to make the handwriting."

Her assistant returned and led them to a small writing desk and two chairs concealed behind one of the screens. With the confidence of someone who had gone through this process numerous times before, Sonya opened a drawer in the desk and removed several sheets of bond paper, which she placed on the desktop along with a leather pen cup containing what appeared to be some fine writing instruments.

Sonya straightened, and darted a quick look at Avram before she sashayed away. The special smile she directed at him didn't escape Claudia's notice, nor Grusha's, as Claudia could tell by the way the matchmaker narrowed her eyes in disapproval.

"I come back when you are finished," Grusha said, stalking after her assistant.

"I think that young lady is in trouble," Claudia said, taking one of the chairs.

Avram Cohen raised brows as thick as two black caterpillars. "She's very young," he said with a slight accent. "Young girls like to flirt, and men like them to do it."

Claudia glanced at his handsome face and had no

trouble understanding Sonya's attraction to him. "No doubt. Okay, this will be painless, I promise. It won't take long at all."

"It's okay. I've done this before. In Israel, graphology is used to select kibbutz members."

"Is that where you're from?"

He said that it was. Claudia said, "In that case, I'd like you to include a paragraph in both Hebrew and English. I expect you know that it doesn't matter *what* you write about—maybe what you're looking for in a woman?"

There was a glint of humor in the look Avram gave her from under the fringe of dark lashes. "I think the baroness has her own ideas about what sort of woman is good for me."

"I expect you're right about that."

She watched him spurn the selection of pens that Sonya had offered, reaching instead for a distinctive Waterman fountain pen from an inside pocket of his jacket. Placing the nib at the right margin, he began to write, moving his hand rapidly across the paper to the left, then back again on the next line, the strokes forming Hebrew words. He followed up with a few lines written from left to right in English with almost the same degree of fluid rapidity.

His choice of pen had already told Claudia something about him. Even before she began to analyze the handwriting, she knew that he cared about the way things looked, that he had an eye for color and texture. And it was unnecessary for her to read the text of what he had written to understand what the symbolism meant in terms of the movement of the writing across the paper, the spatial arrangement, the writing form.

Avram finished writing and laid down the pen,

looking up at Claudia with the magnificent brows raised. "Will that do?"

She glanced at the specimen from across the desk. "Yes, that's fine. I don't do an instant analysis, but I'll examine this later and give the baroness the results for you. I'm sure you'll come out with flying colors."

He tipped his dark head just a little, which gave him an air of courtliness and made him seem older than his years. "I'm sure you're right."

Grusha reappeared just as Claudia slid Avram Cohen's handwriting sample into her briefcase. The timing made her wonder if the matchmaker might have a video feed that allowed her to watch them from her office.

"Finished, my pets?" said Grusha.

"Baroness Olinetsky, perfect timing." Avram rose from his seat and took her hand, covering it with his own. "I hope to hear from you soon."

Claudia would not have been surprised if he'd clicked his heels. She watched his retreating figure, admiring the graceful way he moved as he crossed the loft, sartorially splendid in a charcoal pinstripe suit. He took the time to stop and say good-bye to Sonya before exiting the office.

Grusha gave a suggestive quirk of a penciled eyebrow. "A lovely little bottom, don't you think? If only I were ten years younger, I vould keep him for myself. But no. Avram is very vealthy client. He pay one hundred thousand dollar for me to make him perfect match."

"A hundred thousand dollars? I didn't realize matchmaking was so—"

"Profitable," Grusha inserted with a self-satisfied smile. "For someone like me, who is very good at what I do, the money is there. Now, Claudia, ve go into my office and ve talk."

Chapter 3

Grusha Olinetsky might or might not actually be a baroness, but as she motioned for Claudia to be seated in one of the Louis XV gilded armchairs, she exuded the stately demeanor of nobility, and her private office had the character of a grand European palace. She seated herself in a chair, the burgundy velvet back of which was embroidered with her initials and a gold crest. Her desk was elegant rosewood and stood on carved ormolu legs, the front feet formed into lion's paws.

As Claudia sat down and waited for her new client to begin the meeting, her eyes wandered to a curio cabinet against the wall to her left, filled with fascinating objects.

"Copies," Grusha said before she could ask about the collection of Fabergé eggs. "*Imperial* eggs are vorth many million dollar."

"I wouldn't have known the difference," Claudia said, wondering if she ought to have curtseyed. "They're beautiful, copies or not."

"Secret copies my grandfather had made. His father's family work for the Romanovs—you know it was Tsar Nicholas who commissioned the original eggs?" Grusha sat back in her chair and steepled her fingertips, the long fingers coming together prayer-like at her lips. She looked down for a moment, then lowered her hands and leveled her gaze at Claudia.

"So, Claudia Rose. After ve talk last week I read about you on Internet. You are famous expert in your field. Almost as famous as I am matchmaker."

Claudia suppressed a smile. "I'm not so sure, Baroness Olinetsky. I don't have a TV show, and I've never been on Oprah."

"Call me Grusha," she said. "Is true, I am world famous. I make many, many successful matches. They pay me big fee. I give them joy."

"And you've found that graphology is helpful in making good matches."

"*Da, da*, graphology is good test, tells me what the person want to hide." She gave a self-congratulatory grin. "I introduce many couple who get married, live happy, like fairy tale."

"That's wonderful," Claudia said. "Obviously, you're very successful. But . . . I think you wouldn't have brought me here if *everybody* was happy. You mentioned that your previous graphologist had made some mistakes?"

The grin instantly vanished and Grusha's lips pursed in contemplation. Her hand strayed to a smoky Lalique paperweight on her desk—a nude kneeling Venus—and she began absently stroking a manicured fingertip along the figurine's delicately sculpted back.

In the end, she ignored the question altogether. "Come, Claudia," she said, rising. "I show you what ve do."

Claudia followed her across the room to a black walnut cheval bookcase, its shelves filled with rows of slim leather-bound folders.

"These are my client files," Grusha said, brushing

her finger across the folders at eye level. The titles appeared to be names embossed in gold leaf along the spines. She scanned them and, finding the one she wanted, removed it and handed it to Claudia. "Here is Shellee. A beautiful girl."

The name *Shellee Jones* was printed in a decorative font on the title page. The next page showed a glamour shot that could have been captioned *All-American Girl*. The button nose and mischievous smile invited you to like her. Burnished blond curls tumbled over her shoulders.

A series of candid snaps followed: Shellee Jones, lounging on the deck of a yacht, perfect body in a string bikini; seductive in a business suit; exquisite in evening dress.

Next, her vitals: twenty-nine, born in Lincoln, Nebraska; five-six, a slender one-twenty. There was a one-page bio and a summary of what Shellee desired most in a life partner.

Thumbing through the pages, Claudia skimmed past a letter from a physician, reports from a private detective, a credit agency, a psychologist, not taking the time to read any of it in detail. Near the back of the folder she came to a report signed by Andrew Nicholson, and what she was most interested in seeing—Shellee's handwriting sample.

Rich blue ink had been lavished on cream-colored paper in thick, sensuous strokes. This was a woman who appreciated her creature comforts and drew them to her naturally, expending as little effort as possible in the process. The handwriting was large, the lower loops wide, which suggested to Claudia that Shellee enjoyed an active social life. She was the type of person who lived to have fun and who lived life to the fullest.

Lifting her eyes from the file, Claudia found herself under Grusha's scrutiny. "Is this one of the problem clients?" she asked. "Where mistakes were made in the analysis?"

Grusha brushed off the question. "You vill take it vit you. Read report, look at handwriting, then you vill tell me what you think."

"I'm not sure I understand what it is you want from me, Grusha. Am I supposed to critique Andy Nicholson's work, or do you want me to write up a new analysis, or just give you a verbal opinion?"

Grusha returned her attention to the bookcase, behaving as if Claudia had not spoken. "Sonya vill put these files in box and you vill take them back to your hotel and analyze handwriting," she said, engrossing herself in selecting several folders from the shelves. "My driver vill take you. But before you go, ve have wine. Come."

She dumped the stack of folders on her desk and they went to another corner of the spacious office. A low hexagonal table held a silver tray set with two balloon wineglasses and a decanter with the brilliance of fine cut crystal.

"What an unusual table," Claudia said, taking a small armchair, thinking that it was a little like sitting in an antique shop.

"Is very, very old design," Grusha said. She sat on a sofa upholstered in a silky striped material, its mahogany arms fashioned into high curves. "Too bad you cannot see the painted top under the tray. The tsars make these tables a thousand year ago." She removed the stopper from the decanter with a flourish and began to pour. "You like wine, yes?"

"It's a little early in the day for me."

"Come, I insist. You vill enjoy this very nice Cabernet." Grusha raised her glass in a toast. "To our successful partnership."

Wine might be de rigueur for a continental afternoon business meeting, but it didn't feel quite right in Manhattan. Of course, Grusha Olinetsky wasn't a run-of-the-mill client.

Claudia touched glasses with her hostess and took a sip. What she knew about wines wouldn't fill a thimble, but something told her that this one was top quality. She thought she could actually detect a delicate berry flavor with a hint of spice. She set the glass back on the tray. "Grusha, about these handwritings you want me to—"

The matchmaker held up a hand like a traffic cop, letting her know that it was still not time to talk business. She leaned down and produced a gold foil-wrapped box from under the cocktail table. As Grusha removed the lid, Claudia noted the Godiva logo embossed on the top. Nestled inside were a dozen or so multicolored chocolates of various shapes and colors.

Grusha slid the box across the table and pointed a French tip at an amber-colored piece. "You must try the Wild Bolivian. Goes very good vit the wine; you vill see."

Feeling slightly decadent, Claudia took the chocolate she indicated and bit into it. She nearly moaned as rich cocoa flavor melted and slid down her throat like liquid velvet. *Mouthgasm.* She popped the rest of it into her mouth, acutely aware of how easily one could be seduced by these little luxuries; sidetracked with fine wine and fancy chocolate.

She dabbed her lips on a cocktail napkin. "That was amazing. Thank you. Now, I'd really like to hear about your concerns with Andy Nicholson's work. What kinds of mistakes did he make?"

"You must have another sweet." Grusha picked up the box of chocolates and offered it to her again, tempting her like the Edenic snake offering forbidden fruit.

Wondering why her client was so reluctant to discuss the business she had brought Claudia here to handle, and at great expense, too, Claudia shook her head. "No, thank you, Grusha, really. I think it's about time I got a better understanding of what my assignment here really is, don't you?"

Grusha pushed to her feet, her hands stretched out, her tone almost angry, as if Claudia had breached some social etiquette. "Your assignment is to tell me what you find in the handwriting of these clients I give you. Forget about Nicholson! I know he is your enemy. This is why you agreed to come, yes? I do not care about that. Does not matter what Nicholson think."

Her vehemence was startling. She had obviously investigated Claudia's background and learned of her ongoing animus with Nicholson. "Any bad blood between Andy Nicholson and me won't contaminate the work I do for you, I can assure you," Claudia said firmly.

"You must make sure it does not. I cannot have you distracted by your hatred for this fool. I am not going to influence you. Just tell me what you find—no report. When you can give me answers?"

What have I gotten myself into now?

"If you just want a few notes about the personalities, tomorrow afternoon," Claudia said. "I can give you something at least preliminary on these samples by then."

A bellman brought the heavy box of file folders up to her hotel room on a luggage cart. Claudia tipped

him and unloaded them onto the bed. Her meeting
with Grusha Olinetsky had left her with more questions than answers. She had felt all along that there
was a subtext to the conversation with the matchmaker. Clearly, there was something important that
Grusha wasn't sharing with her. And her instincts
told her that whatever the matchmaker wasn't saying went beyond a simple desire to avoid biasing her
opinion.

She thought about Jovanic's suggestion that something illegal might be going on. Maybe something
that had gone off the tracks and now Grusha needed
a fixer. Claudia decided that since Grusha had investigated her, she would eat a little crow and ask him
to do a background on Elite Introductions and the al-
leged baroness who ran it.

As if he had caught her thoughts across the miles,
Jovanic called on her cell phone. "How's it going with
the mad Russian?"

Hearing his voice made her long for him. She reminded herself that she needed some distance. "You
mean my new best friend? She plied me with Cabernet and Godiva."

"Is that all it takes to lead you astray? I'll have a
bottle of Cab and a box of chocolates waiting. When
are you coming home?"

Claudia laughed. "I only just got here. She's already introduced me to one of the clients and she's
given me a whole load of samples to analyze."

"So, why did you have to go to New York?"

"You know, she's kind of a character. I was wondering whether you could—" She checked the phone
display as the call waiting beep sounded in her earpiece. "Hey, Annabelle's on the other line. Can I call
you back in a minute?"

"It's okay. I gotta go meet Alex. I'll call you later if I get a chance."

Alex was Alexandra Vega, his partner. His leggy, blond partner, upon whom Annabelle had offered to spy. Alex, who, in the last couple of weeks, Claudia had begun to suspect wanted to share more with Jovanic than detective work.

"How can you let him *do* that to you?" Annabelle Giordano's voice held the kind of indignation only a teenager can muster, somehow overlooking the fact that she was the reason Claudia had ended her call with Jovanic. "Alex *is* a babe," she added sagely.

"Knock it off, Annabelle. I told you, there's nothing personal between them."

Annabelle's snort was worth at least a dozen words. "Well, if it was me, I wouldn't be so laid-back about it. He's your dude. Even if he *is* a cop."

"I'm on the East Coast right now. What would you suggest I do?" She immediately regretted asking the question. Knowing Annabelle, she might suggest phone sex, just to be outrageous. The girl had been through so much in her short life. She'd had far more experience than her fourteen years warranted.

"I could scope out his apartment for you," Annabelle offered, as if they hadn't already had that conversation.

"Don't even *think* about it. You promised you'd stay out of trouble while I was away. Spying on Joel and Alex is not what staying out of trouble means."

"But he deserves it if he's being a manwhore."

Claudia rolled her eyes, even though Annabelle wasn't there to see the gesture. "*Manwhore?* He is *not*—where'd you get that word? Never mind. I don't want to know. Tell me how it went at school today."

She spent the next ten minutes listening to an account of who the biggest badasses were at the school Annabelle was attending with Monica. She understood that the choice of topic was deliberate. Annabelle was letting her know that she wasn't about to give up her rebellious habits without a fight.

Before they ended the call, she extracted a weak promise from the girl not to get in Jovanic's face. After a rocky start, he and Annabelle had formed a truce and Claudia couldn't bear to see it broken. Besides, she really did trust him. Alex she wasn't so sure of.

Chapter 4

Before settling down to work on the handwriting samples, Claudia called room service and ordered a hideously expensive French dip and fries. She switched on the laptop and waited for it to boot up, beginning to feel the effects of the long day of travel. Apart from the traffic noise from down on the street, the room was too quiet, the stillness making it too easy for her mind to wander into areas where she would rather not go. TV would be too much of a distraction. Deciding on music, she selected an Il Divo playlist on the laptop and sat there, listening to the voices of the four men soar. *In my fantasy I see a just world, / Where everyone lives in peace and in honesty.*

Like poking at a sack of snakes, something in the soulful words of "Nella Fantasia" awakened the feelings that Claudia had been struggling so hard to keep buried.

It's a fantasy all right, she thought bitterly. *This is a world where good people are kidnapped and murdered. Where's the justice in that? Someone you care about can be here one moment and gone the next. Some murky evil force in human form can change the direction of your life in a nanosecond.*

Nothing. You control nothing . . .

The long-suppressed emotions felt alien, agonizing,

like nerves coming to life after being burned. Tears welled up and coursed down her cheeks, splashing onto her knit top and leaving little wet splotches.

Anger was easier to deal with than sadness, but Claudia couldn't seem to stop weeping. "What the *hell* am I doing?" she muttered at the empty room. *Crying is a useless waste of energy. It won't bring back the dead.* She stomped into the bathroom, trying to get back to the anger, and snatched a tissue from the holder. She scrubbed it roughly over her face, blew her nose, and was ordering her blotchy image in the mirror to knock it off when room service arrived.

Averting his eyes from her tearstained face, the kid who brought the food set up the meal and departed. It smelled good, and Claudia munched on the sandwich, delaying the time when she would have to open the file folders and begin her analyses.

Deciding that a long, hot shower was what she needed to get back into work mode, she stood under the pulsing massage head until the water worked the kinks out of her neck and shoulders. She dried off quickly with the skimpy hotel towel and threw on a pair of flannel drawstring pants, a long-sleeved T-shirt, and woolly socks, then went back into the bedroom and folded back the bedspread.

She piled the pillows high and settled on the bed. Despite the generally dismal tone of the room, the pillows felt soft and welcoming. At this moment, what Claudia wanted most was to lie back against them and think of nothing at all. Another five minutes and she would be so relaxed that she would fall asleep. But that was not why she had spent the day flying almost three thousand miles, and that was not what Grusha was paying her to do.

She grabbed Shellee Jones' folder from the top of

the stack at the foot of the bed and turned the pages to the handwriting sample. A more detailed inspection affirmed the initial impression that she had formed earlier at Grusha's office. Shellee's gregarious personality leapt off the page.

The strong rhythm and showy capital letters reflected a love of life. The inflated loops on her l's and h's pointed to a flamboyant but sensitive personality. Her feelings could easily be hurt. The loops on the g's and y's were long and wide, symbolic of strong physical drives and a need to be center stage. The handwriting portrayed Shellee as the type of woman who did not simply walk into a room; she danced in. Life was a party to be enjoyed and shared with as many friends as she could cram in.

In her handwriting sample, Shellee Jones had written,

> *I want someone who recognizes all of my wonderful qualities and is supportive of all the creative things I do. This man must see life as a great adventure and he will have to understand that a relationship with me is a blessing that is worth fighting for.*

One important piece of data Claudia noted was that the upper loop of the personal pronoun *I* had been formed with a sharp angle. When added to the other characteristics, this feature suggested to her that Shellee carried long-term frustration directed at her mother. That could be translated to anger and expanded to include other women whom she perceived as being in a position of power over her. *Like Grusha?*

She flipped the page to Nicholson's analysis of Shellee's handwriting. The bulk of his report dealt with her social style and her potent sexual needs, but precious little else. He hadn't said anything about her potential for conflicts with women in authority, which was an important omission.

Claudia closed the file, concluding that his analysis wasn't balanced. His comments made Jones sound like an airhead bimbo. He had omitted any reference to her intelligence, which she had in abundance, or her ability to plan ahead, or anything else of much substance.

She was surprised to find that the next folder belonged to Avram Cohen. Why had Grusha requested her to take a sample from this client when she already had his handwriting? Here was the original in the folder, along with Andy Nicholson's analysis. Was Avram one of the problems she had alluded to?

He was smiling in the picture, but the three-quarter pose he'd adopted gave him a shade of mystery, as if he were saying, *I see you, but I will not allow you to see all of me.*

Reaching over to the armchair where she'd left her briefcase, Claudia retrieved the handwriting sample Avram had prepared for her that afternoon. Placing the two specimens side by side to compare them, she observed that the handwriting in both tended to be small and simplified. *A scientific mind*, she thought. The samples were congruent with no major changes between them, so why the need for a second analysis?

The spatial arrangement of the words and lines was wide, the margins large. Unique connections strung one letter to the next, which attested to Avram's innate intelligence. His biographical notes indicated that he was the CEO of a computer graphics company. In light of the handwriting, that made sense.

Since she'd already met him, Claudia knew that

Avram had charisma and was at least outwardly comfortable in social situations. Seeing it in black and white only verified what she had felt at their meeting. Now she was able to add to that intuitive sense the knowledge that, as charming as he was, Avram was more of an intellectual than a social creature.

The way he had arranged the handwriting on the page, the way he laid out the margins and spaces between the letters, words, and lines, were all symbolic of his need for what Claudia thought of as elbow room. He was not the type of person who would take kindly to someone hanging over his shoulder, breathing down his neck. Getting to know him on more than a superficial level would not be easy.

Like peeling the layers off an onion, Claudia decided. It would take a long time and not a little effort to gain his confidence to the degree that one would be allowed into his trust.

Something jumped off the page at her: The punctuation looked too heavy, too round.

Getting off the bed, she laid the sample on the desk and withdrew from her briefcase the small padded velour bag that contained the pieces of her portable inspection microscope.

She unzipped the bag and quickly assembled the microscope. After removing the protective lens cap, she placed the scope over the sample Avram had written in English and slowly moved the objective lens from left to right until it came to the end of a sentence. When the lens was positioned exactly where she wanted it, she took a penlight and pointed it into the rectangular cutout in the acrylic base to illuminate what she was seeing through the eyepiece.

What Claudia had eyeballed now became clearer as she adjusted the rotary focus ring. She followed the same procedure throughout his English sample, moving the scope around until she found several heavy-pressured commas and periods. Dot grinding. The result of spending too long with the pen pressing on one spot.

The Hebrew script had a different kind of punctuation, but the pen pressure on the points and accents was as heavy as it had been in the English sample. Claudia slid the microscope off the page, feeling a keen disappointment.

She didn't deceive herself into believing that a person's handwriting could reveal *everything* about them, but one thing she had learned from her years of observation and experience was that handwriting did not lie. Dot grinding was a red flag that was often a demonstration of guilt feelings, and it pointed to the potential for abusive behavior, even violence. It could be that he had been harshly treated as a child and as an adult would take out the unresolved feelings on others. Coupled with the wide spaces between words, which meant that he didn't feel strongly attached to other people, the dot grinding hinted at potential problems.

Had Avram Cohen used a different type of pen, she might not have as readily picked up on the dot grinding. A roller ball or gel pen would have been less apt to produce the same level of intensity on the ink line. But given the amount of pressure she was seeing in those dots, a fountain pen nib would have been wrecked. If she had asked to examine his pen after he wrote the sample, she would without question have been able to see the damage.

As Claudia continued her microscopic examination of the handwriting, something else came to her notice: tiny tics at the bottoms of the letter g that indicated sexual frustration and often pointed to problems with impotence.

Avram was a young man for that type of problem, yet there were many causes of impotence. She leafed through the pages until she came to Andy Nicholson's analysis, expecting to see some mention of the red flags she had spotted. But as he had done in Shellee Jones' report, Nicholson focused largely on Avram's sex drive, which he had concluded was about average. There was no mention of anything troublesome, like possible violent acting out or sexual frustration. Had Andy not noticed the heavy punctuation or the tics? Or had he noticed and put a different construction on them?

If the potential for violence was something he had observed and for some specific reason failed to mention, his rationale was lost on Claudia. Part of the handwriting analyst's job was to alert the client to possible problem areas.

If Grusha was going to make a successful match for Avram, it would be important for her to introduce him to an independent woman who would not expect him to make her a whole person. Because his locus of control was internal, Avram would have less interest in making the emotional needs of a demanding partner a high priority. He might know how to behave in social situations, but he was more likely to give the bulk of his time and energy to intellectual pursuits.

And there was the larger, more important issue: Under stress, he might well strike out physically at someone weaker. If indeed he was experiencing sexual potency problems, his frustration level was already high. A woman who was particularly emotional and demanding might be attractive to him at first, but she would soon press his hot buttons and then the situation could be dodgy.

Claudia continued to graze on her sandwich as she thought about Avram's handwriting. She asked herself, given the level of aggression she was seeing, what sort of problems a woman might face in a relationship with a man like him.

It would have been helpful if she could see into handwriting like a crystal ball, but the truth was, handwriting reflected past behavior and the *potential* for future behavior. There was no way to know for certain whether all the conditions needed for the writer to act on that potential would come together in just the right mix at just the right time.

She recalled a client who had submitted samples of her own and her future husband's handwriting for analysis. The droopy rhythm in the bride's handwriting had marked her as having emotional dependency of a type that attracted her to abusive partners. The groom's rigid, muddy-looking writing was that of an explosive personality seeking someone to abuse. True to type, the bride had ignored the warnings in the handwriting analysis report. When she later contacted Claudia, hysterical and running for her life after coming close to being beaten to death by this man, it came as no great surprise.

There was no surefire way to predict that someone would in fact become violent, but the fact that such a strong potential for violence existed in Avram Cohen's handwriting was crucial information for Grusha to have.

Again Claudia asked herself—was this one of the mistakes Andy had made, that she had been brought in to find? She thought of how suave and smooth Avram had been that afternoon. Could she be wrong in her evaluation? She was certain that she was not. Her final assessment was that, thanks to the important information Andy Nicholson had left out of his report, Avram had probably acted badly with a match Grusha made for him and it was now coming back to bite her.

The two of them had appeared quite chummy in her office, but it was possible that the hundred thousand dollars the Israeli client had paid for Grusha's services might have had something to do with that.

She scribbled some notes and stuck them in Avram's file. When they met the next afternoon, she would have some pointed questions to ask the baroness. Claudia had not yet seen the matchmaker's handwriting, which was a foolish omission on her part. If there hadn't been such a rush to bring her to the East Coast, she would have insisted on first seeing a sample.

Deciding that she had earned a break, Claudia left the files on the bed and went to check her e-mail on the laptop. She found one from Peggy Yum, the producer. It looked like Yum had been serious about wanting to have her appear again on *Hard Evidence*.

> *Grusha Olinetsky's people called me for your number. Is she using you on her show? We're planning a segment on "dating services—are they safe?" Call me as soon as you get this. It's a winner!*

Claudia looked over at the clock. Eight fifteen. Three hours earlier in L.A. Yum might still be in her office.

"*Hard Evidence*," Yum's voice chirped on the other end of the phone. "Peggy Yum, segment producer, speaking. How may I help you?"

"Peggy, hi. It's Claudia Rose. I just got your e-mail."

"Claudia! Fantastic; we were just talking about you at the production meeting. We want to schedule this segment ASAP. Can you be here Thursday morning? We'll talk about—"

"Wait, Peggy, I can't. I'm in New York for a few days, so this week is out. And listen, it's a problem for me to talk about dating services right now."

"So, Olinetsky *is* using you? That's way cool! It'd be perfect, like, you'd be undercover. You can give us the scoop on what goes on behind the scenes."

"I didn't say she was using me, but if she were, don't you think it would be a little unethical for me to accept this kind of assignment?" Claudia's reflection in the mirror behind the desk mouthed back at her, *Can you spell conflict of interest?* "You're probably looking for dirt on her, right? I'm not interested in being part of an exposé."

"It doesn't *have* to just be dirt." Yum's self-righteous indignation made it sound as if she were pouting. "I guess we could use some success stories, too. Look, Claudia, I really want to do this segment, and you'd be perfect for it. You're so great on camera. You have bunches of credibility. This could be a really awesome segment."

"Thanks for the compliment, Peggy. I appreciate it; really, I do. If it were any other time, I'd jump on it, but for now, I think you need to find another story if you want me to be involved. How about one on handwriting analysis for employers? That's mostly what people use graphology for."

"That's not sexy." Yum was now into full sulk. "Just forget it. Talk later."

Claudia was left listening to dead air, debating

whether she wanted to work with the young producer at all. Their conversation had left her feeling old and cranky, but as long as Grusha was her client, she didn't see how she could accept an assignment such as the one Peggy Yum was proposing. She would think about it, see if she could find some sort of compromise, but she refused to bend her principles.

A few stretches of stiff muscles to help refocus her attention; then she settled back on the bed with the next client folder and a couple of cold French fries.

The glam shot in the next folder in the stack showed a sloe-eyed gamine beauty with black hair cut short and punked into spikes. Heavy black eyeliner and purple shadow made pale cheeks paler. Heather Lloyd, a fashion model. Twenty-five, five-nine. With those looks, Claudia guessed, probably successful in her field.

A selection of snaps that were supposed to be informal had obviously been posed for maximum effect. One scene had been shot on Ellis Island with a backdrop of Lady Liberty, Heather's skirt billowing in the breeze, à la Marilyn Monroe. In another she was dressed in cutoffs and a halter top, sitting on the steps of a brownstone, blowing an exaggeratedly puckered kiss at the camera. A third showed her on a fashion show catwalk in filmy lingerie, revealing legs that were close to being anorexic thin.

Before she turned to the handwriting, Claudia tried to imagine what it might look like. From Heather's modeling photos, it was clear that she spent a lot of effort creating her appearance. Chances were the same was true of her handwriting.

When she came to the sample page, the stylized script told Claudia that her educated guess had been right, and the content agreed.

I want a certain kind of lifestyle, so I am seeking a very successful gentleman who is financially secure. I want a man who is kind and lovable who will take care of me. He wants a woman to love and worship, always and forever. He wants me to be that woman.

The text described what Heather wanted, but she had written nothing about what she might have to offer a mate. Even without the narcissistic sentiments she had expressed, her painstakingly constructed handwriting with its many arcaded forms revealed a woman who would make security and financial reward the highest priority in her life. It was all about image and how she projected it. The way others perceived her was of paramount importance, so she would take pains to hide anything about herself she believed flawed. For anyone to see her as less than perfect would give her a sense of shame.

The handwriting had one uncommon characteristic: Several of the lower loops were twisted into something resembling a bow. In handwriting, lower loops were connected to, among other things, biological urges.

In virtually all cases Claudia had examined, the particular form Heather had adopted was made by victims of sexual assault. The convoluted path that Heather's loops followed was a strong indicator that, like Avram, she had sexual issues. The question was, would that affect her ability to form a healthy intimate relationship? In Claudia's opinion, it would.

Had Andy Nicholson explained all this to Grusha?

She read his report, which said little of substance: "She is a cumulative thinker who builds one idea upon another. She has the trait of yieldingness, but there is some resentment."

He'd written about her gregarious personality and generosity. What Andy's report failed to state was that the handwriting painted a portrait of a sweet-natured but naive girl who acted younger than her years, whose self-image was tied in with her beauty. That would all make sense if she had been the object of unresolved sexual abuse.

Cumulative thinking, gregarious, yieldingness, resentment—a superficial laundry list of traits that meant little in the big picture of Heather Lloyd's ego-centric self-absorption or the sexual implications of those lower zone bows.

Claudia glanced over at the clock and saw that the hour was getting late. Time always seemed to surge forward when she was immersed in handwriting samples. What felt like ten minutes was in reality an hour.

She knew she should get some rest so she would be ready for her meeting with Grusha tomorrow, but her body was telling her it was three hours earlier than the nightstand clock claimed it was. If she went to bed now, she would be awake by three a.m.

Her eyes went to her cell phone on the nightstand. She wondered how Jovanic and Alex were doing on their stakeout. Would he call? He usually did when there was little action. She gave a small sigh and reached for the next folder.

Over the next half hour Claudia reviewed three files where the clients' handwriting was not particularly noteworthy or remarkable. She made a few notes, but the samples looked normal and emotionally healthy enough that she didn't bother to read Andy Nicholson's reports. She knew instinctively that these were not problem clients.

Another short break. She took a small bottle of

white wine from the minibar and poured it into a
water glass from the bathroom. It wasn't up to the
standard of Grusha's Cabernet, but it was drinkable.

The next client was a man named Marcus Bernard. Thirty-six, he'd listed his vitals as six two, two-
ten, but Claudia was sure he must have fudged his
weight by about ten pounds. In his head shot he wore
a red baseball cap. His smile, hidden behind a full,
graying beard, seemed open and affable. Something
about him reminded her of the actor Sean Connery at
a younger age, though Marcus Bernard's lips tended
more to thinness.

In his biographical notes under *Occupation*, he'd
entered "real estate developer, hotels." Several snap-
shots showed him outdoors in natural settings—
hiking with a tall walking stick; standing in front of
an open pit at a groundbreaking. In one he wore a
tuxedo, a silk scarf draped with studied carelessness
around his neck.

Claudia turned to his handwriting sample in the
back of the folder. He had scrawled only a couple of
lines that said he was looking for a woman who was
sexy in the boardroom or the bedroom. *How original.*

"Someone who is fun to be with," he had penned.
"Loyal, passionate, adventurous, and flexible."

The word *flexible* was underlined several times.
That kind of heavy underlining often meant that the
writer was dogmatic and tended to pontificate. What
kind of flexibility did he expect to find? In the context
of this handwriting sample, she thought it might be
referring to a partner who would be tolerant of indis-
cretions. Or maybe his desire was for a woman who
would participate in exotic activities, such as group
sex. That was something his handwriting couldn't
tell her.

The sample displayed many of the hallmarks of a smooth talker: slack rhythm; thready, indefinite letter forms. Some words were illegible. Bernard had left little space between words and lines. The upper loops were too tall, the long lower loops too long and pulling to the left.

In some ways, the handwriting reminded Claudia of another writer—Lyle Menendez, who had been convicted of helping his younger brother murder their wealthy parents back in the mid-1990s.

The capitals in Bernard's signature were large and tall, which indicated that he thought very well of himself—maybe too well. The final stroke on the capital M in Marcus plunged below the baseline and curved under the a, which was the next letter to the right. A long beginning stroke on the a crossed the downstroke, creating a form that resembled the letter X.

Claudia had researched this "X formation," and had discovered that in most cases, those who made it had a fatalistic attitude or had been close to death in some way. She wondered whether Bernard had lost someone close to him.

What she saw in the handwriting suggested that he was something of an action junkie who threw his energy around, sticking his fingers into a dozen pies. He needed excitement and stimulation, but small details were unimportant to him. He would need a strong support staff to follow behind and pick up the pieces. Experience told Claudia that he would use diffuse activity to help him avoid dealing with things he would rather not face.

By this time, she figured she knew what she would find in Andy's report: sex, sex, and more sex. This was one case where she couldn't disagree with him.

With the disproportionately long lower loops as part of the whole picture, Marcus Bernard would constantly be seeking new experiences and possibly new partners, but emotional satisfaction would elude him. The question was, knowing that, would Grusha have taken him on as a client?

The wine and the fatigue from the long day were kicking in. Claudia yawned as she scribbled more notes, then moved on to folders number seven and eight. Seven was a rather boring sample; nothing stood out. Ron Gibson, twenty-nine, an advertising executive. The writing meandered along without a lot of energy. Claudia thought he was a little depressed, but he would be okay once Grusha hooked him up with the woman of his dreams.

Number eight was an elfin woman with massively large, artistic handwriting. Her bio notes described her as Penelope Mendes, a twenty-seven-year-old writer from L.A. The handwriting was block printed but the letters touched, which suggested that while she wanted to be independent, Penelope really needed closeness.

The last folder in the pile belonged to John Shaw, award-winning professional photographer and world traveler. At thirty-nine, he was a little older than the other clients she had viewed. He had a clean-cut, wholesome look, with springy ginger hair and blue eyes—unusual for a redhead, she thought. When she came to his handwriting sample, the news was not so good.

The writing style was a conventional school type, except for a serious problem with the upper loops. Some of the l's were twisted, while others were shaped like a candle flame with bulging sides and soft angles at the apex.

While twisted lower loops like the ones in Heather Lloyd's handwriting pointed to sexual issues, in the upper loops the twists could indicate serious medical or psychological problems. Claudia couldn't diagnose a specific illness without a medical license, but she knew that physiological problems could sometimes be seen in handwriting.

If a physical illness was not the source of the flame-shaped loops, then John Shaw had an idiosyncratic view of life; he was not on the same wavelength as the rest of the world. The baselines also pointed down, a sign of depression, illness, or fatigue.

Claudia stacked the folders on the desk and went into the bathroom. She began her evening rituals to prepare for bed, thinking about what she had learned. So far, several of the male population of Grusha's matchmaking club had monumentally failed to impress her. She had observed enough red flags in the handwritings of three of the male clients to believe that any of them could have engaged in behavior that might come back to haunt the matchmaker. And Heather Lloyd was a self-involved egotist, so she could be a problem, too. She guessed that the other clients had been thrown in as ringers, to test her.

She got into bed and was switching off the light when her cell phone rang.

Chapter 5

"Claudia? Hey, how ya doing? It's Susan Rowan—sorry to call so late, but I figured you'd be up. I know you—you're always working."

The Long Island accent on the other end of the line was one that was hard to mistake. Susan Rowan was a colleague who lived in Manhattan. Claudia didn't know Susan well enough to view her as a close friend, but they had crossed paths several times over the years and shared meals at a couple of handwriting analysis conventions.

"Susan. Good to hear from you."

"I just heard you were in the city, so I was hoping we could get together while you're here."

"Where in the world did you hear that?"

"Oh, you know. A little bird told me."

"What little bird might that be?"

"I'll tell you about that later. How long are you gonna be here? Do you have time to meet?"

"Of course, Suze, I'd love to see you. What's your schedule like?"

"How about breakfast tomorrow? There's a good bagel shop up a block from your hotel. Go out the front door, turn left and start walking. You can't miss it."

Claudia pressed the end button and crawled back under the covers, wondering where Susan had obtained the information on her whereabouts. Besides Jovanic, she hadn't told anyone except her close friend, Kelly Brennan, that she was going to be away.

Susan Rowan had commandeered a table in a secluded spot at the back of the noisy café. A stylish redhead, she wore a tweed jacket over a turtleneck sweater that attempted to cover loose folds of skin on her neck. Her Levi's bagged a little at the seat on a body that was all angles and planes.

She smiled with genuine warmth and brushed Claudia's cheek with her own. "They'll kill you as soon as look at you to get a table," she said, slipping out of her jacket and draping it over the back of the chair. "I'll order for us if you'll stand guard."

Noticing her sallow complexion, Claudia remembered hearing that Susan had been receiving cancer treatment. She could see that her friend had lost considerable weight since their last encounter at a seminar a couple of years earlier.

Claudia watched Susan elbow her way to the counter, ignoring the grumbles of other customers. The humidity from the bagel kettle, the warmth of the oven, the steam from pots of fresh coffee had all conspired to fog up the windows, creating a sense of cozy seclusion that was more imagined than real. Savory aromas perfumed the air, making her stomach gurgle. It all felt very *New Yawk*.

Susan reappeared five minutes later, bearing a tray laden with bagels in a plastic basket. Claudia reached for a cinnamon raisin and a single container of cream cheese. "These smell wonderful. I'm glad you phoned me. And not just because of the bagels."

Susan cracked a smile as she began layering lox

and cream cheese on a water bagel. "Oh, sure, I know where I stand."

"I heard you'd been ill. I hope that's all behind you now."

"It's been a long haul," Susan said, grimacing. "But I'm great now, really great. I'm done with chemo, got my hair back, and the docs have given me a clean bill of health. I've been planning what I want to do with the rest of my life."

"And have you got it all figured out?"

"As a matter of fact, I have. I finally got divorced— it's the damn marriage that made me sick. Never marry a doctor, Claudia, I'm telling you, they're only good for the alimony."

"I'll keep that in mind."

"You got a boyfriend?"

Claudia nodded, but she didn't feel as sure of herself on that count as she used to. Jovanic had not called back the night before. She had to wonder how late he and Alex had stayed out on their stakeout. "He's a detective," she said. "LAPD."

Susan laughed. "Just as bad, I'm sure. I think it's the male persuasion that's the problem, not the career."

"I like the male persuasion myself. Not ready to give up on them just yet."

"Me, I'm ready to travel the world. Maybe I'll find my soul mate out there somewhere."

"Wouldn't it be more fun to find the soul mate first and travel the world *together*?"

"True, Claudia, so true. And I've got some ideas about that." They chatted on for a few minutes about men and relationships; then Susan set her coffee cup in its saucer and showed her hand. "So, you wanna know who the little bird was? The one who told me you were in Manhattan?"

"Hell, yeah. Spill the beans."

"Grusha told me."

"*Grusha?*"

"You didn't know? I used to work for her before I got sick. I was the one who told her you were on that show last week—the interview show."

"That's news to me. She never told me."

"Typical. She plays her cards close to her vest."

Claudia was busy trying to figure Susan into the equation, but wasn't immediately able to see where she fit. "What was she like to work for?"

Susan flapped her hands. "She's a hoot if you don't take her too seriously." Claudia raised a questioning eyebrow, and she added, "Well, you've met her; she's a big drama queen, not to mention paranoid. Everyone's out to get her—know what I mean?"

Claudia knew *exactly* what she meant. "What's her handwriting like?"

"She doesn't let anyone see it. Claims she's functionally illiterate, but I don't believe that for a minute. Makes you wonder, doesn't it?" She put her finger to her lips. "Shhh, don't tell anyone, but I have seen it. I'll dig out the sample for you."

"I heard she'd been using another graphologist." Claudia made an effort to sound casual, but she needn't have worried about giving away confidential information.

Susan's face scrunched into a grimace that made no bones about what she thought of her successor. "Andy Nicholson. That awful, awful man. I warned her. Told her he's a first-class fraud, but she still hired him. He tells the most outrageous lies and he gets away with it, too."

"I worked with an attorney who's thinking of filing perjury charges against him for lying about his credentials," Claudia said.

"Never stick. You know how experts get all kinds of immunity when they testify. Grusha was crazy to use him and I do believe she's lived to regret it."

"Then why didn't she come back to you? Why call me, when I live on the other side of the country?"

"She knows I have no intention of going back to work," Susan said. "I can afford to enjoy life. It's about time I had some fun." She reached for her purse and dug through it, getting out a compact and lipstick. Holding the tiny mirror with one hand, she squinted into it, applying coral pink gloss and blotting her lips on her paper napkin. "Nothing good can come of getting involved with the Andy Nicholsons of the world. Grusha should have listened to me."

"Maybe she thought what you told her was out of professional jealousy," Claudia said, remembering Grusha's warning not to allow her own animosity toward Andy to interfere with her judgment. "She couldn't have checked out his creds very well. Most people are willing to accept what's on a Web site at face value without doing any research."

"You know he's a friggin' hired gun. She used him because he'll say anything the client wants to hear."

"But how would that benefit Grusha? I mean, doesn't she want to know the truth about the people she's matching up?"

Susan reached over and patted her hand. "Yeah, dollface. *Her* truth."

Claudia's thoughts drifted to Grusha's phone call voicing her concern that Andy had made errors in his reports. If what Susan had just said was true and Grusha had used Andy to make it *appear* she had screened potential club members, and she had kept negative information about their personalities out of their files, she was now backtracking to cover herself.

"I mean," Susan was saying, "to hear her tell it, there's nothing the least bit disturbing about two of her clients dying so close together. But you have to admit, it really is pretty strange . . ."

"Uh-huh," said Claudia absently, her moment of introspection broken. Then, "*What* did you just say?"

"Hel-lo!" Susan snapped her fingers in front of Claudia's face. "Welcome back. I said, isn't it strange that two of her clients have died so close together?"

Claudia frowned, sure that she must have heard incorrectly. "*Two* of them? I didn't know *any* of her clients had died."

Susan gave her an odd look. "I guess it's not something she'd want to broadcast, though it had nothing to do with her. They were both young, too."

"What happened?"

"The second one was only a couple of months ago. She was one of the last clients I did for the baroness before I got sick and quit. It was kinda creepy. I just happened to see the article about it in the *Times* and made the connection. She was a young model—not so well known, but . . ."

"What was her name?" Claudia interrupted.

"Heather Lloyd. She was only—"

"Twenty-five," Claudia finished for her, stunned. She sipped her coffee, not tasting it. "Grusha gave me Heather Lloyd's handwriting to analyze. Why would she do that if she's *dead*? She must have given it to me by mistake." She thought of the photo of Heather Lloyd playacting the coquette—Marilyn Monroe on Ellis Island. It was hard to believe. "What happened to her?"

"Skiing accident," Susan said. "She went up to Vermont over the holidays and skied herself right into a tree."

Claudia's mouth dropped. "Oh, man! Are they sure it was an accident?"

"Yeah, it was just one of those things. The article said she was an experienced skier, but for some reason—I guess no one will ever know why—she left the trail and hit a fallen branch or a tree trunk or some bizarre thing like that."

"Was she with someone?" Recalling Heather Lloyd's handwriting, Claudia knew that it was highly improbable that she would have taken off for what she presumed was a classy Vermont ski house without an audience in tow.

But Susan shook her head. "The article didn't mention anyone. It's a crying shame, with her being so young and all. But you know, these things do happen. Remember Sonny Bono? He died the same way."

"Of course." Who could forget the former husband and mentor of the legendary singer, Cher, and later, mayor of Palm Springs? He had skied to his death in the late 1990s.

But something wasn't adding up. "In Heather Lloyd's file there was an analysis by Andy Nicholson. Why would Grusha have both Andy and me analyze Heather Lloyd's handwriting when she's dead?"

Susan gave an eloquent shrug. "That, my friend, is a mystery. The baroness has her own way of operating."

"I intend to ask her about it."

"Good luck with that; she can be a cagey devil. And don't tell her I told you."

"I won't mention you. But what about the other one? You said *two* deaths?"

Susan leaned forward and lowered her voice. "Yeah, get this—it's even creepier. The other one was *another* client whose handwriting I'd analyzed. He was a medical student named Ryan Turner. Drowned in the Bahamas, scuba diving."

The name meant nothing to Claudia. Cheered by the knowledge that Ryan Turner's was not among the client files Grusha had given her, she was still puzzled. "Let's back up the bus a minute. You did say *you* had analyzed Heather Lloyd's handwriting, too?"

"Yeah, I remember it. She had persona writing. You know, that superstylized script."

"Right. But there was only *one* analysis in her file—Andy Nicholson's."

"Well, I certainly wrote a report," Susan said, her penciled brows forming an arch. "So where the hell is it?"

Claudia returned to her hotel wondering what other important information Grusha Olinetsky might have held back. She could understand why the matchmaker wouldn't wish to publicize the premature deaths of these two clients. But what was the point of asking a third person to analyze Heather Lloyd's handwriting? Unless, as Claudia suspected, she hadn't liked what she had seen in the first two reports and was hoping for something more favorable in the third.

The red message light was blinking on the twentieth century phone as Claudia entered her room. She kicked off her shoes and tossed her coat on the chair, dialed the message center. The recorded voice of Grusha's assistant, Sonya Marsi, held a hint of reproof.

"You didn't answer your mobile, so I hope you get this before you come to the office, Ms. Rose. The baroness wants you to meet with our club psychologist, Dr. Pollard, and our physician, Dr. McAllister, this morning. I've already made appointments with both of them for you, so call me back ASAP."

Claudia fished her mobile out of her purse and checked the screen. Sure enough, there was one missed call. She hadn't heard it ring over the din in the bagel shop.

When she returned the phone call, Sonya informed her that she had made the first appointment for eleven. Grusha's driver would fetch Claudia from the hotel at ten forty-five and transport her to the offices of the medical doctor and the consulting psychologist who vetted Grusha Olinetsky's clients. That left a little more than an hour for Claudia to take a second look at the files and collect her notes.

"Oh, and Ms. Rose," Sonya added, "I've messengered you a file the baroness forgot to give you yesterday. It should be there any minute."

No more than two minutes after they had rung off, the front desk called to say there was a package waiting for Ms. Rose. She asked for it to be brought up to her room.

After handing the bellman a tip, Claudia closed the door and ripped open the flap of the thick envelope. With a sense of inevitability, she removed the folder and read the name of the client: Ryan Turner. The medical student who had drowned while scuba diving.

She took the folder to the desk and sat down, opening it first to the head shot, then flipping to the photo gallery. Her first impression of Ryan Turner was of movie-star quality looks: thick black hair, strong jaw, six-pack abs, muscular legs.

I wonder what his bedside manner was like.

As with Heather Lloyd, she didn't want to accept

the fact of his death; it was just too sad to contemplate. Yet Grusha had sent her his file so she could examine his handwriting. Heather Lloyd's file might have been given to her by mistake, but two mistakes of the same kind stretched the boundaries of credulity to the breaking point.

When she turned to Ryan Turner's handwriting, she was intrigued to note that of all the Elite Introductions client files she had examined so far, his sample had the greatest emotional maturity. Firm, swinging rhythm, good spatial arrangement and simplified forms equaled a smart, adaptable guy with the ability to plan ahead. Not far enough ahead to avoid his own death. *Scuba diving*. *Huh*.

Maybe comparing the handwritings to each other would provide some answers. Claudia smoothed the bedspread over the unmade bed and set out the leather folders in two rows of five, each one opened to its handwriting sample.

Her practiced eyes traveled over the handwritings, searching for something in common between the scripts, or something in the personalities of the clients that might clue her in to Grusha's motive for giving her this mystifying task.

She found that two of the women—Heather and Shellee—shared some similar personality traits. The men's handwritings were all over the map, but three of them—Avram, Marcus, and John—had red flags for pathological behavior. Ryan Turner's handwriting was emotionally healthy, but he was dead.

In the next phase of her examination she considered the demographics: four women, six men, aged from their mid-twenties to late thirties. Their careers were varied. From the information in the files, there was no connection that she could see.

Except that two of them are dead. It kept coming back to that.

Why would the baroness want me to analyze the hand-writings of two dead clients?

She opened her laptop and signed on to the hotel's wireless Internet connection. Opening a browser window, she Googled "Heather Lloyd + model + dead" and found a handful of links to minor articles featuring the young woman, most of them covering fashion shows.

Two recent articles mentioned her tragic death. One added an important detail that Susan Rowan had been unable to provide: Heather had been skiing with an unnamed companion when she left the trail. Only minutes later, she was dead from severe head injuries.

Who had her companion been—a match made by Grusha Olinetsky? Since Lloyd had evidently plunked down a big fee to join Elite Introductions, chances were she would be dating a member. Maybe it was her companion's handwriting that Claudia should be analyzing. Or maybe she already had. She made herself a note to ask Grusha whether Lloyd had dated any of the men in the group.

A search on "Ryan Turner" produced a short article about his drowning death in Nassau, the Bahamas.

According to the reporter, the young doctor was new to scuba diving. The spokesperson for the hotel where he was staying indicated that he had taken a quickie course with their instructor and was not adequately prepared for the difficulty he ran into. He had been strongly warned not to dive alone. *That's the hotel covering its ass.* It was assumed that he had ignored this advice, as no one came forward to claim the body, which was found by other divers, trapped underwater in seaweed.

It all sounded on the up-and-up, but Claudia found herself wanting to discuss her questions about the two deaths with Jovanic. She considered phoning him, but if he had been up all night on stakeout, he was probably catching up on his sleep. She would have to wait for him to call. Meanwhile, there was still time to take a look at the other clients. She opened a new browser and Googled Shellee Jones.

She was staring at the words on the laptop screen when "Bad Boys" sounded on her cell phone.

Chapter 6

The *Cops* television show theme was the one Claudia had chosen for Jovanic's ring tone. "Hey," she said, "how's it going?"

"Hey," Jovanic said. "It's going fine here. How's it going with Anastasia?"

"Grusha. I haven't seen her yet today. She's sending me to talk to some of the other consultants she uses before we get together later."

"What's the point of that?"

"I haven't had a chance to ask her. I guess she just wants all the consultants to get to know one another."

"How about you come home soon and consult with *me*?"

"Is that your way of saying you miss me?"

"You know, it's not nice to force a guy to say stuff like that, but . . . okay, yeah, I miss you." She could hear the grin in his voice.

"I miss you, too." *But I'm liking the space a little bit.*

"So, how are you doing, all alone in the big city?" He knew her well enough to detect the nuances.

"I'm fine. Great."

"You sure? You sound—"

"Stop being so protective, Joel, I'm fine. How's Alex?" That just slipped out before she was even aware that it had been on her tongue.

When he hesitated, Claudia got a sharp impression that she wasn't the only one who wasn't telling all. She thought about pressing the point, but she wanted to see his eyes when she asked him what was up. And she was convinced that something was.

"Alex is fine, you're fine, we're all fine." He sounded fed up, with a weariness that probably had little to do with the number of hours he had worked. "Are you pissed because I didn't call last night?"

"Of course not. You were working."

"I got in late, didn't want to wake you." He added quickly, "You know how it is on a stakeout."

"Yeah. Did you get your man? Or woman?"

"No, we're on again tonight. So, how's the job *really* going?"

She told him what she'd learned from Susan Rowan.

"Two dead clients?" he repeated.

"Two *young*, dead clients."

"Both accidents, unrelated."

"There doesn't seem to be a connection, just a weird fluke."

"You know what I think about coincidences."

Jovanic had block-printed writing. That meant he expected things to have a sound, logical reason or he wouldn't accept them.

"I don't much believe in coincidences, either," she said. "But maybe this is one of those times when a cigar is just a cigar."

"It *stinks* like a cigar."

Claudia laughed. "That's funny, coming from a re-formed smoker."

"Cigarettes smell better than cigars. Maybe I should take it up again."

"Not if you want to kiss these lips, Columbo."

He made a huffing sound that passed for a chuckle.
"I haven't had a chance to check out this baroness
character yet, but when I get back to the office——" He
hesitated as someone in the background called his
name. Claudia thought she recognized Alex's voice.
"Gotta go," he said. "I'll let you know what I find
out."

She clicked end on her cell phone and went back
to her laptop with her stomach churning. *Why is Alex
with him when he's off duty?*

Put it aside, think about it later.

The article she had pulled up about Shellee Jones
before Jovanic's phone call was waiting behind the
screen saver. She ran her eye over the short piece,
looking for anything that would add to the scant
information she already had. Her hand went to her
mouth. *Oh crap.*

*While dining out at a trendy restaurant in the East
Village, Shellee Marie Jones, youngest daughter of successful hedge-fund manager Donald Jones, apparently
ingested a substance to which she was severely allergic.
Anaphylactic shock caused Jones to stop breathing, and
although paramedics were called to the scene within a
few minutes, they did not arrive in time. Friends and
family were at a loss, claiming that Jones was always
scrupulous about making sure she touched nothing that
contained peanut products. An autopsy is pending.*

It wasn't a common spelling of the name, but
Claudia might almost have convinced herself that the
article referred to some other Shellee Marie Jones if
the head shot published with the article had not been
identical to the one in the leather folder on the bed
behind her.

Another coincidence?

She located the publication date. What she read unsettled her further. Jones' death had occurred only three weeks earlier. The article made no mention of the dating service, but according to her Elite Introductions file, Shellee Jones had been a member of the club only since January. Even if Susan Rowan had seen the article, she wouldn't have made the connection to Jones, as the young woman had joined well after Susan ceased working for Grusha.

Three dead clients.

"Yep," she said aloud. "That's one coincidence too many."

She ran over in her head what she knew of the men whose files the matchmaker had given her. At least she knew that Avram Cohen was alive.

He was yesterday, anyway.

She didn't have the same knowledge about the other clients. One by one, she typed in their names and information. She browsed their Web sites and Googled them. Finding nothing alarming on the clients whose handwritings had raised no concerns, she went on to Marcus Bernard, one of her red flag handwritings.

Copying from his file, she keyed into the search field "real estate developer, hotels."

Several links came up to East Coast projects that had been developed by Bernard's company—a four-hundred-room hotel in Boston whose top floors contained luxury condos; a similar one in Philadelphia; another in Jupiter, Florida.

Navigating to his company's Web site, Claudia clicked through the links until she found one for a photo gallery. The sixteen thumbnails led to glossy photos of Bernard's buildings and high society events he had attended. The bearded, tuxedo-clad Marcus Bernard matched his Elite Introductions file photo.

As she skimmed through photos that had been shot at a charity fund-raiser the year before, her gaze caught on another familiar figure at the black-tie event: Grusha Olinetsky, recognizable despite platinum blond hair rather than her current jet-black, but twisted into the same French roll she still favored.

Pear-shaped diamonds dangled from her ears and glittered across her throat. A clingy gold lamé strapless gown showed off pale shoulders. Grusha's gloved arm was tucked possessively through Bernard's and his hand covered hers.

Claudia clicked the back button and paged through some of the other links without finding anything of interest. What she had discovered about Ryan Turner and Shellee Jones left her with the almost certain knowledge that she had been duped into coming here. She went and poured herself a glass of tap water from the bathroom faucet and downed a vitamin.

What game is Grusha playing with me?

It was a question Claudia intended to ask her client. But first, she would keep the appointments that Sonya had made for her with the club's doctors. She intended to glean whatever information she could arm herself with before the inevitable confrontation with Grusha Olinetsky.

Returning to the laptop, she tried one last search, this time on John Shaw, whose file was the last in the pile. But even with the additional demographics she entered, the name was too common to bring up anything useful.

Maybe no news is good news for him, she thought, contemplating the array of perplexing information she had accumulated so far.

Ten fancy leather file folders, three dead clients.

Chapter 7

Yellow cabs and honking horns. Steel-colored skies and overcoats. Grusha's town car at the curb, the chauffeur at the car door, his cheeks chapped red in the biting cold.

Claudia left the hotel, the lower half of her face wrapped in a woolen scarf, and hurried over to the town car. She sank into the backseat and ripped away the cloying fabric, the sheer numbers of people thronging the midtown sidewalks making her feel claustrophobic. An unexpected yearning to be home in L.A. struck her and she laughed at herself. Sitting in her car on the 405, bumper-to-bumper with a million other motorists, would hardly be an improvement.

About ten minutes later, the car stopped before a stately building on Central Park South. The driver informed her that both Dr. McAllister and Dr. Pollard maintained their practices there. She figured it made sense that clients who were paying a steep membership fee would expect to see the club's physician and psychologist in an exclusive office.

Apart from two pretty nurses in neat blue scrubs sitting behind the front desk, Dr. Ian McAllister's third-floor waiting room was empty. The nurses were a matched pair with long black hair and exquisite skin. Either could have posed for a cosmetic surgery brochure. Claudia had a suspicion that they might have been hired as much for their attractive appearance as for their medical and clerical skills.

One of them jumped up right away and said she would let Dr. McAllister know that his visitor had arrived, and to please have a seat.

Expecting to be kept waiting as she inevitably was at her own doctor's office, Claudia began riffling through a glossy upscale fashion magazine on the coffee table. There wasn't an item in it that wouldn't crush her budget, but it was interesting to see how the other half dressed. The doctor's appearance at the reception room door just a few moments later took her by surprise and made a good first impression.

In his mid-forties, McAllister was tall and imposing. Claudia took in the neatly trimmed gray-streaked beard and moustache that gave him the look of a college professor; the classic blue dress shirt with a mauve patterned tie worn under a pristine white lab coat; the lock of chestnut hair that flopped onto his forehead. A faint squint had chiseled vertical lines between his brows. Although his smile was welcoming, the squint made it seem as though he were frowning at the same time, creating a disturbing disharmony. He took the hand she offered in a firm grasp. "Delighted to meet you, Ms. Rose."

The doctor led her to his private office, asking all the right questions: Where was she staying? Was she rested? Was this her first time in New York? His politeness felt a little forced, as if making small talk might be uncomfortable for him.

Dr. McAllister installed her in a comfortable leather guest chair across from his desk, then moved around the desk and seated himself, clasping his hands on the blotter in front of him.

"How long have you been acquainted with the baroness?" he asked.

"I actually met her just yesterday," Claudia said. "She saw me on a TV show on Sunday morning, gave me a call, and voilà! here I am. How about you?" She thought he looked startled at the question. Maybe as a doctor he was unaccustomed to the person on the other side of the desk taking an active part in the conversation.

"Well, let's see." He wrinkled his brow as if he really had to think about the answer. Even with that perpetual half scowl he was attractive in a rather serious way. "I've worked with the baroness for about three years now. We met at a social function just as she was starting her business. She said she was in need of a consulting physician. As you've no doubt discovered, she's rather particular about the members she accepts into the club. Needs to make sure they're in good shape, no communicable diseases." He gave a slight smile. "It wouldn't look good if someone got AIDS or syphilis from a match she had arranged for them."

"I suppose it wouldn't. So you screen the clients for STDs?"

He inclined his head. "That's part of it, along with their general state of health. The applicants also have to pass a psychological examination, and of course, a handwriting analysis. Apparently you are the new graphologist."

"Apparently I am," said Claudia. "The latest in a succession, from what I hear."

"Yes, the baroness puts great stock in graphology. She won't accept a new member into the club without having their handwriting analyzed. The last graphologist was a Mr. Nicholson, the short-lived fellow who followed the woman—I can't think of her name—she unfortunately fell ill."

One of the nurses arrived with a tray bearing a bone china coffee service. She poured for them without speaking and glided silently away. Claudia spooned sugar into her cup with a tiny silver teaspoon. "You're thinking of Susan Rowan. It just so happens I had breakfast with her this morning. I'm happy to say she's recovered from her illness and seems to be doing quite well."

"That's excellent news," McAllister said. "She was supposedly quite a good handwriting analyst, but I must say, *your* résumé is impeccable. The baroness was so impressed that she called to share it with me."

Claudia smiled, dismissing the compliment. "Thank you, Dr. McAllister, but I know better than to believe my own PR. I've worked in the field a long time, that's all. I've accumulated a lot of experience."

"You're too modest, Ms. Rose. Tell me, are you single, as well as modest?"

The personal question startled her. The commitment between her and Jovanic was unspoken, taken for granted. Yet, despite his protectiveness since the murder and the events that had followed, there had been that undeniable distance between them lately. She had started noticing it since Alex's unwelcome presence had become a constant in their lives. So far she hadn't mentioned it to Jovanic, just kept an eye on the way Alex looked at him. Then there were the phone calls and text messages that arrived from her several times during evenings and days off with some excuse or another about work.

Oh hell, maybe it was all in her head. She was well aware that it was the barriers *she* had erected that kept Jovanic from asking for more from her. But bottom line, she was less certain of him than she had been and she was questioning her own judgment a lot these days.

She stammered, realizing that McAllister was waiting for a response. "I'm, uh—" She felt her cheeks color up. "I'm seeing someone."

Ian McAllister threw her a sardonic smile. "You should be careful; you'll have the baroness fixing you up with the man of your dreams."

"Maybe I've already found him."

"Mmm, perhaps. Or—"

"Has she tried to fix *you* up?"

When the doctor smiled, his lips went up only on one side, giving him a cynical look. "*That* is possibly her fondest desire." He glanced down at the gold wedding band on his left hand. How had that escaped her notice? He said, "My wife has been gone a long time. I've spent most of my time outside of work hours raising our daughter. I must admit, it wasn't always easy, maintaining a busy practice and being a single parent. But now . . ." He trailed off.

Claudia was curious about the reference to his wife. Since he was still wearing a wedding ring, she assumed he must be a widower. "How old is your daughter?" she asked.

"Eighteen last April," he said abruptly. "But I'm alone these days." He'd brought up the subject, but she got the feeling that he didn't want to discuss his daughter after all.

Maybe she's a problem, Claudia thought, thinking of Annabelle. She hoped the girl wouldn't take advantage of her absence and ditch school. It wouldn't be the first time she had gone in search of more interesting pursuits than geography or computer science. She gave herself a mental shake and got down to the business at hand. "Dr. McAllister, I need to ask you—"

"Call me Ian," he interrupted, the dark eyes resting on her speculatively. "We're working together for the same company, no need to be so formal, *Claudia*—is that all right?"

"Of course." She found him disarming, but starting a flirtation with him wasn't part of her plan. "Ian. I'm not quite sure how to ask this but—" She paused. "It's just—Grusha gave me several handwritings to analyze of members who are—well, they're not alive."

McAllister's eyebrows went up. "Not alive?"

"Dead . . . they're dead."

"I know what *not alive* means, Ms. Rose. They covered that in medical school."

It was so ridiculous, she had to laugh. "Oh, good. I'm glad we got that straight because for a moment, I wasn't sure. Ian, seriously, do you have any idea why she might do that?"

"Maybe she was testing you."

"Testing me? A moment ago you said she brought me to New York because I have a good résumé, so she already knows I'm competent. Any other ideas?"

Dr. McAllister looked over at her without speaking and Claudia wished she'd kept her mouth shut. He must have thought she was challenging him. She was just trying to understand Grusha's motivation.

Still silent, he took a black Mont Blanc pen from his breast pocket, held it up and inspected the gold nib, then snapped the top back on. He sighted down the pen barrel and lined it up dead center on the leather desk blotter, making small adjustments until he was pleased with his efforts. When the ritual was finished, he glanced over at Claudia. "I'm afraid I must have left my tarot cards at home today. You'll need to ask the baroness herself." He moved his pen a quarter inch to the left with his fingertip.

"I intend to." Claudia set her cup in the saucer and began to gather her briefcase and coat. "But first, I have an appointment with Dr. Pollard. I believe her office is also in this building."

"Yes, she's up on fifteen. Do give her my best."

"I will. Thank you for the coffee, Ian. It was a pleasure meeting you." Claudia stood and held out her hand. "Though I have to say, I'm not entirely clear on why Grusha felt it was important for us to meet."

Rising, McAllister held on to her hand for a split second longer than he needed to. "Before you go, Claudia ... er ..." He looked down and began fiddling with the few objects on his desk, although the blotter already made a sharp perpendicular line to the left edge of the desk, and the business card holder and prescription pad were at acute right angles to each side of the blotter. The pen remained a dividing line at the center.

He said, "The baroness hosts a monthly cocktail party. It gives some of the more select members and potential members a chance to look one another over in a neutral environment. Dr. Pollard and I usually attend because the members have already met us, so they don't feel like total strangers." He paused and Claudia noticed that he was blushing. Obviously, the attraction was mutual. He cleared his throat. "As it happens, this month's event is this Saturday evening. I suspect it's one reason Grusha sent you to meet us today. She'll want you to attend. So, what do you think?"

"What do I think of—you're asking me out?"

"No need to panic. Remember, we're on the same team. Do you have any objection to going with me?"

"No, of course not, but I don't expect to be here that long."

He smiled faintly. "Oh, knowing Grusha, I suspect you will be."

Chapter 8

She took the stairs up to Dr. Pollard's suite, examining the little fizz of interest that had bubbled up at Ian McAllister's invitation. No denying he was an attractive man who had an intriguing air of much left unsaid.

She stepped from the stairwell into a quiet hallway and hooked her cell phone earpiece over her ear. Giving a voice command, she moved over to a window for privacy. Below was Central Park, the bushes and trees still laden with snow, making a pretty Currier and Ives picture.

On the third ring, Kelly Brennan, her best friend since childhood, answered in a sleepy voice. "Yo."

"You're still asleep? It's nearly noon."

"Aw, hell, Claudia, who gave *you* a grasshopper suppository? Or have you forgotten you're in the Big Apple?" She could hear Kelly yawn. "I was up all night, going through briefs."

"Fruit of the Loom or Jockeys?"

Kelly snickered. "That's just wishful thinking. So, are you waking me up just to remind me that you're gadding around New York while I'm stuck here, prepping for trial, or was there actually something on your mind?"

"Right now, I'm looking at Central Park. It's been snowing and . . ."

"Tell me that's not why you called."

"No. I think something's going on between Joel and Alex."

"No freaking way!" Kelly was wide awake now.

"*Yes* freaking way. Every time I talk to him she's there, too, but he avoids talking about her, and . . ."

"Jeez, Claudia, you've been bitching about him *hovering* over you and being too protective. Time to make up your mind."

"I know, I know. Maybe it's just . . . Maybe I'm feeling a little guilty."

"Guilty? Whatcha been doing, hoochie mama?"

"Nothing. I just, well, I had a . . . reaction . . . to a man I just met. I'm not going to pursue it, but . . . would I have a *reaction* if I were really in love with—"

Kelly wouldn't let her finish. "You're human, aren't you? You can love Joel and still get your knickers in a twist over another guy—trust me."

"That's not quite the right cliché, but thanks for the thought."

"Okay, Claud, cut the bullshit. Really. What's going on over there?"

"Actually something pretty strange *is* going on. I just found out . . ."

The elevator doors opened across the hall and a woman and child stepped out, the child chattering loudly. Claudia swivelled back to face the window and lowered her voice. "Sorry, can't talk about that right now. Later."

"Okay, so tell me about the guy."

"He's a doctor who works for my client. Kind of reminds me of Alan Rickman, the actor."

"You mean *Professor Snape*?"

"Rickman isn't Snape in real life, you dork. He doesn't have long, greasy hair."

"If we're doing Harry Potter bad guys, I'll go for luscious Lucius Malfoy."

"We're not *doing* anyone—I'm just noticing. He invited me to a party."

"Well, go, for fuck's sake; enjoy yourself. You don't have to *sleep* with him."

Claudia thought of the meticulous way Ian McAllister had arranged the accessories on his desk. His almost-mocking demeanor. "No, I certainly won't do that. Anyway, I'm really not sure what I think about him. He has a couple of quirks—" She glanced at her watch. "Hey, sorry I woke you. I've gotta go see a psychologist."

"My god, Claudia, you went all the way to New York to get shrink-rapped?"

"Not *me.* She shrinks the applicants for my client."

Kelly's voice was always as expressive as her face. This time, it held a laugh. "If you say so, Grasshopper. Just don't let her give you any lotions, potions, or untowardly motions."

Unlike Dr. McAllister's fashionably appointed waiting room, Donna Pollard's had the ambience of a homey den. You could imagine friends and family members gathering for an informal chat on the high-end home-style sofa. On the wall opposite the entry door, a soft-focus Kinkade painting drew the eye: a rose-festooned stone stairway that led upward into unknown places. Cutesy symbolism for someone engaged in self-exploration?

The air was at least ten degrees warmer than the hallway, and three times as stuffy. Feeling as if she stepped inside a marshmallow bunny, Claudia slipped out of her trench coat and folded it over her arm. She crossed to the interior door and followed the instructions on a small card to ring the doorbell upon arrival for an appointment.

The thick pile carpeting muffled the sound on the other side of the wall, but she thought she heard a faint ring. A few seconds later the door opened, framing a short, slender woman who looked like a middle-aged schoolgirl from the fifties: gray hair clipped back into barrettes, a light blue twin set and plaid woolen skirt with sensible black pumps.

Claudia held out her hand with a smile. "Dr. Pollard? I'm Claudia Rose. I'm the new graphologist for Elite Introductions."

The woman didn't smile back. Her body language was stiff, protective—elbows held close to her sides, putting up barriers. "I'm not Dr. Pollard," she said, keeping a grasp on the doorknob and ignoring Claudia's hand. "I'm her secretary, Dorothy French. Unfortunately the doctor is not going to be able to see you."

"I don't understand. Grusha Olinetsky's assistant said she'd made an appointment for me. Is Dr. Pollard not here?"

"She *is* here, but there's been a . . . a situation." The muscles around the woman's mouth bunched into a tight grimace. "We had a break-in this morning. It's all very upsetting. The doctor is lying down."

"Someone broke in?" Claudia echoed. "Is she okay?"

"That all depends on what you mean by *okay*. She needs some time to herself."

Borrowing from Dr. McAllister's "same team" reasoning, Claudia urged her. "Ms. French, please, if there's something I can do, let me help. We're both consultants for Elite Introductions."

Conflicting emotions played out across the woman's face. Longtime habit of maintaining professional distance probably made it difficult for her to share her concerns. Claudia nudged a little more. "It's okay, you can talk to me. I'm not a client."

Dorothy French's small frame shuddered, and the act seemed to release something in her. She stepped into the waiting room with Claudia, shutting the door behind her, and moved over to the sofa. She sat on the edge, her back so straight she could have held a stack of books on her head. Finishing-school straight. Tension straight. But the hands clasped in fists on her lap betrayed her agitation.

Claudia could see that if she wanted to learn what had happened she would have to let Dorothy French ease into the story on her own. She sat at the other end of the sofa, allowing the woman time to gather her thoughts.

"All right," Dorothy said at last. "All right." Having decided to unburden herself, her words came tumbling out. "As I said, there was an intruder, and Dr. Pollard *has* been hurt." At Claudia's indrawn breath, she put out a restraining hand. "Not *seriously* hurt. At least, not in a physical way as far as I can tell. I mean, he struck her, but . . . As you can imagine, it was very upsetting for her. For us both."

"I'm sure it must have been. Did she walk in on someone?"

French gave an impatient shake of her head. "No, no, it was the other way round. She was in the kitchen, making herself a cup of tea. If I'd been here, he wouldn't have escaped, I can tell you that!" The fierce spark of anger in her eyes was convincing.

Claudia said, "Lucky for him you *weren't* here. He must have been pretty brazen to just walk in."

"It was very early. He wouldn't have expected

anyone to be here at that hour. When Dr. P has trouble sleeping, she comes here to the office and works on her progress notes. It's dead quiet early in the morning, no phone calls or appointments." Dorothy paused to take a breath. She continued to squeeze her hands tightly together, as if holding on to them gave her a sense of security.

"That's what she'd done this morning, arrived before five o'clock. As I said, she was in the kitchen. She heard the back door open—the private entrance. It was locked, of course, but that lock *was* a bit flimsy. In fact, I've been at the building super for ages to have it seen to. This fellow must have used a credit card or some such, if the television shows are to be believed. Poor Dr. P was literally *petrified* when she heard him. She couldn't move a muscle."

"I don't blame her," Claudia said. "It sounds very frightening. What was he looking for? Drugs?"

"Heaven knows what he was after. We don't keep anything of that sort here, other than our own prescription meds. Dr. P hid behind the kitchen door and then she heard him going through things in her office. She thought it would be safe to go out the back, the way he'd come in. Unfortunately, he heard her and came rushing out into the hallway and knocked her down. Bashed her over the head. I don't know what he hit her with, but it was heavy enough to leave her senseless. He got away while she was unconscious, the bastard."

"Was she able to describe him to the police?" Claudia asked.

But Dorothy French had reached the end of her willingness to dispense information. "As I told you earlier, the doctor is resting," she said, rising from the sofa. "And now that you know the circumstances, you must understand why she's unable to keep the appointment."

Claudia was getting a bad feeling. She didn't believe in coincidences any more than Jovanic did. She stood. "Ms. French. Dorothy, wait. I do understand, believe me, I do. But I need to speak to Dr. Pollard now, more than ever. It's urgent. There's a very serious matter I need to discuss with her before I return to the West Coast."

"Out of the question."

"Look, three people are dead. I think it's entirely possible this break-in you've had could be connected to their deaths."

Dorothy French stared at her. "What on *earth* are you talking about?"

Claudia struggled to put her suspicions into the right words. There were just too many bad things happening to people connected to Elite Introductions, too close together. But if she was wrong, and what she said got back to Grusha Olinetsky, she could find herself on the butt end of a defamation lawsuit. "Would you *please* just ask—" She broke off as the interior door opened and a woman appeared in the doorway, holding an ice pack to the base of her skull.

Chapter 9

Dr. Donna Pollard reminded Claudia of Mrs. Santa Claus. Her eyes were the blue of stonewashed denim, and a halo of white-blond cotton candy hair framed the round face. Two high spots of color blotched a complexion that was currently a light shade of pale. Claudia's grandmother would have described the doctor as *zaftig*.

Pollard adjusted the ice pack and reached out to grasp Claudia's hand in her own. "Come along with me," she said. "We'll talk."

Behind them, Dorothy French made a huffing sound in protest. The psychologist turned to her and put a hand on her shoulder. "It's *all right*, Dorothy. Stop fussing. I'm fine."

They went to a small room with subdued lighting. Furnished more simply than the anteroom, it contained a low-slung easy chair and a love seat, a coffee table crammed between them. On the table, a box of tissues had been strategically placed for emotional clients. The walls were a muted shade of cobalt with matching drapes. Framed abstract artwork looked like Rorschach inkblots, waiting to be interpreted by the viewer.

Donna Pollard lowered herself into the easy chair and gingerly laid her head back, cushioning the ice pack behind her neck. "Please, sit anywhere."

"That looks pretty painful," Claudia said, opting for the middle of the sofa. "Are you all right?"

The psychologist's lips twisted into a crooked smile. "Well, it's certainly no fun, but it'll heal. I'm sorry for the misunderstanding about your appointment."

"You've had a very upsetting experience. Under the circumstances, I wouldn't have pressed to see you, but there's an urgent—"

"Dorothy is just being protective," Pollard interrupted. "It's her job."

"I understand. Sometimes we need to have someone protecting us, but—"

"Do you have someone who protects you?"

"Uh, yes, I do. Dr. Pollard—"

"Something bad has happened to you, hasn't it, Claudia?" Dr. Pollard removed the ice pack and laid it on her lap, her head tilted attentively, nodding slightly in encouragement.

Claudia felt her heart lurch. "What makes you say that?"

"I'm trained to recognize such things. There's a deep sadness in you. I feel it."

"Somebody I knew was murdered a couple of months ago."

Why am I telling this to a total stranger?

Pollard made a sound of distress. "What a terrible thing!" She lowered her voice and leaned forward. "But as terrible as that is, I think there's more, isn't there? You've been sad for a long time. Far longer than a couple of months."

The walls closed in. For a fleeting moment, Claudia actually considered getting up and running from the room, running from the intrusive questions. But then she wouldn't get her own questions answered.

"Dr. Pollard, I really don't think—"

"Why don't you tell me about it." Pollard's voice was soft, almost hypnotic.

"Thank you for the offer. I appreciate the thought. But why don't we stick with Elite Introductions business."

"I can see that you're hurting, dear. Talking about it would help so much. You'll see."

The insistent way Pollard was coming at her was unlike any therapist she had ever met, especially since she wasn't a client. And why was the doctor behaving as if nothing had happened to her that morning? Claudia shook her head, bent on getting the meeting back on track. "Talking about me is not what I'm here for, Doctor."

"But it could be . . . well, all right then, if you're sure. But if you change your mind . . ."

"I'll remember that."

Pollard nodded, giving in with a knowing smile. "Well, okay. Welcome to the Elite team."

"Thank you. I've just come from having a chat with Dr. McAllister," she said, relieved to have turned Pollard's attention away from her.

At the mention of McAllister's name, something changed in Pollard's eyes. What did *that* mean? Claudia plunged on, interested to see where it went. "He mentioned the party on Saturday night. I'm looking forward to meeting some of the clients whose handwritings I'll be analyzing."

"I'm sure they'll be very interested in meeting you, too."

"Do you think you'll be up to going to the party?"

"Oh yes, dear, a little knock on the head isn't going to stop me." Donna Pollard gave a bright smile to underscore just how fine she was.

"A little knock on the head? You were attacked by

an intruder. That's nothing to shrug off. Have you been checked for concussion?"

Dr. Pollard reached over and patted Claudia's hand. "The baroness expects me to attend these things. She needs me to help facilitate, since I've already met everybody who will be attending."

"Why do I have the feeling that you don't want to talk about the break-in?"

"You're right. I can't say I do."

"Well then, there's something I'd like to ask you about a couple of the dating club clients."

Pollard's face closed down. "I'm sorry, Claudia, but I can't discuss clients. It goes against professional ethics. You should know that."

"Even though we're consulting about the same people for the same company?"

"Even though. It's just not allowed."

"Dr. McAllister wasn't willing to help, either." There it was again. That look. "Does it make a difference if these people are dead?"

There was a gasp from the other side of the coffee table, then a deafening silence.

"Are you *aware* that three of Grusha's clients are dead?" asked Claudia, Pollard's posturing and pretense that everything was fine and dandy wearing thin. "Are you aware that those clients were all under thirty, and that they all had accidents, and—"

"Stop," Pollard protested in a faint voice. "I know about them. But I don't see the point in talking about it."

"Can you help me understand why Grusha would give me the handwritings of dead clients to analyze?"

"I have no idea. As you said, there were a couple of very unfortunate accidents. But that's all they were."

"No one suggested they were anything else." Claudia wondered why Donna Pollard was being defensive. "Since you've mentioned it, though, don't you think the odds are a bit high for *three* deaths to be chance occurrences?"

"Stranger things than that happen all the time," Pollard answered quickly. "I don't know why Grusha wants you to analyze their handwriting, but why don't you just do it? That's what you're here for, isn't it?"

"Is it?"

"How would *I* know? I've just been hit on the head; I probably do have a concussion. I need to lie down."

Something had touched a raw nerve. What was Pollard guarding so closely?

"Did you call the police about the break-in?"

Pollard hesitated.

"Why didn't you?"

"There was nothing to tell them." Petulance. "Why create a big fuss and upset the neighbors? I didn't even see him, he came up on me from behind."

"What about fingerprints?"

"I'm sure he wore gloves."

"But you don't know for sure?"

"He didn't take anything. Nothing was missing."

"What do you think he might have been after?"

"Drugs and money, of course. It was . . . just a random break-in."

"You don't really think that, do you?" Claudia shifted to the lip of the sofa and leaned toward Donna Pollard, putting herself into her space. "What are you afraid of, Dr. Pollard?"

"You mean, besides confronting an intruder?"

"You know that's not what I meant."

"What else would I be afraid of?"

"That's what I'd like to know. Let's see, I've been in New York for less than twenty-four hours and I've discovered that three young people are dead, all of whom you've met as Grusha's clients, and now you've had a break-in. Don't you think those things just might be connected? I do. And I think you have an idea of who's responsible."

"Does Grusha know that you know about all this?"

"Not yet, but she will soon. So why don't we just move on and pool our resources? Maybe we can get a clearer picture of what's going on here."

"Nothing's going on, I tell you."

"Dr. Pollard, I'm not leaving until you tell me what you know, or think you know."

"I don't know *anything*, I really don't. It's just a very unfortunate series of coincidences."

Claudia didn't move. Donna Pollard's face scrunched into an expression of irritation and she gave a loud, resigned exhale. "What is it you want to know? Just tell me."

"There are two women and one man who have died. Let's start with the women. What do Heather Lloyd and Shellee Jones have in common?"

Pollard gave it some thought. She spoke with marked reluctance. "You're asking the wrong question."

"All right then, what *should* I be asking?"

"It might be more effective to look at whom they dated."

"That information wasn't in their files. Do *you* know?"

"New clients are introduced to three potential matches. There are crossovers."

"What do you mean, crossovers?"

"Several women are introduced to the same man, or vice versa," Pollard explained. "You have to understand, I may not know how everyone was matched up. Grusha doesn't always keep me in the loop—it's not necessary. But I do know that Shellee Jones went out with three men: Avram Cohen, John Shaw, and Marcus Bernard. Heather was also introduced to John Shaw. She went out with him once, but she didn't like him, said he was too old for her, and she was absolutely right. She had asked to meet a man who was a *little* older, but it makes no sense to introduce a twenty-five-year-old girl to a man who's nearly forty. When Heather died, Grusha was in the process of interviewing some younger men for her. She'd also dated Avram Cohen and Ryan Turner, but according to her, there was no chemistry with Avram. I don't know what happened with Ryan."

Ryan Turner was dead. Shellee was dead. Heather was dead. But Avram, John, and Marcus were not. What did it mean? She was trying to assimilate the news when Dr. Pollard dropped another bomb.

"I suppose I should tell you that three of the same men also dated Jessica McAllister."

That stopped Claudia cold. "Who is Jessica McAllister?"

"Ian's daughter, of course."

Chapter 10

Having opened this new can of worms, Donna Pollard decided it was time to withdraw and refuse to say anything further. She closed her eyes, put the ice pack back on her neck, and called out for Dorothy French to escort Claudia to the door. The meeting was at an end.

Grabbing a cab over to Elite Introductions, Claudia felt her head swim with questions. Why hadn't Dr. McAllister mentioned his daughter's involvement with some of the men at the dating club? It seemed a major omission when he knew of the deaths of two female clients. Two female clients he had examined.

Grusha Olinetsky was late again. The matchmaker flashed a toothy smile as the door to her office opened and she came out, but Claudia could have sworn there was something sad in her walk as she came toward her.

I sound like Donna Pollard, she told herself. But she couldn't shake the impression that Grusha's cheerful demeanor was merely a mask.

"Claudia!" The matchmaker's hands were outstretched in welcome and she took Claudia's shoulders, pressing one cheek to her own, and then the other, continental style. "I have been so much looking forward to seeing you again and hearing everything you have to report to me. But first, I have here someone who is very eager to meet you. Please, to come into my office."

Across from Grusha's desk, a man sat in the chair Claudia had occupied the day before. He rose when they entered, an impressive figure in a leather bomber jacket over V-necked cashmere, khaki cargo pants and military boots. *Indiana Jones in Manhattan.* And as easy on the eyes as Harrison Ford in the films. Short brown hair shot with gold highlights, glossed into hip spikes. Six feet, broad shoulders, probably mid-thirties. Indy's whip and battered fedora would have completed the picture.

Something familiar . . .

Claudia struggled to place what it was, returning her gaze to the squarish face with its sexy cleft chin. The picture in her mind's eye sharpened and came into focus. *Wow.* He was clean-shaven now, but in his file photos he'd been sporting a graying beard and wearing a baseball cap. She guessed that he'd also shed some pounds since the photos were taken. The devilish grin was what had clued her in to his identity.

He offered a deeply tanned hand. "Marcus Bernard," he said at the precise moment his name popped into her head. "I've been looking forward to meeting you, Claudia."

"Marcus vants to hire you," Grusha interrupted. "He needs you to analyze the people who go to vork for him."

"Construction, right?" Claudia said, remembering his bio. "You build hotels."

"You got it." He blasted her with the full force of the smile. "Hotels, condos, shopping malls, office buildings, you name it, we build it."

"I am taking a suite in his new building," said Grusha. "Dr. Pollard and Dr. McAllister will have consulting offices there."

"Sounds convenient, everybody together in the same space. The clients should like that."

"Precisely," said Grusha. "The building is scheduled to open in July. It's simply gorgeous, the Bernard Building."

"It's not *quite* Trump Tower," Marcus said with mock humility. "But I'm pretty proud of it. I'd love to show it to you, Claudia."

"If I'm here long enough, I'd love to see it." She recalled his handwriting: smooth talker, abundant energy, the type who found it hard to keep still. Even now, he was tossing his keys from one hand to the other. That could get on your nerves if it went on too long.

"I hire a lot of people," he said. "In this business, they're not always on the level, so I'm looking for something to back up the drug tests. The baroness here says you can help me with that. Considering how savvy she is, I'm willing to listen."

Claudia nodded. "I work with a lot of employers, analyzing their job applicants. I'd be happy to work with you."

He caught her eye and sent her a boyish smile that probably melted harder hearts than hers. "How about lunch? We can discuss the possibilities over a nice Scottish salmon. Have you been to the Gotham?"

It had already occurred to her that Marcus was one of the men who had dated both Shellee Jones and Heather Lloyd. She did want to talk to him and find out what he knew. But right now, it was more important for her to marshal her thoughts and figure out where Dr. Pollard's information fit. She returned his smile. "It sounds wonderful, but I really have to talk with Grusha right now. A rain check?"

She caught Grusha's disapproving frown. "No, no, you go vit Marcus now," Grusha said, flapping her hands at them. "Go, eat! The Gotham is fabulous. Ve talk later. I have some free time later this afternoon."

"This can't wait," Claudia said. "I'd rather make it sooner than later."

Marcus reached into his pocket and handed her a black and gold embossed business card. "Are you free for dinner? Call my office when you're finished here and I'll have my secretary make arrangements for my car to pick you up at your hotel." He gave her a salute and leaned in to brush Grusha's cheek with his lips. "Be sure to let me know as soon as you've found Ms. Right for me, Grusha. I'm gettin' horny."

Well, that was crass.

Grusha gave him a sidelong glance from under her lashes. "Ah, Marcus, I doubt that you lack for someone to relieve your distress in the meantime. But yes, dahling, of course. I call you soon. You know I have someone in mind, perfect for you. I have to vait for the results of the background check and the doctors. Then I vill give her handwriting to Claudia for analysis. And when ve know she has passed the test, you vill meet this beautiful young lady and ve vill vatch the chemistry begin to bubble."

"Okay, okay, just don't make me wait too long."

As Marcus Bernard strolled out of the office, Grusha turned on Claudia with an irritated glare. "You should have gone vit him. Is not good to refuse a client like Marcus when he shows interest in talking to you. He is always hiring and firing people, and he pay vell. He can be very good client for you."

"I appreciate the referral. Thank you, Grusha, I will

see him later. Now, could we close the door please? I really do have something important to discuss with you."

"Fine. Sit down; ve talk." Content to have made her point, Grusha leaned out the door and called to Sonya to bring coffee. She closed the door and took her seat behind the desk, giving Claudia an arch look. "So, how did you like Ian?"

"Ian was fine. But before we get into that, I'd like to know what made you choose the particular files you gave me."

"What do you mean? I vanted to see what you vould say about their personalities. Do you have a report for me?"

"Yes, I have a report. Three of them are dead. Now you tell me, what's wrong with this picture?"

The matchmaker's face paled. Her eyes grew big and round. "How could you possibly know—who told you that?"

"What difference does it make how I know?"

"Which one of them? Was it Donna Pollard? Or was it Ian? Who—"

Claudia's patience was beginning to wear thin. "What's really going on here, Grusha? Why are these people dead? Tell me honestly: Why did you bring me to New York?"

"Stop shouting at me! You are making me nervous."

"I'm making *you* nervous?" Claudia echoed, getting to her feet, prepared to walk if she didn't get some immediate answers. She had been through too much, and her fuse was shorter than it used to be. "How do you think *I* feel? You've been playing me for a fool, bringing me here for some secret purpose of your own. That makes *me* pretty damn nervous. I want to know why you're using me."

"No, no, Claudia, vait—that's not it! You are not a fool. You are very smart voman. *That* is why I bring you here."

"If that's what you really think, then please don't insult my intelligence anymore. Stop this blatant attempt to manipulate me. I want the truth this time."

Grusha held up her hands, placating. "All right, please, sit down. I tell you everything."

Claudia hesitated, then dropped back into the guest chair waiting for the explanation. She felt skeptical that what she would hear would be the truth.

"Ve talk confidential, yes?"

"Yes, of course."

"So. Is like this. I had business in another place a few years ago. A girl who vork for me make trouble. She vant me to pay her more money. I say no. She quit. Is okay; I don't need her vit the attitude! But she call my clients and she tell them things about me—lies. I run legitimate business, but this girl, when she lie, she get some people to go to court and testify against me." Grusha's expression darkened. "Cost a lot of money, a lot of my life. That thing hurt my business very bad, very bad. So I move to East Coast, I vork and vork to build again, make new clients, new business." The deep-set eyes had traded warmth for flat black intensity. "I cannot afford *anything* to interfere this time. You understand me, yes? I have to make sure things are done right."

As she listened, Claudia resolved to research the story on the Internet for herself. There might be some articles about Grusha and her court case. She said, "I understand that you had problems before, and that *something* is apparently going on now. But what does this have to do with the mistakes Andy Nicholson made? Or did you just make that up to get me here?"

"No! Is true." The matchmaker's lip started to tremble. She took a folded tissue from a pocket of her dress and pressed it to the corners of her eyes. "Somebody *is* trying to sabotage my business, but I do not yet know who or why . . ." Her voice trailed away and she spread her hands in resignation. "So. Claudia, I need your help. You have good reputation, you can save me."

"Let me understand what you're telling me—that Andy Nicholson failed to identify red flags in the handwriting of a client who is now trying to sabotage you?"

"Yes, yes, that is it," Grusha said with evident relief.

"And you've identified some people who you suspect could the culprits. That's what those files are?"

"Suspects, I—I am not sure."

"If you're saying that you want me to pick the most likely suspect from this group, there are a couple who concern me. But that doesn't answer why you gave me the handwritings of dead people."

Grusha hesitated. "It is true what you say, that some clients have died in terrible accidents, but . . ."

"*And* Dr. Pollard's office was broken into this morning."

"What? What you are talking about?"

"I guess you haven't heard. She was attacked in her office early this morning. That didn't feel like a coincidence to me."

Grusha's brows knit in a worried frown. Claudia could see that the news had shaken her.

"*Attacked*? Donna was attacked?"

"Yes. Hit over the head, in fact. I think she has a concussion. Yet, for some unknown reason, she's refused to call the police. I don't suppose you have any idea why that might be."

"What did this person vant from her?"

"He didn't stick around long enough to let her know. So, Grusha, tell me: What is *really* happening here?"

"Too many bad things, too close together. *Something* is very wrong. Someone is behind all these things; I am convinced of it."

"Well, yes, it's pretty obvious that someone is. But why? *Why* would someone do this? There has to be a motive."

Grusha groaned. "I vish I know. Someone is trying to sabotage me again. This much is clear."

"And there are people dying, so you have to go to the police. *That* much is clear."

"No! I *cannot*! I vill be ruined if it comes out. *That* is why I ask you to come. I need you to find this person for me. Their *handwriting* vill show who it is, and why these people are dead."

"Grusha, I hope you understand handwriting only reveals someone's potential. It can't predict for sure what the writer is going to do. But what I can do is describe the behavior that the handwriting reflects on the page. Guessing games are out."

"I thought—I thought if you could find something in their personality that connects them . . . Claudia, I have faith in you. Remember, I read all about your reputation."

Claudia gave her a thin smile. "That's all well and good, but I'm not psychic. What made you pick those particular clients?"

"I gave you the files of the men who dated the two girls and I put in some other ones as a—what do they call it? A test, some kind of test."

"A blind test."

"Yes, that is it. Andrew Nicholson give them all

good reports, but I had some questions about them; that is all." Spots of color rose in her cheeks and her eyes moved to the left.

She's lying about something.

"Why do you think Nicholson was wrong about these particular men? What have they done to make you suspicious?"

Grusha hesitated. "I have no reason to suspect them. Just that some of them dated the same girls."

"Grusha, for heaven's sake! If you believe there's a killer loose, targeting your business—"

"Claudia, please, you have to help me. The police vill not believe me."

"Why not?"

Another long pause.

"Why not, Grusha?"

"Because . . . because I have trouble vit them in the past."

"What kind of trouble?"

"It has nothing to do vit this. But once the police know you, you are never again free. If I go to them, they vill immediately suspect me of something, and it vill get into the media, and then—"

"I'm not a private detective," Claudia interrupted. "And I'm not interested in being part of some *Mission: Impossible* investigation. I've been close to murder before, very recently, and I don't want to be anywhere near it again. If that is what's going on here, you can count me out."

"Vait! Please look to see if anything from the handwriting vill give a clue about these people. If you find something that connects them—if ve find some proof, I vill go to police. That is all you have to do. What do you think?"

"I think I don't like it; that's what I think. The police

need to be made aware of—I'm sorry, excuse me." A beep from Claudia's cell phone signaled the arrival of a text or picture message. Murmuring an apology for not switching off her phone during the meeting, she removed it from her pocket and looked at the screen. The number was Annabelle's cell phone. *What now?*

The LCD screen said she had a video message and gave the option of viewing it now or later. She clicked view now.

Grusha's voice came at her from a long distance. "Claudia? Are you all right? You've gone pale. Is bad news for you?"

Chapter 11

Even on the small cell phone screen, Claudia was easily able to recognize the woman with the blunt-cut blond hair: Detective Alexandra Vega, her arms wrapped around Jovanic, her body pressed up against him, her lips on his.

He wasn't fighting it.

After a moment, Alex stepped away and they both got into a car. The video had lasted only fifteen seconds, but Claudia felt sick. She may have had her suspicions for the last several weeks that there was something going on between Alex and Jovanic, but having it stuck in her face this way was a body blow. It was one time she had desperately wanted to be wrong.

There had to be an explanation.

It won't be good enough.

Learning to trust him hadn't been easy. Not that he had done anything to make her doubt him, but because painful past experience had taught her not to allow any man to get too close. Until this moment, she'd believed she had come a long way. The video unraveled her hard-won assurance. As she sat there, trying to look and act normal, her feelings were running the gamut from disbelief to anger to jealousy to grief.

After leaving Dr. Pollard, Claudia had intended to give Grusha the news that she was quitting the assignment and returning to the West Coast as soon as she could get a flight. She would repay the generous retainer. Now Annabelle's cell phone transmission had changed things. There was no point in rushing back to L.A.

In her heart, she questioned whether she was making the rational choice—maybe this was not the best time to make rash decisions. But before she could change her mind again, she turned to the matchmaker. "You just want me to analyze handwriting, right, not get involved in any investigation?"

"Yes, yes, just handwriting. I give you bonus, too."

"I don't need a bonus. Let's just get on with it."

Sonya was given instructions to order sandwiches from the deli on the ground floor of the building, and they prepared to brainstorm. The thought of food held no appeal for Claudia, but her decision to remain and help seemed to have renewed Grusha's energy and she was now bustling around her office, making space for their lunch.

Claudia took a break to tidy up. Annabelle's defiance of her order not to spy on Jovanic angered her, and she wanted to throttle Alex. She hadn't yet begun to think about what she would like to do to Jovanic.

She dampened a paper towel and dabbed it over her face, repaired her makeup. A little lipstick and blush made her look less like death warmed over. If she was going to stay on in New York, this was not the time to be depressed. She had a suspicion that despite her promises, Grusha might have been less than forthright. It was going to be important for Claudia to be alert during their conversation and listen for anything that was being communicated between the lines.

Before returning to Grusha's office, she gave herself a stern talking-to and forced the cell phone image out of her head.

"So, three of your clients have died—unless there are any *other* dead clients you haven't told me about?"

Grusha looked aghast. "God forbid!"

"Okay, then, two of the clients—Heather Lloyd and Ryan Turner—died in sporting accidents. One—Shellee Jones—had an allergic reaction to peanuts. It's too much to believe that all three of these were really accidents. But is it possible that any of them might have been genuine? The anaphylactic shock, maybe? Could that have been just a horrible coincidence?"

Grusha pounced on the suggestion. "Yes, of course! How could someone arrange such a thing at a restaurant? Poor Shellee does not belong vit the others!"

Her eagerness sent Claudia's guard up. For someone who had insisted that she come all the way across country to participate in this situation, Grusha seemed far too willing to drop part of it.

"For argument's sake," Claudia continued, "we'll take the worst-case scenario and assume that all three were deliberately killed. My question is motive. Why *these* particular people? The victims were of both genders; this isn't necessarily sexually motivated. From what I've read in their files I couldn't find anything that seemed to tie the three of them together, personality-wise. Both Heather's and Shellee's handwriting looked pretty typical of a lot of young women of their age and their position in life. Since they were club members, they must have had financial means. Ryan had especially good handwriting in the sense that he was emotionally mature and had a healthy self-image. So, what can you tell me about them?"

Grusha's hand automatically moved to the Lalique nude on her desk. "They were beautiful girls. Heather was a little airheaded, but she was beginning to be successful in her modeling career. She come to me for introduction because she was afraid men vanted her for the way she looked." She gave a rueful chuckle. "Is true—it was not her brains they were interested in. Men do not really vant those skinny girls, but I did not tell her that because I can sell the whole package. I give Heather what she vanted—three handsome rich men to choose from. She like Ryan best because he was sexy doctor. He was fourth-year resident and she saw potential for very nice future. He had family money, too. He was going to do very vell in plastic surgery. Poor boy."

"What about Shellee Jones?"

"Ah, that Shellee. Her father is suing the restaurant where she die. She had horrible death." Grusha grimaced. "Choking, could not get air. Poor Marcus, he feel so bad that he could not save her."

"Marcus?"

"All he could do was vatch her die."

"You mean he was there?"

"They were having dinner together. Was beautiful match. They were falling in love; vould have been vonderful vedding. He was devastated."

"He didn't look devastated just now. She only died three weeks ago and he's already complaining about being horny?"

Grusha gave a fatalistic shrug. "It was terrible thing, but he cannot go along wearing sackcloth and ashes for the rest of his life. They went out few times, that is all. Life goes on."

Just now, you had the wedding planned.

"Does Marcus have a motive to destroy your business?"

"Nobody have motive that I can think of." Grusha's mouth turned down. "Believe me; I have thought about it very much."

"The surviving men whose handwritings have problems," Claudia persisted. "Avram, John, and Marcus. There were red flags in all of them. Do you suspect them?"

"I told you, I do not have suspects. I give the files to you because these men I introduce to both Shellee and Heather. What problems do you see?"

"Okay, we'll review the problems." Claudia had brought the problem files in her briefcase. She pulled one out and riffled through the pages to the handwriting sample. "Let's talk about Avram Cohen. He has the potential for violent behavior."

"Cannot be. He is gentleman."

"He may be a gentleman when things are going well, but what about when he's under extreme stress? I believe he could lash out in a physical way and hurt someone."

"I cannot believe it," Grusha said, shaking her head again. "He is like a kitten."

"Kittens have sharp claws. Did he pass the psychological exam?"

"Sure, he did okay. Dr. Pollard never said anything wrong. And neither did the one before you—Nicholson."

"Yes, well, that's why you called me in, isn't it?" Claudia pointed out the tiny tics on Avram's lower loops. "These are indicators of sexual problems. Were you aware of that?"

A look of dismay crossed Grusha's face. *"Sexual*

problems? How could that be? He is virile young man. Cannot have sex problems."

"His handwriting shows sexual frustration. He could be having problems with impotence. He didn't discuss that with you?"

"Of course he did not! Maybe he tell Donna something, or Ian, not me. I don't take someone into the club who could not perform in bed!"

"Well, neither of the doctors is willing to discuss the clients with me, so that's something you'll need to follow up on. What about Marcus?" Claudia pulled out his file. "Charming con artist. He knows how to manipulate his way to success."

Grusha gave an indulgent smile and a little nod of acknowledgment, maybe even approval. "I see what you mean about Marcus; he is playboy. He love the game, the chase. He is good at—what is that vord—he *exploit* people's talents."

"In other words, he's a ruthless user who turns someone's strengths and weaknesses to his advantage."

Grusha's plump lips pursed into a rueful pout. "He is very good at getting what he vants."

"So, if he's not a suspect, you gave me his file because—?"

"Because he dated both girls."

It was a reasonable explanation, but was it the truth? Her body language was open, but Susan Rowan's words echoed: *She can be a cagey devil.*

"Let's take John Shaw next," Claudia suggested, watching for her reaction. So far everything she'd said, Grusha had shot down.

"Heather liked John. She vould have gone out vit him again, but he was not so attracted to her after the first date. Said she was too—let me think—superficial.

"Shellee vent out vit him a couple times, too, but

something happen between them. She vould not tell me what it was, just said he was too old for her."

"Why do you think something happened?"

Grusha tapped her temple with her fingertip. "Intuition, dahling. The vay she look at him, it was not the same, after." She nodded, sure of herself. "Something happen."

"Do you think he could be capable of—"

"John—I am not so sure about him. Another one that idiot Nicholson said was good. What did you see in his handwriting?"

Claudia leaned down to remove a lighted hand magnifier from her briefcase. After pulling Shaw's sample from his file, she switched on the light and let the lens hover over some of the upper loop letters that had indentations near the apex. "These dents suggest to me that at some point he's probably sustained a major blow to the head." She rotated the file so that Grusha could see what she was talking about. "See this? If I'm right, that kind of injury could affect the way he thinks. Seeing how he's in the population of suspects, that's worth serious consideration. But whether he has a head injury or not, he's definitely marching to his own drummer."

"I see." Looking thoughtful, Grusha hit the call button on her phone and asked Sonya to freshen their coffee, then peered through the magnifier again. "John is famous photojournalist. He photograph the soldiers in Iraq. A bomb vent off near him. He is lucky to be alive."

"So, at the very least, he might have had a concussion," Claudia noted, filing away that interesting piece of data to mull over later.

"I am having a little soiree on Saturday. You can ask him about it when you meet him there."

"I heard about the party. Dr. McAllister offered to take me."

"Is vonderful idea! You vill like Ian, trust me."

Claudia started to protest that she was in a relationship; then she remembered the video Annabelle had transmitted to her cell phone. "You're matchmaking, aren't you, Grusha? I'm not looking for a new man in my life."

A broad grin spread over Grusha's face. "I cannot help myself. I am very good *svacha*—matchmaker. Ian is fascinating man; you enjoy him. Now, my dahling, I have to meet vit a new client. You go; think about what ve need to do next. Ve talk later."

During the ride back to the hotel, Claudia thought about the video. She resolved that when she spoke to Jovanic about it she would be calm and self-possessed. She would not jump to conclusions. She would practice trusting him, and she would allow him to explain.

Back in her room, she called his number, but the voice that answered was not his.

"Detective Joel Jovanic's phone."

Her self-possession deserted her faster than she could blink. "*Alex*? This is Claudia. Where's Joel?"

"Oh, hi, Claudia. He's in the shower. Do you want me to have him call you back?"

"What's he doing in the shower when you're there?"

Alex gave a little laugh. More like a purr. "My bad. I spilled coffee all over him. He wanted to clean up before we went back to the office. It's all totally innocent, Claudia, nothing to worry about."

"Who's worried?" *Liar, liar.*

"Wait a second, I think he just turned off the water." Claudia heard her call out, "Hey, JJ."

JJ?

The blood was pounding in her ears as she clicked the end button.

Jovanic called back a few minutes later, but she let it ring through to voice mail. She couldn't trust herself to speak to him right now. Instead, she phoned Marcus Bernard and arranged to meet him for dinner later.

Stay busy; don't think about Joel and Alex.

Easier said than done. She threw herself into Internet research on Heather Lloyd. That would eat up some time. She looked up the ski lodge in Stowe, Vermont, that had been mentioned in the article about Lloyd's death. She called the number and asked to speak to the manager.

The manager's manner was obsequious until he learned the reason for her call. As soon as she told him she was inquiring about Heather Lloyd's accident, his attitude did an about-face. "You're a reporter," he accused her with disdain.

"No, I'm a, er, a friend of the family," Claudia said, fumbling over the lie.

"Our insurance company is handling the matter. Why don't you call them, or the police? They both took a report."

After a couple of abortive attempts to get him to talk about the skiing accident, she gave it up as a bad job. Maybe she would get better results in person. If she went to the ski lodge and checked in as a guest, she could question the staff about the death. If she appeared as someone who had read about Heather Lloyd's accident in the newspaper and was curious about what had happened, she might get a better reception than with the more direct approach, which had gotten her nowhere. Would Grusha spring for a trip to Stowe?

Maybe I should get a PI license. She quickly rejected the idea, laughing at herself. She would do better to stick to her assignment, which was to analyze hand-writing and give her opinion on the personality traits she found there.

The latest batch of e-mail contained one from Peggy Yum, the *Hard Evidence* producer.

Sorry you weren't willing to work with us on this seg-ment. We found someone who didn't have a problem with it.

Does everybody *have to have an attitude today?*
Claudia shot back an e-mail, asking who they were going to use. Yum must have been at her computer, as her reply was as fast as an instant message.

Andrew Nicholson. Do you know him?

Shit! She knew she would have to warn Grusha about his upcoming appearance on the show. She knew from personal experience that Andy had no scruples. There was no telling what he might say to Peggy Yum about Grusha and Elite Introductions now that he had lost the account.

It hadn't taken him long to find another job—*her* job. Claudia clicked back to her in-box, wondering what dark forces had prompted Yum to seek out her nemesis.

Some handwriting samples had arrived by e-mail attachment from one of her major clients, an employ-ment agency. They were seeking to fill the position of project manager of a large hotel being constructed in Portland.

The remainder of the afternoon passed quickly. One by one, Claudia analyzed the samples of the top three candidates and typed up her report. One candidate in particular stood out as having the personality traits required for the job. She was happy to give the positive feedback, and clicked the send button with a sense of satisfaction.

There was still some time before she needed to get ready for dinner. The work had left her tired and she stretched out on the bed. The moment her eyes closed, the mind chatter began: Joel and Alex. Heather Lloyd's death. Shellee Jones' death. Alex and Joel. Ryan Turner's death. Alex and Joel. John Shaw's possible concussion. All the other players in Grusha Olinetsky's drama. Alex and Joel. Alex and Joel. Alex and Joel.

The room had darkened and fat raindrops splattered against the window like bugs on a windshield. Even after she'd gotten up and switched on all the lamps, the light didn't help to lift her spirits. She felt as gray and gloomy as the winter afternoon sky.

Her eyes kept roaming to the desk, to the cell phone tempting her to pick up the voice mail she knew Jovanic had left. She started toward it a couple of times, but something stopped her. What could he possibly say that would make her feel better about what she'd seen? She had allowed him to get too close, and now it felt as if he had betrayed her.

She fought the impulse until it had swelled and taken on a life of its own. When the battle had finally given her a headache, Claudia gave up and dialed voice mail.

Jovanic's recorded voice was normal, no inflection of guilt or worry in his tone. Not as though he had double-dealt her. "Hey, babe," he said. "I saw your number on my phone. Why didn't you leave a message? Call me back."

She hooked the wireless headset over her ear and tapped the button for voice command. "Call Joel."

He picked up right away, as if he had been waiting for her. "Hey, babe. I've been waiting for you to call. Where are you?"

"Didn't Alex tell you I called?"

"*Alex?*" Was his tone guarded, or was it her imagination, playing overtime? She'd churned it over so much, she could no longer be sure.

"Alex didn't tell me anything. When did you talk to her?"

"When you were in the *shower*," Claudia snapped, then added a sarcastic, "*JJ.*"

The sarcasm went over his head. "What the hell is she doing answering my cell phone?"

"What the hell was she doing at your apartment while you were in the shower?"

His hesitation went on a tick too long, leaving Claudia to wonder whether he was cooking up a story intended to mollify her. She had never known him to lie to her, and it came as a small relief when his account matched Alex's.

"Alex spilled coffee on my shirt. It was easier for her to wait for me here while I cleaned up. Otherwise, I would have had to dump her at the office, come home, change, and then go back over there to pick her up again."

"It might be easier for me to buy that if you two hadn't been liplocked this morning. So, what's the explanation for that?"

"What? Where did you—"

"Annabelle took it upon herself to play shutterbug, so don't bother denying it."

Through the phone, Claudia heard an angry exhale. "Annabelle is a royal pain in the ass. There's nothing to deny. We were staking out this house over on Sawtelle. I stupidly drank too much coffee and had to run down to the gas station on the corner to take a leak. I was almost back to the car when the suspect came out of the house and started walking in our direction. Alex jumped out of the car and *pretended* to kiss me so the guy wouldn't see my face. That's all it was."

"Really? It looked pretty convincing to me. You didn't even notice there was a kid taking video of you."

"Hey, *you* try sitting on a stakeout three nights in a row. Your mind starts to numb out, not to mention your ass. After a while you lose your sharpness. And we were focused on the suspect, which *wasn't* a teenage girl with a cell phone."

"Yeah, you were focused all right. I could see that for myself."

"She's twenty-eight, a baby. Anyway, if I was doing something bad with Alex, don't you think I'd be more careful about it?"

"Gosh, honey, that's a *big* comfort." Claudia packed as much irony as she could into her words.

"Listen, I have something else to tell you," Jovanic said, apparently finished with the subject of Alex, even if she wasn't. "I did a background on this Olinetsky character you're working for. She—"

Claudia angrily interrupted. "Do you think I want to talk about Grusha right now?"

"But you've really gotta hear this—"

"No, Joel, I really don't. Seeing you kissing someone else kind of ruined my day. I had a feeling Alex had the hots for you, but—"

"Ahh, fuck it, Claudia. I haven't done anything wrong."

"Now you sound like Annabelle."

"Well, *shit.*"

"Look, I don't want to talk about our relationship over the phone, but we have to talk about it when I get back home."

"What's there to talk about? Hold on a sec . . ."

It was not a good moment for her to hear Alex's voice close to the phone. Claudia clicked end and flipped the phone shut.

Chapter 12

Marcus Bernard sent a car for her. His driver, dressed in a dark suit and tie, was a thirtyish, wiry guy with a crew cut. After he'd told her that his name was Mike, he remained silent for the duration.

He looked more like a marine than a chauffeur, and Claudia wondered whether he did double duty as bodyguard. Her Internet search had given her the impression that Marcus was a big player in the world of construction. She'd found his name on several lists of charitable contributors—always in the Golden Circles, which meant he had donated large amounts. Because his handwriting had showed him to be a smooth operator, she wondered how much quid pro quo he received from his contributions.

Mike stopped the car outside a classy restaurant with potted palms in front, and wide rough-hewn wood doors. Refusing to allow her dour mood to keep her down, Claudia had dressed with care for the meeting with Marcus. He was a sexy guy and, more important to her, he was a potential new client.

Under her coat, the black silk of her suit felt cool and smooth against her skin. Claudia was an impatient shopper, but she knew the suit had been a good purchase. Accessories toned it up or down. To go out for dinner, she had added diamond stud earrings and a necklace with three diamond teardrops. The teardrops felt appropriate after her conversation with Jovanic.

She hid her melancholy behind a bright smile as Marcus opened the car door and gave her his hand to help her out. The appreciative flicker in his eyes told her what he thought of her appearance, even before he said she looked terrific.

Inside the restaurant, the maitre d' greeted Marcus with the kind of deference accorded a longtime customer.

"Mr. Bernard, madam, good evening. How are you this evening?"

Marcus helped Claudia out of her coat and unwound the fine cashmere scarf from his neck, handing it, with their overcoats, to the coat checker. Indiana Jones of this morning had disappeared, leaving a well-turned-out gentleman in his place.

The indoor dining room gave the impression of an airy patio on the Riviera: pillars and arches; a stone fountain and potted orange trees; chandeliers with low lights. The conversation was subdued, the mood music barely audible. Nothing casual here. The servers were dressed almost as well as the diners.

Each table was generously spaced from other diners and ensured a sense of privacy.

"The food is excellent," Marcus told Claudia as the maitre d' guided them to their table. "I hope you like it. It's next to impossible to get a reservation."

The maitre d' made a subtle show of drawing out Claudia's chair and helping her into it. "Most of our guests have to call three months ahead," he interjected, whipping a white linen napkin from the dinner plate that was already in place, and laying it across her lap with some ceremony.

Claudia looked at Marcus, wearing an innocent expression. "You've had a reservation for months?"

"Oh, not Mr. Bernard," said the maitre d' before he could answer. "We always make room for him."

"Tomás is very accommodating," Marcus said, taking his seat. He nodded at the man, who promised that their waiter would join them momentarily, and glided away.

"Too bad for the people on the waiting list," Claudia said, not altogether comfortable at jumping to the head of the line.

Marcus gave a naughty-boy grin and rubbed his fingertips together, suggesting the exchange of a healthy tip for the good table. "I love this place. I come here a lot. They know me. And money talks. "

The grin saved his remark from complete crassitude, but wealth notwithstanding, Claudia could see that Marcus Bernard was a little rough around the edges.

The sommelier joined them, and he and Marcus began an animated discussion of the wine list while Claudia listened in, hoping to learn something. Then she and Marcus made desultory small talk until the wine arrived and Marcus made a ceremony of tasting it before giving the sommelier the go-ahead to pour.

Claudia thought it a shame to spoil the artful design by eating the starters they had ordered, but Marcus had no such qualms. He dug into his sea scallops, decimating the art in one bite.

"You're very attractive, Claudia," he said after swallowing. "I don't usually find myself drawn to older women, but—"

"We were going to talk business," she interrupted, piqued at being called "older." Forty was the new thirty, wasn't it? And besides, he was thirty-eight.

Claudia picked at tortellini with chanterelles and a savory sauce, reminding herself that Heather and Shellee, both of whom he had dated, had been in their twenties. "You did say you need a handwriting analyst?"

"I do, but what's wrong with mixing a little pleasure with business?"

"Not a good idea, I've found."

He put on a contrite face. "I can see I've offended you. I didn't mean to suggest that you were *old*. I just—"

"I'm not offended, but it doesn't make any difference how old I am."

"The mixing business with pleasure thing, eh?"

"That's right. Why don't we do what we came here for?"

"We are," said Marcus. "I wanted to get to know you better."

"Getting to know people is *my* job," Claudia retorted. She smiled to take the edge off. "You don't need to know me to have me analyze handwriting for you."

He laughed. "Maybe I should have your handwriting analyzed before I hire you."

"I have no problem giving you a handwriting sample. I'll even refer you to a good analyst. But it could become like a hall of mirrors—you have someone analyze them, who analyzes them, who—"

"That could get out of hand, fast," Marcus agreed with a chuckle. "I guess I'll just have to trust that Grusha knew what she was doing when she picked you. Has she given you *my* handwriting?"

"Of course."

"Well, come on, what did you say about me? Did you tell her I'm a perverted ax murderer?"

"Yes, I did, and the cops are waiting right outside to pick you up." She grinned at him. "You have no idea how many people ask me that very question. They're so afraid I'll uncover their deepest, darkest secrets, they have to make a joke of it. Is that why you asked?"

"You're not big on tact, are you?"

"Nope. But I don't think you are, either, so I think you can take it."

"You're right. And I don't have any deep, dark secrets. I'm an open book. Just ask me."

"Actually, there *is* something I wanted to ask you—it's a little delicate."

He looked more interested than concerned. "Go right ahead."

"I understand that you and Shellee Jones were dating."

Marcus let out a breath that sounded like air rushing out of a balloon. "Dating. Yeah, I guess that's what we were doing. Obviously you must know what happened. The restaurant is being sued. Tomás swears they never use peanuts or peanut oil, but—"

"Tomás? You mean it was *here* that she died?"

"Grusha didn't fill you in?"

"No. She certainly didn't tell me where it happened." There was something distasteful in his bringing her to the very place where the woman he had been dating expired only a few weeks earlier, and she didn't like it.

"We were having dinner," Marcus went on, not seeming to notice her coolness. "Just like you and I are right now. We were talking about me taking her to see a new condo site where we were having a groundbreaking. She said her throat was hurting; she thought she was catching a cold. Then a couple of minutes later, she starts wheezing. All of a sudden, her eyes get big, she's trying to say something. I thought she was choking on her filet. I jump up and run around the table, trying to help. Next thing I know, she's on the floor and her face is all swelled up. She's clutching at her throat, gasping for air like a—a landed fish."

Marcus set his wineglass on the table and Claudia saw that his hands were trembling. "God, it happened so fast! Someone called 911, but she was dead before they got here." He shook his head, as if he couldn't believe what he was saying. "Later, I heard she had an epinephrine kit in her purse that could have saved her. She was probably struggling to get it while I was trying to give her the Heimlich. You can't imagine the guilt."

"You can't blame yourself for her allergic reaction."

"You know what's really crazy? Dr. McAllister was here that night—you know, the club doctor? He'd stopped by our table only ten minutes earlier, on his way out. If he had still been here when it happened, he might have known what to do. He might have been able to save her."

"Ian McAllister was here when she died?"

"He was with some guy. When he saw us he said hello, kissed Shellee on the cheek, messed around with her silverware—then they walked out."

"What do you mean, he 'messed around with her silverware'?"

"I guess he thought Shellee's salad fork was tilted, so he straightened it up. You probably don't know him, but he's what you might call a real anal type. Personally I think he's more than a little nuts. And he was jealous; he wanted her. She was one hot chick."

"You think Dr. McAllister had a crush on Shellee."

Marcus grinned. " 'A crush'? I haven't heard that one since high school. I guess you could call it that. But he couldn't have her because she was Grusha's client. And, of course, she was seeing me." The grin faded. "And now she's—"

"I'm sorry you had to go through that," Claudia said, her brain racing through this new information. Could *McAllister* have had something to do with Shellee's death? More pieces of the puzzle would have to surface before that question could be answered. She would like to see his handwriting.

"You dated Heather Lloyd, too, didn't you?"

"Is that why you won't have a personal conversation with me? You think I'm the angel of death?"

"I just prefer to keep my business and personal life separate. Anyway, you could just as easily be afraid to get near me. I've been close to death myself a couple of times."

"There are very few things I'm afraid of, and I can tell you one thing—getting near you isn't one of them."

Marcus reached out and took her hand. She withdrew it.

"Marcus, please. Let's not. I've got too much happening in my life for any more complications. Now, what about Heather?"

"What is this, the third degree?" He was getting irritated. "Sure, I dated Heather a couple of times. So what?"

"What was the problem with her?"

"We just didn't hit it off—nothing particular. She started seeing someone else."

"Someone from Elite Introductions?"

"You'd have to ask Grusha," Marcus said, drumming his fingers on the table. Two servers arrived and uncovered plates of spiced chiboust and chocolate fondant in front of them at precisely the same moment. *Fancy.*

After the servers had departed, Marcus said, "Okay, so Shellee is dead and Heather is dead and yes, I dated them both. It's like a bad joke and the joke is on me."

Claudia spooned rich chocolate fondant into her mouth. *Comfort food*, she told herself. "Do you ski?" she asked.

"One of my passions," he said. "I have a ski house on Lake Rescue near Killington. I guess next you're going to suggest I helped Heather into that tree?"

"You don't have to get defensive. I was just thinking about going to Stowe. I've never skied myself. In fact, I've seen snow only a couple of times in my life—when my parents took us up to Big Bear Mountain when I was a little kid."

"You don't know what you're missing. Let's drive up to my place tomorrow. There's still plenty of snow. Maybe I can talk you onto some skis, show you the ropes."

"Thanks for the offer, Marcus, but I'm not quite ready for that." She grinned at him. "Remember, I've seen your handwriting."

Chapter 13

"I want to know how you got that video of Joel and Alex." Claudia flopped onto her hotel bed, earpiece in place, and prepared to listen to Annabelle's story.

Grilling the girl felt wrong. She suppressed a flicker of shame for using Annabelle to back up Jovanic's version. Wouldn't a good surrogate mother make it clear that what the girl had done was unacceptable, and then refuse to listen to the explanation? But the gnawing pain of betrayal felt even worse, and she *had* to know.

"It was so easy," said Annabelle, sounding smug. "I hooked up with my friend, Scooter, before school, and he drove me over to stake out Joel's apartment. We just waited till he came out. When he did, we followed him." She snickered. "He's supposed to be a detective, but he didn't even see us."

"Wait a minute; who's Scooter? What's his real name?"

"Scooter's one of my old homies. They just use nicknames. When I was hanging out with them before, they used to call me Baby Brown Eyes."

"Jesus, Annabelle! You're not hanging out with gang members again?"

"Scooter's cool."

"I don't care how cool he is, this is *not* happening.

You cannot socialize with gang members! Do you understand me?"

"Well, you're not here and . . ."

"Don't lay a guilt trip on me, Annabelle. I'll be back in a few days. Please don't make me worry about you any more than I already do." Claudia took a deep breath and refocused. "You still haven't told me how you got that video."

"We followed him to this gas station over by Sawtelle and Washington. He met that girl there, Alex. She brought him some Starbucks—it was a venti, too. She's such a suck-up."

"Enough editorial comments. Just tell me how it went down."

"Okay, fine. They both got in his Jeep and drove up the street; then they parked. Scooter parked down the block across the street and we watched them for a while, but they were just sitting there. I can't believe they didn't see us."

Maybe he was preoccupied with Alex.

"You had absolutely no business being there."

Again, the smug snicker. "It's like those videos on YouTube, of cops who get caught doing all kinds of stupid stuff. They never even saw the person videotaping them."

"Joel didn't expect you to be spying on him."

Why am I defending him? It was an old feeling that reminded her of things she didn't want to remember, and she didn't want to connect it to Jovanic.

Claudia got up and went into the bathroom and shook four ibuprofen from the bottle she carried in her travel kit. A pain like an ice pick hacking at the back of her right eye warned of an impending migraine. "What happened next?" She gulped the caplets with a glass of water from the bottle she kept on the nightstand.

"After they sat there for a while, Joel got out of the Jeep and went back to the gas station." Annabelle giggled. "He was walking fast. I guess he shouldn't have drunk that whole venti. Alex stayed in the Jeep, but right as he was coming back, she got out and ran over to him and they started kissing. I knew you wouldn't believe me, so I took the video with my cell phone."

The girl could be so infuriating!

"Believing you is not the point. You weren't supposed to be following him. You were supposed to be going to school with Monica."

"Don't you even *care* that your boyfriend is swapping spit with some other chick?"

Claudia bit back the sharp retort that was on the tip of her tongue. She knew that in Annabelle's mind she was just trying to help. "Look, kiddo, my relationship with Joel is something I have to work on myself, okay? I don't need to have you spying for me. I need you to behave yourself and stay out of trouble."

There was an exaggerated "tch" at the other end of the line. "What*ever.*"

"By the way, where was Monica while all the spying was going on?"

"She wanted to go with us, but I didn't want her to get in trouble if we got caught."

"Well, that was semiresponsible of you," Claudia said. "I wish you'd applied it to yourself."

"You know she's my BFF. I couldn't let her get in trouble."

BFF? It took her a second to remember the twenty-first century teen jargon stood for Best Friend Forever.

Claudia could hear her brother's voice in the background. Annabelle said, "Pete's calling me. I have to go do my homework."

"Excellent idea. Remember to do your graphotherapy exercises, too."

Annabelle mumbled something that sounded suspiciously like "Love ya," but Claudia knew better than to ask her to repeat it, and they rang off. She lay back on the pillows, waiting for the ibuprofen to kick in.

After a restless night filled with unhappy dreams of Jovanic telling her that he wanted to be free to play the field, Claudia woke in a funk.

She made herself some lukewarm coffee in the coffeemaker on the dresser. *Ugh, powdered creamer. Nasty.*

While she was in the shower, she decided to call the police department in Stowe.

The detective who had investigated Heather Lloyd's death was out of the office, she was told, attending a seminar in Manhattan.

"Could I speak to another detective?"

"We don't have another detective," the voice on the other end of the line informed her. "We're a very small department. Except for the detective sergeant, who's not here, either, Jim Gray is the only one we've got. You could call him on his cell phone. The seminar finished last night. I imagine he's on his way back up here by now."

Claudia jotted down the number as the woman recited it. She thanked her, clicked off, and punched in Jim Gray's number. The detective answered on the second ring.

"Gray."

"Hi, Detective Gray, my name is Claudia Rose. I got your number from your office." She hesitated. "I was hoping to speak with you about the death of

Heather Lloyd a couple of months ago. I'm just visiting New York."

"And how might you be connected to Ms. Lloyd?" His New England accent flattened the vowels to a hard edge.

Claudia explained that she worked with Elite Introductions and that she was looking for information on the progress of the case.

He seemed to deliberate for a moment. "ME's office ruled it an accident. There's nothing to progress on."

"Detective, do you think you and I could get together and talk about this?"

"Not sure what there is left to talk about."

"If you're still in the city, how about letting me buy you a cup of coffee and maybe we'll find something?"

He admitted that he had not yet left Manhattan. "I'm in a cab," Detective Gray said. "On the way to meet the Vermonter."

"The Vermonter?"

"The train. There's only one a day back. Leaves at eleven thirty."

"What station are you leaving from? I'll meet you there."

"Penn."

"Perfect, it's just a few blocks from my hotel."

His scheduled departure allowed Claudia plenty of time to get dressed and make the twenty-minute walk to Pennsylvania Plaza to meet him—down to the underground level of the busiest train station in the country via escalator; another five minutes to locate the Starbucks where she'd arranged to meet the Vermont detective at eleven o'clock.

*   *   *

Detective Jim Gray was a compact man in his fifties with thinning brown hair and dark eyebrows, frameless eyeglasses, a square face and just the hint of a moustache. He waved her over to a table at the back of the noisy coffeehouse as soon as she walked through the door.

She'd told him she would be wearing a black pantsuit with a pink top. The description had been sufficient for him to recognize her. "Good detecting, Detective," she said, taking a seat across from him.

He wore a cranberry-colored polo shirt, with a slate gray sport jacket draped neatly over the back of his chair. He was nursing a cardboard cup with the familiar green logo. "Get you one?" he offered.

"I thought *I* was buying."

"Nah," he said good-naturedly. "Against department regs."

"I appreciate you agreeing to meet with me on short notice," Claudia said after the social niceties were out of the way. "I won't take up much of your time."

"'S okay," Gray said. "My train's delayed. One a day to Vermont, and it's got the worst on-time record of any of 'em. Might as well have a little company while I wait. What can I get ya?"

He made his way to the counter and ordered the Breakfast Blend she had asked for. When they both had their coffees in front of them, he asked, "What's your interest in the Lloyd case again?"

Claudia tore open two packets of sugar and stirred them into her cup. "As I mentioned on the phone, I'm working for a dating service that Heather had joined. I'm analyzing the handwritings of some of the members."

"Handwriting analysis, huh?"

She prepared herself for skepticism, but his next words pleased her.

"Hey, that's fascinatin' stuff. Back when I was working for Boston PD we had a girl come in once, claimed she was raped. Had her write out a statement and took it to a handwritin' expert. The expert said she was lyin' about what happened. Turns out the expert was right. In the end, she admitted she just wanted to get back at this guy she'd been dating. So, what do you want to know about the Lloyd accident?"

"Just wanted to make sure it really was an accident."

He gave her the eagle eye. "You got reason to believe otherwise?"

Claudia thought about it and tried to decide how much to say. He was a cop, so talking to him wouldn't breach any professional ethics, but she was certain that Grusha wouldn't thank her for revealing her suspicions to him. Besides, she had not seen any direct evidence of murder. She shook her head no.

Gray leveled a look at her that said he was doubting her answer. "Then why would you be all fired up about meetin' me here? You think something else happened to that girl, you'd best tell me what it is."

"I *don't* have any information. Honestly."

"Lady, I've been a detective for twenty-three years. I know bullshit when I hear it and right now, my bullshit meter is on tilt."

"I'm not bullshitting you, Detective. It's just, well, I was under the impression that she was a good skier, and it seemed odd she'd go off trail like that."

He finished his coffee and balled his napkin into the cup. "What's a handwriting analyst need this information for?"

Claudia sipped at her coffee, trying to figure out how to make the story sound anything other than bizarre. She decided to come clean.

"Three young members of the dating club have died in a short period of time. The deaths appear natural and I don't have any evidence to say they're not. It just seems there are too many of them in a short time."

Behind his glasses, Gray's eyes narrowed. "What do you mean, 'appear natural'?"

She told him about Heather, Shellee, and Ryan.

"Were they all investigated by the local authorities?"

"Yes, but—"

"Were they all autopsied?"

"As far as I know."

He looked unconvinced. "Means, motive, opportunity," Gray said. "That's what it takes to prove guilt. You got those?"

Claudia quickly shook her head. "Nothing conclusive."

"Well, then . . ."

"Can you at least tell me what the medical examiner said about Heather?"

"Sure, it's public record. There was a bunch of antihistamine in her system—cold medicine. That stuff'll make you sleepy. Shouldn't have gone out after taking it. Slows the reflexes." The detective took off his glasses and breathed on the lenses, wiped them with care on a paper napkin and replaced them. "She'd taken a double dose."

"A double dose? Isn't that suspicious?"

"Not particularly. We went all through her room; the box was right there on the nightstand. Prob'ly forgot she'd taken one, took another and went out groggy. No sign of foul play at all."

"What about the man she was with?"

"We asked around. Far as we know, she went out alone that day," Gray said. He drew his brows together and he showed some uncertainty for the first time. "I do recall hearing about a fella she was seen with at the lodge one night, at the bar. Tried to get his name, but no luck. Nobody registered with her and nobody remembers anyone being with her the day she died."

"I don't suppose anyone had a description of this fella she was seen with?"

"Matter of fact, they did. Tall, brown hair, bearded."

"That's pretty nonspecific," Claudia said.

"Your typical eyewitness description."

A description that matched Ian McAllister, or Marcus Bernard's Elite Introductions photo before he shaved his beard.

Chapter 14

Detective Gray had nothing further to add and was disinclined to pursue the matter. So Claudia walked back to the hotel thinking about cold medicine and antihistamines, which she knew were also used to treat allergies.

Antihistamine made her think of anaphylactic shock and Shellee Jones. Then her thoughts jumped to Ryan Turner, the young doctor who had perished in the Bahamas.

Scuba diving.

Scuba diving. Skiing. Anaphylactic shock. Instinct told her that there was a connection somewhere, but where? The available information wasn't providing the answer.

What the hell am I doing?

She reminded herself again of what she had so emphatically said to Grusha: She was a handwriting analyst, not a private investigator. The smart thing to do would be to pack up and get on the next plane to L.A.

She thought of the fee Grusha was paying for her services. And she thought of the roof repairs that her house needed, and the quarterly taxes that would soon be due. Did it make her a sellout if she stayed on for the money against her better judgment?

It couldn't hurt to make one phone call to the hotel

in Nassau where the young resident had been staying. It just might turn up something new. She thought about that as she stopped at the bagel shop and picked up a take-out turkey and Swiss sandwich, no mayo, and a latte for lunch. But by the time she returned to her room to track down the article on Ryan Turner's unfortunate demise, she still didn't have a satisfactory answer to the sellout question.

The Paradise Reef hotel's Web site portrayed a luxurious beachfront resort: stunning views of pellucid green water teeming with manta rays; a glass-walled dining room that gave diners the sense of being underwater along with the marine life that swam by in its own lagoon. The glossy pictures oozed opulence.

Grusha had said that Ryan Turner's family had money. Was *that* the connection between the dead clients? Shellee Jones' father was a hedge-fund manager. That meant money, too.

What about Heather Lloyd? Nothing had been mentioned about the model's financial status, but as an Elite Introductions client, she would have had to come up with the membership fee—a not insignificant amount.

Calling the Nassau hotel, Claudia got routed to the marketing manager, who spoke in a British accent. "We can't possibly discuss our guests," the manager said in a clipped tone that brooked no argument. "They expect us to maintain strict privacy, and we do."

Claudia argued anyway. "I'm not actually asking about your guest," she said. "I'm asking about his companion. Can't you at least tell me whether anyone else was registered with him, even if you don't divulge the name?"

"Our hotel discharges its responsibility when it offers guests a dive guide and warns them not to dive alone. The hotel has no liability in this matter *whats*oever." Parroting what the newspaper article had said.

"I'm not looking to sue your hotel," Claudia said, irritated by the stonewalling. "I don't think you're hearing me. All I'm asking is whether Dr. Turner was with anyone on that final dive."

"Ms. Rose, I cannot help you any further."

"You haven't helped me at all," Claudia said to dead air as the marketing manager hung up. The better part of an hour down the tubes and she'd gotten nowhere.

Jovanic had phoned a couple of times, but she'd let it ring through to voice mail. What was the point in answering? He would protest again that there was nothing between him and Alex and Claudia would not believe it. She couldn't remember trusting anyone—even her ex-husband—in almost thirty years until Jovanic. She'd thought she was safe with him. Her heart hurt from thinking about it.

Nibbling a few bites of the turkey sandwich, she decided that she needed to do something active. Easier to play private detective for Grusha Olinetsky than to deal with her own life.

Aside from Grusha, she knew that two people had knowledge of all the dead clients: Ian McAllister and Donna Pollard. Ian was now on her suspect list, so he was out. But Dr. Pollard might hold a key to this mess. Claudia just had to get the psychologist to talk to her again.

The doorman hailed her a cab, and fifteen minutes later Claudia entered Dr. Pollard's office. There were no clients in the waiting room.

Dorothy French opened the interior door when Claudia rang the bell, and made it clear that she was not happy to see her visitor. "What now?" she asked with no pretense of courtesy.

Claudia offered her most winning smile. "Any chance the doctor could spare a few minutes for me?"

"Have you considered making an appointment? Wouldn't you expect that she might be with a client?"

"From your answer, I'd guess she's not. Besides, it's lunchtime, so I was hoping she might be free."

"Why can't you leave her alone?"

Why are you so hot to protect her?

"Dorothy, please ask Dr. Pollard if she'll see me. I'll be going back to the West Coast soon, and you'll never have to deal with me again. But today, right now, I need to ask her a couple of questions. It's really important."

The secretary huffed in annoyance. "Wait here." She stepped back into the hallway and yanked the door closed behind her with a sharp snap.

Dorothy French left her waiting for ten minutes before she let Claudia know that Dr. Pollard had agreed to meet with her. Knowing she was lucky that the psychologist had agreed to see her at all without an appointment, Claudia thanked her and followed her to the womblike room where Pollard conducted therapy.

"Come in, dear, sit down." Donna Pollard smiled benevolently at her, as if they hadn't parted on strained terms at their last meeting. She wore a fern green hand-knit turtleneck sweater and a long brown woolen skirt with lace-up Uggs, as if she might be planning a hike in the snow.

She appeared relaxed and at ease, unlike on the previous visit, when nervous tension had vibrated through her. "You look tired, dear," she said as Claudia sat down. "Aren't you sleeping well?"

The love seat was familiar in an uncomfortable way. Maybe therapists all shopped at the same love seat store. "Strange bed," Claudia said, disliking the feeling of being under the microscope. She reminded herself that she was not there for therapy, and she felt better, more in control. "How are *you* feeling, doctor? Any more problems?"

"None at all. As I told you, it was a random break-in. I'm fine, no concussion. No ill effects." Pollard smiled with more warmth than was warranted for the occasion. "So, Claudia, what brings you here today?"

"I've had some quite interesting conversations since I saw you last."

The doctor leaned forward a little in her chair, her lips parted. "Yes?"

"I had dinner with Marcus Bernard last night. I learned that he was present when Shellee Jones died."

Wariness came into Pollard's blue eyes. "I can't tell you how bad I felt. A terrible thing to happen."

"Do you think there's anything odd in the fact that he dated both Shellee and Heather?"

"Not at all. The dating service isn't large. Marcus has been a member for a while now, and Shellee and Heather were both fairly new. He wasn't the only one who dated them both. Why? What do *you* think it means, Claudia?"

"I don't know whether it means anything, but I thought maybe you would."

"I'm sorry. I can't say as I do."

"When I was here the other day, you mentioned Dr. McAllister's daughter."

"I shouldn't have done that."

"Why not? Was she your patient?"

"You probably know, Claudia, that I can't give you the answer to that. It would be unethical to divulge who my patients are."

"But you can talk about Elite Introductions clients because Grusha has given permission. You said Jessica McAllister had dated three of the men we were discussing. Which ones?"

When Pollard hesitated, Claudia took the advantage and prodded her. "You might as well tell me."

"I really don't think I should."

"Fine, I'll ask her myself."

"That would be—difficult." Pollard hesitated. "I'm afraid Jessica passed away a few months ago."

Claudia heard herself gasp. "Oh my god."

"I suppose it doesn't matter if I tell you. You could find out for yourself. Jessie committed suicide."

"Suicide! Ian said he had a daughter, but he didn't say she was dead, let alone a suicide. What the *hell* is going on?"

Pollard looked down at her hands clasped in her lap. "Everyone in Elite Introductions has something to hide."

"What do you mean?"

The psychologist raised her head. "What?" She seemed confused to see that she wasn't alone in the room.

"You said everyone has something to hide," Claudia said, overwhelmed by the news that there was another young person to be added to the dating club's death tally. "What did you mean by that?"

"I said that out loud?" Pollard squeezed her eyes shut. "Please forget it. I shouldn't have said that. It's the knock on the head. I'm still having headaches. I don't know what I'm saying. I shouldn't even be here."

She appeared so agitated that Claudia didn't have the heart to remind her that only a few moments earlier she'd said she had suffered no ill effects from the attack.

"Was there any question that Jessica's death was suicide?" Claudia asked.

The psychologist spoke quickly as if to get it over with. "She took a bottle of Tylenol. Then she slit her wrists and sat in a tub full of warm water, waiting to die."

"Two methods. It sounds like she wanted to die very badly."

"She was only just eighteen," Pollard said, her eyes bright with tears. With her own emotions playing so close to the surface, Claudia wondered how she managed to conduct therapy with vulnerable clients.

"Why do you think Jessica would do something like that?"

"I can't discuss it with you."

Claudia struggled to keep her voice even, but she was fed up with being thwarted. She could hear the anger coloring her words as she spoke. "Who were the men she dated, Donna?"

"Please don't ask me that."

"I *am* asking."

"It's confidential information."

"How confidential can it be? She's dead! You and I both know there's something wrong here."

"But the men are still alive, except for Ryan."

"If someone else dies and you don't tell what you know, you, Dr. Pollard, will be an accessory after the fact."

That jolted her.

"All right, all right, I'll tell you. Jessica dated Avram Cohen, Marcus Bernard, and Ryan Turner." Pollard swallowed hard. "Now, I think that's enough. There's nothing we can do about it now. You'll never be able to prove—" She stopped midsentence, her face contorted in alarm.

"Prove what, Donna? Look, I know you're frightened, but you've got to tell me what you know."

"You need to leave. Now."

"No, *you* need to tell the truth. If these deaths are all connected and you think you know how and why, you could be in danger yourself. You've already had a break-in. Somebody thinks you know something. Isn't getting knocked on the head enough of a warning for you?"

As the two women looked at one another, realization slowly dawned in the eyes of the psychologist. The seconds ticked past and Pollard seemed to come to a decision. She got out of her chair and crossed the room to a lateral wooden file cabinet in the corner. Taking a key from her pocket, she stared at it in her hand for a second or two, as though hardening her resolve.

Finally, she leaned down and inserted the key in the lock, where she left it hanging; then she straightened. "It would have been unthinkable if the intruder had gotten into my patient files. I always keep them locked up tight."

She gave Claudia a long, meaningful look. "I'm going into the kitchen to make us some tea, Claudia. I'll be about five minutes; you can wait right here."

The instant the door closed behind Donna Pollard, Claudia leapt up from the love seat and dashed to the file cabinet. No question about the tacit message Pollard had telegraphed to her: Get Jessica McAllister's file.

She found it in the bottom drawer.

Chapter 15

It was a tremendous breach of ethics for Dr. Pollard to make the file available; it almost certainly held something of vital importance for the psychologist to take that kind of legal risk. Claudia opened it and began to riffle through pages upon pages of densely written notes. There would never be enough time to read through the thick sheaf of papers before Pollard returned with tea.

She stuffed the papers into her briefcase, fumbled it closed, her heart racing. Replaced the empty folder in the drawer and locked it, leaving the keys dangling.

Claudia tiptoed into the hallway and listened. The sounds of tea-making could be heard coming from what she presumed must be the kitchen. Thanking the file-stealing gods that Dorothy French was nowhere in sight, Claudia slipped through the back door and made a headlong dash for the elevator.

Before Dr. Pollard could change her mind, Claudia raced out of the building and stepped off the sidewalk, looking for a taxi. Luck seemed to favor her as a vacant yellow cab appeared almost immediately. She raised an arm and waved. The cabbie stopped a few feet ahead of her.

As she started toward the vehicle, a tall figure in a long overcoat stepped in front of her, smooth as glass, and opened the taxi door.

"Hey!" Claudia objected, ready to launch into a diatribe about its being "her" taxi. She bit back the angry words in surprise. "Dr. McAllister?"

The doctor turned to her, extending a hand, and invited her to get in. "Ian," he reminded her. "Where may I drop you?"

Claudia scooted to the far side of the backseat, leaving room for Ian McAllister to slide in beside her. She gave the driver the name of her hotel and angled to face her accidental companion. "Fancy meeting you here."

"I do have an office in the building, if you recall," he said in that deadpan way he had. He clasped his hands, which were encased in black kid gloves, and let them rest on his lap. "I just came off the elevator and saw you running out of the building as if it were on fire. Is everything all right?"

She thought of what she had just learned from Dr. Pollard about Jessica McAllister, and of the file in her briefcase. How could she approach him to discuss his dead daughter without revealing where she'd gotten the information? The words refused to come out. Instead, she said simply, "I was visiting Donna Pollard. Did you know she'd had a break-in yesterday?"

"No, I wasn't privy to that information." Ian unbuttoned the gorgeous alpaca coat and removed his gloves. "The building needs to improve its security."

Claudia darted a quick look at him, but he was looking straight ahead and she couldn't tell whether he was being serious. She said, "She was attacked, hit over the head. I wonder whether it had anything to do with the reason Grusha brought me to New York."

Ian inclined his head toward the cabbie, who had left the partition separating them partway open. "Perhaps we shouldn't discuss this just now. How about this evening? Dinner?"

"Oh, I don't—" She was thinking about the fact that he hadn't asked whether Dr. Pollard was okay. It seemed an interesting omission.

"Don't you like me, Claudia?"

"What do you mean?"

"This is the second time I've asked you out and both times, your first instinct has been to refuse me."

"I told you, I'm—I'm seeing someone."

"Do you find me repulsive?"

"Of course not. In fact, you're quite attractive, but—"

"Then have dinner with me. Just dinner. I'll pick you up at your hotel. I have my car garaged in the city. We'll take a run up the Hudson."

"If you have a car here, why are you taking a cab?"

He gave her the odd smile that seemed to stop just short of a sneer. "I wanted to take advantage of the opportunity to see you."

Jessica McAllister's file was thick with Dr. Pollard's handwritten notes. The psychologist wrote in a flowery hand that matched her appearance: a trifle overblown.

A good therapist needs objectivity, Claudia thought, viewing a page crowded with hard-to-read handwriting. That kind of dense spatial arrangement indicated difficulty in stepping back and maintaining professional distance. Many of the o's and a's were open at the top, the loops right-slanted: talkative, emotional, quick to become overinvolved.

Was that what had happened during therapy sessions with Ian McAllister's daughter? Had Pollard become emotionally overinvolved with Jessica?

Once Claudia had familiarized herself with the flow of Donna Pollard's handwriting, reading it was a little easier. But the picture of Jessica McAllister that began to emerge set her teeth on edge.

On the intake form, Pollard had written that Jessica had joined Elite Introductions at the behest of her father. Despite Grusha's insistence that, having turned eighteen a couple of months earlier, the young woman didn't have enough life experience to date the kind of men who joined the club, she had allowed herself to be persuaded. Claudia was cynical enough to think that payment of a hefty fee might have had some influence on Grusha Olinetsky's acceptance of the young woman as a member.

Dr. Pollard and Jessica had immediately hit it off at the initial psychological screening appointment. Pollard learned that the girl's mother had deserted her husband and child when Jessica was just four years old and had never contacted them again.

Jessica, or Jessie, as Pollard tended to refer to her, seemed to be looking for a surrogate mother, and the psychologist was drawn to her. Although most Elite Introductions members saw Pollard only once in the screening process, she and the girl had decided between them that Jessie should enter therapy. As an adult, she did not need her father's permission, nor did she have to inform him of her activities. Pollard decided to see her pro bono, so there would be no audit trail that her father could follow.

Still, she had made clinical notes, from which it became apparent that the process of transference had been completed early on—the client had literally transferred her feelings from her mother to the therapist. The unfortunate truth was, it also appeared from the notes that countertransference—the feelings of the therapist becoming inappropriately intertwined with the client's, and possibly interfering with therapy—had occurred.

Claudia stopped reading for a moment and thought of her own relationship with Annabelle Giordano. She couldn't fault Pollard for caring about Jessie McAllister. Lord knew it was easy to become involved with a vulnerable girl who needed a confidant. But although she had degrees in psychology, Claudia had chosen *not* to become a therapist because she knew that she would be unable to maintain the needed level of detachment to be helpful to clients.

When she'd hit thirty it seemed the right time to look back and examine her life. In her self-exploration, she'd recognized that something was amiss, so she'd found a therapist for herself.

In the first session, she had begun to get an inkling that her inability to trust had interfered with intimate relationships and contributed to the failure of her marriage. Yet confronting the demons of the past had been too painful for her. She'd dropped out after only a couple of visits. Now, ten years later, she was struggling to deal with the issues on her own, but she found that she didn't want to look back and deal with the pain of the past.

She'd discovered that Jovanic had trouble trusting, too. But over the months they'd been together, they had both started to learn how to lower their barriers, little by little. At least, they had until Alex began to show up without warning, phoning him at all hours. Jovanic insisted it was strictly business, but Claudia's intuition was zinging, and she didn't like what it was telling her. And as she had withdrawn, so had Jovanic.

What a pair we are, she thought as she came back around to the problem of Jessica McAllister. No time for her own problems when there was work to be done. There was something to be said for filling her time with work.

"Feels uncomfortable with F," Pollard had written in notes dated half a year earlier. The next few lines pointed to "F" as referencing Jessie's father, Ian McAllister.

F wants to know specifics of her sexual activities. Quizzes her constantly about her body. Claims he's concerned as a physician. J feels uncomfortable with these discussions. I do not believe interest is prurient, but more driven by a need for control.

Later, Pollard wrote, "F jealous of J's boyfriends. Drives them away with superior attitude and controlling behavior."

Claudia read on and learned that Ian had requested that Grusha find Jessie a match with an older man. The notes said that he had judged every introduction she made as unworthy of his daughter. Not wealthy enough. Not powerful enough.

Jessie confided to her therapist that she believed no man would ever attain her father's standards. And, understandably, she didn't want a "made match" anyway.

J perceives F as a control freak. Any man he approves for her will have to further his status, and also be someone he can control.

It struck Claudia that Ryan Turner might have filled the bill on all counts, except, perhaps the requirement for an "older" man. Ryan had been a twenty-seven-year-old second-year resident, at the outer reaches of a reasonable age for eighteen-year-old Jessie. He was a medical man. He came from a wealthy family. He was drop-dead gorgeous. And

his career choice gave him the potential for achiev-
ing status and power.

The notes indicated that Jessie had dated Ryan
twice and was infatuated with him, but her father
had denigrated Ryan's choice of plastic surgery as a
specialty and put the kibosh on the relationship before it had a chance to blossom.

After her father nixed her short-lived romantic
attachment to Ryan, Jessie had gone on a couple of
dates with "AC," whom Claudia deduced must be
Avram Cohen.

"Says she's afraid of him," Pollard had written.

*He hasn't acted out physically, but J complains that he
gets angry easily and blows up. Nothing showed up in
his assessment. She may be overly sensitive.*

Jessie had been introduced to Marcus Bernard, but
indicated that she thought he was way too old and he
turned her off. Late thirties would be ancient to a girl
of eighteen. Still, at her father's insistence, she had
seen him several times before digging in her heels—
with Donna Pollard's secret encouragement— and
refusing to see him again.

Flipping through the pages, Claudia came upon a
handwritten note from Jessica herself.

*Dear Dr. P, what am I going to do? He wants to keep
me under his thumb forever. He thinks I'm one of his
possessions, not a real person with needs of my own.
I'm freaking out. I'm about to break into tiny pieces and
no one will ever be able to put them back together again.
Not even you, Dr. P. Please help me! Love Jessie*

As Claudia read the words and looked at the
handwriting, she felt an aching sadness for the young

woman. Why hadn't she broken away from her father after she'd reached her majority?

Jessica's handwriting held the answer: the "good girl" syndrome. The need for her father's affection and approval was plain in the round letter forms and crowded words, not so different from Dr. Pollard's own. Jessica had missed the nurturing of a mother and Ian had not been equipped to give her what she needed in terms of emotional support. The lack of a comma between *Love* and *Jessie* made the words into a plea.

Love Jessie.

Many letters thrust up against each other, a feature of people who were unsure of their boundaries and had no real sense of their own space or power. Claudia's mind flipped over to Annabelle, who had once attempted to kill herself. Thank god she had been rescued in time.

But Jessica had managed to complete the act. Judging by this handwriting, it would not be surprising to learn that her actions were, in reality, a plea for help, rather than a sincere desire to end her life. When she slit her wrists, had she intended for someone to find her before it was too late?

Or was there a possibility that Jessie hadn't acted alone in her suicide?

Claudia turned to the next page of Dr. Pollard's notes. In a frantic act of rebellion, Jessica reported to her therapist that she had been sneaking out to rave parties when she knew that her father would not find out. Pollard's notes described dangerous drug use and indiscriminate sex. Unprotected sex.

An AIDS test, positive for the HIV virus. Claudia read on, her heart sinking lower with each line.

She wants to throw it in F's face that she has found an area of her life where he has no control. Her diagnosis is something he cannot change. J is euphoric. Delusional that somehow this fixes things.

Pollard wrote that she had tried to talk Jessie out of making this revelation to her father. Her concern was that McAllister, having lost the object of his sociopathic/narcissistic rage—his daughter—would need to deflect it onto someone else.

A month passed between that note and the last one in the file, which indicated that Pollard didn't know whether Jessie had confronted her father or not. Nor did it matter further. The girl had ended her life.

Claudia turned the last page and sat there for a while, just looking at the bundle of papers. What did it all mean in terms of Grusha Olinetsky and Elite Introductions, if anything?

There was a reason why Donna Pollard had directed her to this file, and it wasn't just because Claudia had asked about McAllister's daughter. The manifest answer was that Pollard suspected Ian McAllister of being Grusha's saboteur. But what did that have to do with his daughter?

Okay, what are the facts?

McAllister signed Jessie up with Elite Introductions.

He was dissatisfied with the men she met: Avram Cohen, Marcus Bernard, Ryan Turner.

Jessie slept around with random guys who would never have been accepted into Elite Introductions.

She injected drugs.

She contracted AIDS.

Then came the questions: Did Jessie tell her father that she had the disease? If she did tell him, how had he reacted?

Did she really kill herself?

Chapter 16

Zebediah Gold answered the phone as he often did, in a rather brusque way that made Claudia wonder what she was interrupting and whether she should just hang up. But when he heard it was she, asking him for a few minutes of his time, his voice brightened.

"Sweetheart! I always have time for you; you know that. What shall we talk about? You and me on a desert island with a pitcher of martinis and—"

She interrupted. "If you don't mind, let's talk about OCPD and narcissistic rage."

"I like my idea better. Yours has made my brain go flaccid. Exactly whose obsessive compulsive personality and rage has you concerned?"

Zebediah was a semiretired criminal psychologist and her long-ago lover. She could always count on him to make himself available when she had a knotty problem to gnaw on.

Claudia summarized her meeting with Ian McAllister and told Zebediah what she'd learned about Jessica McAllister's suicide from Dr. Pollard's clinical notes.

Zebediah listened quietly as she spoke. When she was finished, he said, "She slit her wrists?"

"That's what Dr. Pollard said. She took pills, too."

"Cutting oneself is supposed to be one of the most painful ways to end it all."

"That's what Annabelle told me. When she tried it, she cut herself with a broken bottle. She told me that her hands started shaking so badly she couldn't control them. They cramped up like claws. It sounded excruciating."

"God, she's lucky someone came along and found her in time."

"Unlike poor Jessica, who bled out in the bathtub."

"And you think her father might have had something to do with it?"

Claudia faltered, having second thoughts as she faced the enormity of what she was suggesting. "What do you think, Zeb? With the level of controlling behavior Donna Pollard described in her notes, do you think it's possible that he could have killed her and made it look like suicide?"

"The ultimate control," Zebediah mused. "The power over life and death."

"He would have to be crazy, wouldn't he, to do something like that?"

"Not necessarily. Narcissistic rage is a reaction to something—or some*one*—that injures the person's ego. When that happens, some people will act out their rage, yelling and screaming, or through violence. But others turn it on themselves and become depressed. It all depends on the type of person. What you're suggesting is extreme, but it's within the realm of the possible. You say he's a physician?"

"Yes, which means he might know how to fix it to look like suicide. He's smart enough to stage things convincingly." Claudia paused and thought about it, visualizing how it might have happened. "I'm not suggesting he would have done it intentionally, but what I'm thinking is, maybe Jessie confronts him with her AIDS diagnosis, throws it in his face. He flies into a rage, completely loses control, and accidentally kills her. When he realizes what he's done, he sets up the suicide scene to avoid getting caught."

"Except your scenario presupposes that whatever *actually* killed her didn't show up in the autopsy." Zebediah sounded dubious. "You would expect there to have been defensive wounds if he came at her in a threatening way. If he hit her, there would be bruises. I don't know, sweetie. It just doesn't wash. I mean, what did he do, bash her over the head and carry her to the tub? The medical examiner would certainly have caught something like that."

A theory was forming in Claudia's head and she was starting to warm to it. "It could fit in with the other deaths in the dating service. What if Jessie told Ian that she had AIDS, but didn't tell him how she got it? If he didn't know about the drugs and rave parties, he could be taking revenge on Grusha, thinking Jessie had been infected by one of the men she'd dated through Elite Introductions. He would be furious to think of her sleeping with someone and him not knowing about it, too."

"Except that you said his job is to screen all the applicants for that very reason—to avoid taking on someone who has a medical condition that might harm another member."

"True. But if he was pathological, he wasn't looking at it rationally. Narcissistic rage is about revenge, isn't it? I haven't seen his handwriting yet, but to me, he doesn't seem like the depressive type who would turn it inward on himself. It has to go somewhere, so it explodes outward, onto someone else—Grusha Olinetsky and her dating club."

"Okay, my clever detective. How does the good doctor arrange to kill all these other people?"

"He's a medical man. I bet he could do it easily enough. Heather Lloyd had a double dose of cold medicine in her system before she hit that tree. He would have known how much to give her without arousing suspicion, and she would have been easy to control—shove her off the trail and into the tree."

"Whoa! Your suspicious little mind has been busy, hasn't it? Is there any evidence that the doctor went to Vermont with Heather?"

"I phoned the ski lodge, but they wouldn't give me any information. I also talked to the detective on the case, but he couldn't add anything, either."

"What about the others?"

"I don't know how he would have managed Ryan, but Ryan *is* dead. And Shellee—don't you think it's suspicious that she had an attack of anaphylactic shock just a few minutes after Dr. McAllister stopped by her table in the restaurant?"

"Playing devil's advocate, how did he happen to have the very thing on him that would kill her?" Zebediah asked.

"Her allergies would be listed in her medical record, especially one that severe. Since he gave her a physical, he would know what she was allergic to. If he planned far enough ahead, he could have been following her and seen Marcus take her to the restaurant. He pretends to meet up with them at the restaurant by chance, he leans over to give her a kiss on the cheek, and drops peanut dust in her hair or her food."

Zebediah chuckled. *"Peanut dust?"*

"Don't laugh, it could happen. I was on a flight to Seattle a few months ago, to see my parents. After they'd handed out the peanuts, the woman in the seat in front of me complained that her child was so allergic that even the dust in the air could kill him. In fact, she said he was already wheezing. The flight attendant made an announcement and went around and picked up all the little packages."

"Oh my god, a flight with no peanuts?"

"They substituted salted pretzels."

"Well, that's a big relief."

"It's not nice of you to make fun, Zebediah. I might have a date with a killer tonight."

"You'd better hang on to your garter belt, darling. It's going to be a bumpy ride!"

"You're incorrigible and you're not being very helpful."

He laughed. "I'm totally penitent; can't you tell? You should quiz the doctor on his whereabouts when those poor people died. See if he has alibis."

"Okay, I know you're mocking me, but you can't deny they're dead."

"You're so easy to tease," Zebediah said with affection. "Never mind, my precious, I don't think you'll be in any danger over dinner."

"Shellee Jones died over dinner," Claudia persisted.

"True. Look, if you're serious about this, don't go with him."

"I am going. I want to get to know him better, maybe get him to give up a handwriting sample. At least that way I can get a better idea of what kind of person he really is."

"Does Joel know you have a date with a dashing doctor?"

"It's business, just business, and I haven't spoken to Joel today." She didn't mention that he'd e-mailed and texted her on the cell phone, asking why she wasn't returning his calls. She hadn't responded to either.

"The lady makes it clear she doesn't want to have *that* conversation," Zebediah said.

"You're right, she doesn't. Let's get back to the issue of rage. We know that people with obsessive compulsive personality disorder are perfectionists. They're anal-retentive. That's part of the need to feel in control. They always have to be right. Everything is black or white, no gray area."

"You get an A in Psych 101, Claudia darling. The primary need of the OCPD client is to avoid anxiety, and *that* is at the root of the extreme need for control. If they can keep everything predictable, they won't have to feel anxious all the time. In theory, that is. In fact, that's not the way it works."

"Anxiety shows up in handwriting." Claudia tapped her finger on the desk with impatience. "I've *got* to get his handwriting, Zeb."

Chapter 17

Dr. McAllister arrived at seven on the dot. Looking distinguished in a Prussian blue cashmere suit, crisp white shirt, and solid burgundy satin tie, he took Claudia's arm and showed her to a gleaming black Aston Martin double-parked in front of the hotel. She had to admit it was a beauty with its ground-hugging profile and smooth-flowing lines. It had probably cost more than her house.

Ian saw her into the passenger side. "A performance automobile like this deserves to get out of the city and let loose from time to time," he said. "I thought we would drive up the Hudson to a favorite restaurant of mine. You'll enjoy it."

Claudia murmured her assent and sank into a suede and leather seat that might have been molded to fit her body. Relaxing into the voluptuous cockpit made her feel like a pampered movie star.

Ian closed her door and whipped a piece of chamois leather from his pocket, giving the recessed handle a quick polish before going around to the driver's side. Then, using the chamois to open the driver's door, he slid inside.

Watching him, Claudia thought it seemed a little creepy. Then she reminded herself that he was obsessive-compulsive and needed his rituals to feel at ease.

She didn't sense any danger from Ian, but she had to wonder whether the memory of the dead clients had anything to do with his high level of anxiety. The ghosts of his daughter Jessica and Shellee, Heather, and Ryan crowded her mind. Their presence was pervasive and she knew she would never completely forget them.

The twin exhausts roared as the engine came to life, rising above the sounds of post–rush hour Manhattan. Ian held the gearshift as gently as a lover's hand. "It's a DBS," he said with pride, and proceeded to give Claudia a rundown of the car's features.

She turned to him with a smile. "The only thing I know about Aston Martins is that James Bond drives one."

"Call me Bond, James Bond," Ian quipped, his close-lipped smile raising one corner of his mouth.

"You don't have an ejection seat, do you?"

He gave an oblique glance her way. "Only for those who offend me. So far, you're doing fine."

His tone was sardonic, but when he said that, it made Claudia feel creepy all over again. They talked for a while about the differences between life on the East Coast and the West Coast. Then she told him about Annabelle, creating an opening for him to pick up the thread of how to handle a teenage girl, and perhaps bring up the topic of his daughter.

"I have almost zero experience with kids," Claudia said. "I used to babysit my niece when she was a tot, but that's completely different from dealing with a teenager. I'm finding it really tough, having a fourteen-year-old girl to deal with at this stage in my life."

Something in Ian's profile changed, hardened. His voice hardened, too. "All you have to know is teenagers need a firm hand. Especially girls."

"I suppose that's true, but unfortunately, I'm not much of a disciplinarian."

"Too bad. 'Spare the rod and spoil the child' still applies. These days, more than ever."

"Surely you don't mean the literal rod?"

He kept his eyes focused on the road ahead. "Let's not spoil our evening with unpleasant thoughts. We're taking a spin in one of the most fabulous automobiles in the world, and we're going to a wonderful place for dinner. What could be better?"

"I thought you might give me some advice, seeing as you have a teenage daughter yourself."

Ian stiffened visibly. His grip tightened around the steering wheel. "Why do I have the feeling that you already know something about that?"

Shit. What do I say now? She wanted information, but she had no desire to become the object of his rage. They were approaching a highway sign that directed them to the George Washington Bridge and she seized on the distraction. "Wow, look at the bridge! I've never been this way before. How long *is* the GW?"

His head jerked around in her direction and he snapped, "Nearly a mile." Then he lapsed into a morose silence. Claudia was sure that his eyes were glittering in suspicion of her motives, though she couldn't see them in the darkness. Underneath the warm wool of her coat, she shivered. *Oh god, don't tell me the whole evening is going to be like this.*

Using the steering wheel controls, Ian switched on the audio and bumped the volume up. The uncomfortable void was immediately filled with the screaming guitars and pounding drums of AC/DC, as loud and clear as if the band had been inside the car with them. She hadn't pegged him for a rock aficionado, but "Highway to Hell" seemed to fit this trip.

"Tell me about the restaurant," Claudia said hastily after the song ended, before the bass could begin thumping again.

He lowered the volume and answered in a measured way that begrudged every word. "The food is extraordinary. It's fairly small; you might say intimate."

In the distance, the bridge had a festive appearance—blue lights on the cables looked like Hanukkah decorations. As they approached and joined the lines of traffic, Ian's mood began to improve and he started talking about the bridge: It had two levels, the first opened in 1931. It was the fourth largest suspension bridge in the United States. From the upper arch flew the world's largest free-flying U.S. flag, a symbol of freedom.

Listening to him in the role of tour guide, Claudia began to unwind and enjoy his company. He sounded so normal, she could almost convince herself that she had imagined the undertone of anger a few minutes ago. The balance of the drive passed pleasantly enough, and when he opened up the engine on the highway, it was magical, like flying.

The restaurant, a squarish building with fifteen-feet-high windows, stood on a pier at the river's edge. A few intrepid diners huddled around space heaters outside on the wooden deck, but most of the outdoor tables were deserted in the late-winter evening.

They slowed and Ian steered into the parking lot. A valet in black and red came out from under the awning at the restaurant's front door and stepped off the sidewalk in anticipation of taking the car. Ian slammed on the brake and they jerked to a halt, avoiding the young man's feet by inches.

Ian rolled the window down just wide enough to

hiss through it, "You idiot! What the hell d'you think you're doing?"

The valet made to open the door for him. "It's valet parking, sir. I'll be happy to take care of your car for you."

"Get your hands *off* my car. *Nobody* touches this car." Ian stepped on the gas and the DBS leapt forward. The valet's hand flew off the door and he stumbled backward, tripping against the curb and landing on his butt on the sidewalk.

"Stop the car!" Claudia yelled. "Check and see if he's okay."

Ian glanced in the mirror, but kept driving. "He's fine," he muttered, raising the window. "Idiot. He must be new. The regular boys know I won't have their filthy fingerprints mucking up my steering wheel, *or* their muddy boots on the carpet."

Claudia twisted around to make sure the valet had picked himself up. The good impression Ian had made in his office was fast fading. "I'm sure they're trained not to get customers' cars dirty."

"You're too optimistic, my dear."

He drove to the back of the lot, choosing a parking space as far from the restaurant as he could find. He backed into it and climbed out, taking out the chamois and vigorously buffing the area where the valet had put his hand. When he was satisfied, he went around to open the passenger door for Claudia.

After the warmth of the vehicle, the cold air hit her like a sheet of glass. The melancholy sound of water slapping against the dock pilings reached her and she drew her coat tighter around her. If Jovanic were here . . .

Don't go there . . .

*   *   *

Aside from the atmosphere being lower key, the dining ritual was similar to the previous evening with Marcus Bernard. The maitre d' fussed over them and conducted them to a table next to the tall windows overlooking the Hudson. The sommelier brought the wine Ian requested, and they ordered food with exotic names and ingredients.

They made polite conversation, the awkwardness of Ian's outburst in the car still hanging like a pall between them. Claudia could tell that he knew she was disgusted with the way he had treated the valet, and she didn't much care. The wine seemed to disappear rapidly from his glass and he soon signaled for another. Claudia's glass was still more than half full.

"What's it like for you, testifying as an expert in court?" he asked as they waited for the starter course.

"It's not my favorite part of the work; it can be nerve-wracking. Mostly when I testify, it's in forgery cases. Sometimes . . ." She stopped talking and looked pointedly at Ian, who had taken the linen napkin from his lap and was polishing his silverware. She watched him wipe the napkin over his fork, taking great care to polish each tine. He turned it around, holding the area he had just cleaned in one end of the napkin as he worked on the handle. Next, he took the spoon and blew a light fog onto the bowl, rubbing vigorously.

His actions reminded Claudia of what Marcus had told her the evening before: that Ian had been straightening Shellee Jones' silverware just a few minutes before she succumbed to anaphylactic shock.

It took him a few seconds to react to her silence. "Do go on," he said, starting on his butter knife. "I am listening. It's just that, as good as a restaurant may be, you can't trust the kitchen workers to attend to the proper cleaning of utensils. They don't make enough money to care. One can't be too careful."

"Is everything all right, Doctor?" The maitre d' had hurried over and positioned himself discreetly, screening them from other diners who might catch on to what Ian was doing.

Ian continued polishing his knife without looking at the man. "Perfectly."

"May I bring you some new silverware, Dr. McAllister?"

Ian glanced up at the man, then resumed his labors. "Then I would have to start all over again, wouldn't I? You should know by now that I have a particularly high standard of cleanliness."

"Of course, Doctor." The maitre d' offered a big, false smile. "Please don't hesitate to let me know if there's anything I can do for you. Anything at all."

Claudia felt her face get hot. She understood the obsessive-compulsive personality, but Ian's conspicuous behavior embarrassed her.

He replaced the napkin on his lap and gave her a knowing look. "It may seem odd to you, Claudia, but as a physician, believe me, I know something about germs. May I do yours for you?"

"No, thank you. My silverware is clean." She could hardly wait for the meal to be over so they could return to Manhattan. She said, "I'd be interested to hear what brought you to the medical profession."

"Ahh, the medical profession." The second glass of wine had begun to soften the hard planes of his features and loosen his tongue. "Medicine has a long tradition in my family. My father was a physician and so was my grandfather before him, and my great-grandfather before him. There was never any question of what I was expected to do."

The marked absence of affection in his voice struck her. "You make it sound as if you didn't have any choice in the matter," said Claudia.

He showed her a humorless smile. "As a matter of fact, I didn't. What I wanted to do was paint, but that was out of the question. In our house, art was viewed as the height of frivolity. Or perhaps I should say depths. That sort of thing was *not* tolerated. If Father were to catch me being idle—idle hands being the devil's workshop, of course—the punishment was quite severe, trust me."

Claudia thought back to his remark in the car about sparing the rod and spoiling the child. She had no doubt that what he was telling her now was at the roots of the proverb he had parroted.

"Do you mean you were beaten?" she asked.

"Beaten? No, indeed, nothing so uncivilized." Ian's short laugh had a hollow ring. "A beating would have been preferable to the punishments my father could dream up."

"I'm not sure I want to know what you mean by that."

"I'll tell you anyway. His favorites were a cold night locked in the garage or tied to my bed. No meals for a couple of days."

Claudia's sympathies were immediately aroused for the frightened child he must have been. Yet his story also fueled her suspicions. His was the sort of history that might provide fertile soil for a killer who carefully planned ahead. It also occurred to her that the conversation had taken an oddly personal direction considering they had just met.

She saw that he was waiting for her to respond. "I don't know what to say, Ian. It's horrible. Do you paint now?"

He shook his head, and as his eyes locked on hers, she recognized an expression of deep regret. "I gave up on painting long ago. The associations are too difficult."

"I'm sure they must be very painful. Where was your mother while these things were taking place?"

"Poor Mother. She wasn't equipped to deal with him. Mostly she was hiding out in her room, mewling like a baby. Even at five years old, I felt I had to protect *her*. All during the time I was growing up, she would tell me how much it hurt her to see the things he did to me. Unfortunately it didn't hurt her enough to make it stop." He drained his glass, then made a wry face over the rim. "I suppose one can't really blame her. He was a rather terrifying force of nature."

"Is he still alive, your father?"

Ian didn't answer. He was looking past her into those long-ago days, when he had been small and powerless. Claudia reached across the table and touched his arm, moved by the vulnerability she saw in his face.

He jerked away, reflexively brushing at his jacket sleeve as if her fingertips had left dirt on it. His eyes closed momentarily. "I'm sorry. I didn't mean to do that. I just—I have trouble being touched. I mean, when it's unexpected. I've always—"

"It's okay," Claudia said softly. "It's all right."

"You think I'm crazy, and I don't blame you. Since I lost my daughter—" His voice thickened and he broke off.

"The pain must be unbearable."

"Nothing has been the same since Jessica's been gone. She was my life." He stared into the tiny pool of sediment at the bottom of his wineglass as if he were a tea leaf reader and the dregs would reveal something important that he needed to know. "You should be glad you won't be here long enough to get to know me, Claudia. People who get close to me always suffer."

That shook her. "Why do you say that?"

He was silent for a long moment, his eyes downcast. When he looked up, the anguish had been extinguished. Placing his knife and fork on the plate in the exact correct position that would signal their waiter that he had finished his meal, Ian leaned back in his chair. "I must apologize for allowing this conversation to become so maudlin." He trotted out the lopsided smile. "I hope you're enjoying your dinner?"

Was he playing some kind of game with her? If so, she was unaware of the rules. The man was maddening in his quick change of direction and she felt as if she were stumbling around in the dark.

"Okay," Claudia said. "If you want to change the subject, why don't we talk about Grusha. I've never met anyone like her. She's quite a character, wouldn't you agree?"

Ian stared back at her for a long moment. "My dear Claudia, you have no idea just how much of a character our baroness really is."

Claudia had no intention of making herself vulnerable to another rebuff. Her curiosity was piqued, as he must have known it would be, but she just raised her eyebrows.

He took the bait. "She's been to prison, you know."

"No, I can't say I did know that," Claudia said, her interest quickening. "What landed her in prison?"

Ian scrubbed his hand over his beard as if ruminating on how to reply. "I think I'd better not. I've said too much already."

Claudia's intuition told her that this was probably what Jovanic had tried to share with her in their last conversation, when she'd refused to listen. This information was too important to let it go. She would just have to eat crow and ask him.

Chapter 18

Claudia's attempts to persuade Ian to open up about Grusha's past met with failure. He was steadfast in his refusal, placing the blame for loose lips on the three glasses of sauvignon blanc he'd downed. When she pointed out that the cat was already out of the bag and he might as well tell her the rest of the story, he brushed her off, pleading embarrassment over his indiscretion.

She refused dessert, so he paid the bill and they left their table in silence. On their way out, Ian suggested a walk along the Hudson. Claudia, more than ready to call a halt to the evening, gave a quick shake of her head. "It's freezing; let's just go back to the city. It's supposed to snow tonight."

Ian took her hand and tucked it under his arm, ignoring her protest. "I need to clear my head before the drive. Just a short stroll along the pier."

The beginnings of a familiar and unpleasant sense of uneasiness crept over her. For so long, she'd managed to keep it under control, but since coming close to violent death, the sensation had come rushing back with a vengeance. Why couldn't she just say *No, thanks* when she felt pressured by a man? There was something overpowering about Ian that made her hold her tongue.

As they walked outside, Claudia pulled her coat collar up around her neck and pointed out that a light rain had started. Ian squeezed her hand. "I might not have been a Boy Scout, but I am prepared. There's an umbrella in the trunk."

He was steady on his feet and she had no concerns about his ability to drive safely, but she could hardly refuse him the time he claimed that he needed to sober up. She had to admit, her suspicions notwithstanding, it was hard for her to imagine him killing his own daughter. Or any of the other people who had died such awful and untimely deaths. A short walk along the pier was not a big deal, she told herself. There were plenty of other people around.

As they neared the Aston Martin, Ian popped the trunk. A few feet closer, he came to an abrupt halt. "Those *bastards*! Look what they've done!" He dropped Claudia's arm and rushed over to the vehicle.

He was crouched by the front tire, running his hand over the front fender, as she came up behind him. "What's wrong?"

"The valets—they've keyed my car. It's because I wouldn't let them drive it."

Claudia leaned down, the light of a nearby streetlamp illuminating the front fender. She could see nothing more than a few streaks of dirt—a splash of gutter mud by the looks of it.

Ian straightened and spun around. "I'll have someone's job for this." He strode off toward the valet kiosk, leaving Claudia to wonder about his mental stability.

The rain had become a cold drizzle that dampened her hair and numbed her ears and nose. She tried the passenger door, but Ian had not unlocked the doors. She hurried around to the back of the car in disgust.

The umbrella was there, predictably tidy, attached to the fabric of the trunk's inner wall.

She unfurled the big black umbrella and took shelter under it, glad for the protection. Over at the valet kiosk, Ian, who appeared oblivious to the stinging rain, was shouting at the young man. Even from fifty feet, she could hear him accusing the kid of damaging the Aston Martin, and demanding to speak to the manager.

Claudia thought his behavior so obnoxious that she considered asking the maitre d' to order a cab to take her back to the city. Her hotel room might not be five-star, but at this moment she would have warmly welcomed its solitude. Realizing that at this time of night and so far north of Manhattan, the chances of getting a cab would be slim, she quickly gave it up as a bad idea.

She should have refused Ian's invitation to dinner. Reminding herself once again that she was not a private detective, she wished she'd refused the entire damned assignment. A trip to New York was not going to help her avoid dealing with her problems at home.

Claudia started to close the trunk, pausing halfway before opening it again. Her eyes were drawn back to a cardboard box. She had observed the box earlier, but as intent as she had been on getting the umbrella opened and over her head, she hadn't given it any thought. Now something urged her to check it out.

The box was open, so the stack of manila medical file folders that lay inside was in plain sight. A large purple L was stamped on the cover of the top file, and the trunk light was bright enough for Claudia to read the typed label. The patient name on the label was Heather Lloyd.

Despite the cold weather, her palms began sweating inside her gloves, her heart racing as she glanced back at Ian. He was now shouting at a white-haired man who she guessed was the valet manager. The other man was gesticulating, yelling back just as angrily at Ian. A couple of restaurant customers walked outside. Seeing the argument, they hurried back into the building.

Holding the umbrella over the trunk to keep the rain out, Claudia pulled off her gloves. She leaned in and picked up Heather's folder and found several additional files underneath it. The second was labeled *Shellee Jones*. The third, predictably, *Ryan Turner*. The one missing name was Jessica McAllister, for what she thought were obvious reasons.

Slow down, she told herself. This was exceeding the job she had come here to do. Still, the situation was intriguing. She had allowed herself to become involved and now she felt compelled to follow it through. So she asked the question: Why did Ian have these files in his car?

She flipped through the first folder and found a typical patient chart, the type that could be found in any doctor's office. These people had been Ian's patients—long enough for him to screen them for Grusha, at least. That gave him a legitimate reason to have the files.

But it can't be a fluke that he has these particular charts at this particular time in the trunk of his car.

Ian would never give permission for her to take the files as Donna Pollard had done. The small evening purse she carried would not conceal anything for later perusal. Another backward glance told her that Ian's diatribe was continuing unabated. With her heart in her mouth, Claudia opened Heather Lloyd's

patient file and got her first glimpse of the doctor's
handwriting on the chart notes.

Most people thought that all doctors' handwritings were illegible, but after studying the handwritings of thousands of physicians, Claudia knew that
the cliché was a fallacy. Handwriting always told the
truth about the writer, regardless of his or her profession, and many doctors had clear, legible writing. Ian
was not one of them.

Given the minuscule writing size and letter forms
that were simplified almost to the point of skeletal,
the doctor's handwriting was effectively unreadable.
The thick black ink he had used made the words even
more difficult to read. Several ink smudges dotted
the page, which were at odds with his obsessive need
to clean the silverware.

The passing glimpse of the tiny scrawl left Claudia
with a strong impression of a brilliant intellect, impatience, a short fuse, difficulty in connecting empathi-
cally with others. In the short time she had spent with
him, she had already witnessed his acting out several
of those characteristics.

She wanted to take the time to properly examine
his handwriting, but she knew there wasn't a second
to spare. At any moment, he might end the argument
with the manager and catch her spying on him. The
more important and urgent task at hand was to see
if she could learn why these charts were in the trunk
of his car.

Keeping an ear on the situation across the parking lot, Claudia quickly thumbed through Heather
Lloyd's chart. From what she could make out in the
trunk light, the medical chart detailed the physical
examination that Heather had undergone in Ian's
office: blood pressure, temperature, other vitals. But

one item caught her notice: On Heather's visit, Ian had given her sample prescription capsules to treat a head cold.

The blood thrummed in Claudia's ears. Detective Gray had told her that Heather had taken a higher than normal dose of cold medication, which left her groggy and probably contributed to her death. Had Ian done something to the capsules to make them more potent? Or advised Heather to take a stronger than recommended dose?

She moved on to Shellee Jones' file. The words *Severe Peanut Allergy* made her catch her breath. Printed in all capital red letters at the top of the chart, the words were surrounded by large asterisks. Someone had written in the chart notes that at her mother's urging, Shellee carried an EpiPen with her. Claudia knew what an EpiPen was.

A man she'd once known, a friend of her father's who was highly allergic to shellfish, had carried such a kit with him at all times. Once, when this man had gone out to dinner with her family, his throat had swelled after he inadvertently ate food that contained an allergen. A child at the time, Claudia had been horrified and fascinated to see him inject the epinephrine that saved him. He'd stabbed the tip of the EpiPen right through his trouser leg into his thigh. She could still remember his struggle to breathe and how his wheezing respirations had slowly returned to normal after the shot.

Some people shouldn't be saved.

She opened Ryan Turner's folder with shaking hands. Suddenly, she became aware of the strobe of red lights.

Turning, she saw that a police cruiser had pulled into the parking lot and stopped at the valet kiosk.

Those worried customers must have called the cops. Two patrolmen got out and approached Ian and the parking attendant. *Damn!* How much worse could the evening get?

On the other hand, the appearance of the police gave her the gift of a little extra time to browse Ryan's file.

The young med student had been in generally good health, but a note in the chart indicated that he had suffered from bronchial asthma after a bout of pneumonia the year before. Could Ian have somehow used his asthmatic condition to engineer his scuba diving death? She knew there were some big holes in that theory, but . . .

Staccato, angry footsteps were headed in her direction. The red lights were no longer pulsing. Under cover of the umbrella, Claudia carefully replaced the files back in the box and slammed the trunk closed. She spun around to face Ian McAllister.

His eyes blazed in the pale blur of his face, and for a frightening moment she thought his anger was directed at her.

"I'll sue them," Ian said in a voice hoarse from shouting. He took the umbrella from her hand and held it over them both as he unlocked the car and saw her inside. "The manager wouldn't even come over and look at the damage. Insisted they never came near the car, but—"

"Someone called the police?" Claudia interrupted.

He threw her a dark look as if she were at fault, and didn't answer. Thank god he was too distracted to realize how long she had been hovering at the rear of his car.

As soon as they were on the road, the tirade started up and continued in an endless loop throughout the thirty-minute drive: They had damaged his beautiful vehicle; he would sue them; he would never patronize the restaurant again.

"I can't believe they would allow this to happen," Ian ranted. "An Aston Martin DBS! A fine performance machine—do you have any idea what the repairs are going to cost?"

Claudia didn't bother to answer. He wasn't listening to anything but the rasp of his own voice. *Shut up!* she wanted to shout at him. *I don't want to hear any more.* But she wasn't stupid. She suffered the ride in silence, afraid that if she said out loud what she was thinking, he might turn his rage her way after all.

Chapter 19

"Are you out of your mind?"

Grusha Olinetsky sprang up from her desk and began to pace her office. Her respirations, quick and shallow, could easily be seen through her fashionable charcoal and black striped suit. Anxiety had brought her almost to the point of hyperventilation. She swung back to Claudia, her face a mask of despair. "Do you vant to destroy me even faster?"

Claudia kept her tone even. "No, Grusha, I don't want to see you destroyed at all. But you brought me here because you already knew that something was seriously wrong. If Ian is killing your clients—and maybe his own daughter—you can't just let it go on. How do you know you won't be next?"

"Of course I vill not be next," Grusha said bitterly. "The person doing this vants me to suffer. If I am dead, the suffering vill be over. Where vill be the pleasure for him in that?"

Claudia chewed on her lower lip, making a mess of her lipstick. So much for the suggestion she had made, that Grusha talk to the police. Yet she could not sit by and do nothing while the indications—if not actual physical evidence—of multiple murder piled up.

"Why vould *Ian* do this? I have done nothing to him."

"Did you know that his daughter had HIV?"

"*What?*" The matchmaker's mouth gaped open. "But I don't understand."

"Jessica was going to rave parties and sleeping around, doing drugs. She found out she'd contracted HIV, and she planned to tell her father. Then she died."

Grusha looked even more bewildered. "But she killed herself."

"It seems to look that way. But I have to admit, given the deaths of your three other clients, and with him having their files in his car, it does make me wonder."

Claudia had spent most of last night lying awake in bed, thinking it all through. When they had parted company in the hotel lobby, Ian offered a half-assed apology for his shameful behavior. But his extreme reaction to the imagined damage to his car, and his abusive manner toward the valet, had left a sour taste in Claudia's mouth, one that she would not soon forget.

She said, "The level of anger I saw in Ian last night was utterly appalling. And it was over nothing—there were no marks on his car. I dread to imagine how he would react to something serious, like the news that his daughter had been defying him, carrying on a secret life, and had HIV. I have two alternate theories about it, but they end up in the same place."

Grusha dropped onto the sofa and covered her face with her hands. "I did not ask you to develop theories, Claudia," she whined through her fingers. "You said you are not a detective. Why, then, are you detecting?"

"When the shit is hitting me in the face, Grusha, I *am* involved. You involved me, and I allowed it. And,

I'm sorry, but I'm not as dumb as a box of rocks. *I* can see there's a connection between all these deaths, and *you* can, too. Now, when we talked about this before, you said that if I saw anything, you would go to the police."

"But what you are talking about is not the handwriting. We said if you saw anything in the *handwriting*."

"You're splitting hairs. Handwriting shows potential for behavior. It can't predict that someone will kill. Ian's handwriting shows his short fuse and his anger, but I can't say that means he set up these killings and carried them out, just that there are some red flags. Bottom line, the situation has to be brought to the authorities. Let *them* figure it out."

Grusha slumped back against the sofa. Her jittery breathing had slowed and she seemed to resign herself. She sighed. "Tell me about these theories you have."

"Okay, this is with the assumption that Ian is the culprit. One, Jessica told him about having contracted HIV and her secret party life. He was so frantic at learning about it that he went crazy and killed her. Then, realizing what he'd done, he set it up to look like a suicide. It wouldn't be the first time that has happened to someone.

"Two, Jessica did kill herself and he couldn't stand losing control over her, so in his narcissistic rage, he needed to have a replacement to act out on, and you happened to be handy. The second option seems more plausible because of the way it's been done." She floated the concept that she'd discussed with Zebediah. "In his twisted thinking, he could convince himself that you were at fault for her disease, and take revenge by harming what he knows is most important to you—Elite Introductions."

"But this makes no sense," Grusha protested. "He is the one who gives the members a medical examination. If somebody sneaked in vit a disease, it vould be *his* fault, not mine! And from what you just said, it was *not* one of my clients who infected her vit this loathsome scourge. He cannot blame that on me."

"It doesn't have to make sense to you or me, as long as it makes sense to him."

"I did not vant to match that girl," Grusha said, getting heated. "She was far too young—a child of eighteen. Ian insist that I find her a suitable man, and then he complain about everyone I introduce her to. Nobody good enough." She paused, thinking about it. "Do you think he is the one who broke into Dr. Pollard's office?"

Claudia shrugged. "I don't know. The guy was behind her when he hit her, so she didn't see him. It's possible that he was looking for Jessica's file, to see if there was anything in it that might incriminate him—if he is the killer. I know it's a stretch, but Jessica could have told him she had been seeing Donna Pollard for therapy, taunting him, knowing there was nothing he could do about it."

Grusha didn't bother to ask how she knew so much about Jessica and her relationship with her father, and Claudia didn't volunteer the information. What she had read in Jessica's therapy file would remain between her and Donna Pollard. If, indeed, Ian had been Pollard's intruder, he had gotten away without finding what he had been looking for. Unlucky for Donna that she had appeared just then.

"There's something else I want to ask you about, Grusha," Claudia said, determined to bring up the subject that felt to her like the elephant in the room. "You've been adamant about not going to the police, and you've more than implied that the reason is something from your past."

The matchmaker gave her a wary look. "This has nothing to do vit what is happening to my business."

My business. To her, the dead clients represented dollars more than they did lives. It occurred to Claudia that Shellee, Ryan, and Heather were a means to an end to Grusha Olinetsky. She didn't see them as individuals. She needed a steady stream of attractive people to introduce to other attractive people. Their deaths were a threat to her livelihood, and that made them more an inconvenience than anything else.

Claudia hesitated, then plunged ahead. "I'd like to take a sample of your handwriting, Grusha. I should have asked for it before we ever began working together. Under the present circumstances, I'm not going to continue without it."

"I am not going to submit to this—this test!"

"But you don't mind asking your clients to submit to it? What are you afraid I'll see?" It was the same question she had asked of Donna Pollard.

"You already know what I am afraid of, and giving you my handwriting vill not change that." Grusha rose from the sofa, went to the door and opened it. "I have an appointment vit a client. Ve shall have to continue this conversation at another time."

Downstairs in the lobby, Claudia got out her cell phone and punched buttons to pull up the calls that had come in. She scanned through them until she came to Susan Rowan's number and pushed the call button.

"Susan, it's Claudia. I've got a question for you."

"First, I've got one for you: How do you like working for the barmy baroness?"

"That's what I'm calling you about. I remember you told me that she doesn't want anyone looking at her handwriting, but by any chance did you ever find that sample you told me you have?"

Susan chuckled. "She's getting to you, isn't she? As a matter of fact, I did dig up that sample and I am willing to share it with you. Where are you now?"

"I'm just leaving her office."

"How about meeting for lunch?"

They met at Hurley's, a pub in the Theater District close to Claudia's hotel. Having arrived well before the lunch hour, they managed to get in without a reservation. On the second level, the walls were lined with hundreds of books, shelved library style. Susan and Claudia were shown to a crimson velvet–padded booth with ceiling-high paisley-patterned walls that provided the seclusion of a private dining room. An old-fashioned lamp with a fringed lampshade hung over the table, which was set with crystal wineglasses.

"This is very cool," Claudia said, sliding into the booth. "It feels like we should be meeting with Don Corleone."

Susan laughed. "Well, this *is* a sort of clandestine rendezvous, after all. I wouldn't want you-know-who to know what we're doing."

Claudia ordered the grilled portobello mushroom, and Susan the tuna salad. When the waiter left, Susan dug into her purse and took out a folded piece of paper. "It won't be what you expect," she warned, handing it across the table.

Claudia unfolded the paper. Susan wasn't joking. The few words written on it were like nothing Claudia might have imagined Grusha Olinetsky's handwriting to have been. The writing had a childish look, not what a handwriting analyst would expect from a successful businesswoman. She noticed the many covering strokes—strokes that went back over a previous one. People did that when they had something to hide.

"Are you *sure* this is her handwriting?" She was experiencing a little paranoia in case someone heard them, and didn't want to say Grusha's name aloud.

"It's an old sample," Susan said. "But it's definitely hers. I saw her write it. She didn't know I snagged it before I left the office that day."

"How long ago was it written?"

Susan scrunched her eyes shut and turned her face toward the ceiling as she did some mental calculations. "Must be about three or four years. That's right about when I started working for her."

Claudia gave the sample a second look. She had expected to see signs of the Russian Cyrillic script in Grusha's handwriting, and there were some, but the writing was definitely atypical of that culture. But she had learned over the years that handwriting was not always what she expected it to be. It was better to keep an open mind and listen to what a sample told her, rather than to force her own preconceived notions onto it.

"Do you know anything about her background?"

Susan grinned. "I'm happy to say I do. Not her childhood or anything like that. More recent. I made it my business to do a little investigating, and I found some interesting info. Didn't stop me from working for her. Maybe it should have."

"What do you mean?"

"Our baroness is a jailbird."

So Ian had been telling the truth about that. Claudia asked what she had been convicted of, but her loyalties were torn. On one hand, Grusha deserved her privacy. On the other, if she or her clients were being targeted by a murderer, there was no such thing as privacy.

Susan didn't have Ian's excuse of having drunk too much wine, and she showed no reluctance about sharing what she knew. In fact, she looked downright pleased with herself as she leaned forward and said, sotto voce, "She was convicted of pandering. Solicitation of prostitution."

Chapter 20

"Pandering?" Claudia stared back at Susan in shock. "She was a pimp?"

"Not here in New York. This was a while back. She was living in a hick town at the time, running an introduction service. Not a high-priced one like Elite Introductions. From what I could tell, it seemed more on the level of a massage parlor. The way it sounded, someone didn't like her and there was this big exposé. The mayor and his good old boys wanted to run her out of town on a rail—I bet they were probably some of her best clients." Susan paused for breath. She made a moue of disapproval. "Somebody else might have let her off with a warning, but it was pretty clear from the newspaper stories that this prosecutor had political ambitions. Politics and small-town crime—a lethal combination, if you get my drift."

The Theater District lunch crowd had begun to filter in. A dozen conversations boosted the noise level to the sound of a jet engine at full throttle. Claudia leaned in closer so that Susan could hear her question. "What was it that prompted you to investigate her?"

"Oh, you know—Grusha's such a trip. It was just one of those Internet searches. You pay a few bucks and voilà! You get a report that tells you all about the person, practically down to what brand of toothpaste they use. Everything is on the Internet these days; it's not hard to find stuff out."

"That doesn't sound like much of a reason to spend money on an Internet search. Because she's a trip. What else was there, Suze?"

Susan toyed with her salad, digging her fork around in the diminishing mound of tuna. "I always check out new clients on Google. But it's true, I did go further with Grusha than I normally do. I was getting worried about the way she operated." She paused to drink some water before continuing, then took a forkful of her salad and chewed thoughtfully. When she'd swallowed, she said, "Most of the clients she sent me to analyze looked okay. But there were several handwritings that I analyzed from subjects who I thought might cause problems somewhere along the line. Apart from the blatant red-flag ones, I mean."

"Like Heather Lloyd's twisted lower zone loops?"

"You got it. Heather needed counseling, not dating. Someone with sexual issues is the last thing Grusha should have in the club."

"I take it you told her that?"

"Naturally I told her. But she didn't want to hear it. Just argued with me that everything looked good on the background report and the medical; she was a beautiful girl, yada yada. Then I found out that she'd actually changed my report!"

"She redacted it herself?"

"She denied it, but she was lying and I was furious. Told her I wouldn't work for her if she didn't guarantee me that she would never do that again."

"Makes you wonder why she would bother to hire a graphologist."

"Just to cover her ass is my guess. I told her that

it was unethical for her to change even one word of
my report. I also told her that it would be unethical
for me to leave out important information—it's part
of what she was paying for. She freaked about having it in black and white, and the truth is, it doesn't
have to be in writing. As far as Heather's problems
went, I did my due diligence by telling her verbally.
Grusha was my client, not Heather. It was up to her
what she did with the information after I'd given it to
her. I made her sign a contract with a hold-harmless
clause, so that if there were any legal problems later,
I was covered."

"That was smart."

"I've been blindsided before. I learn fast."

Claudia guided her back to the more pressing matter. "So, you found out she had a prison record. I can't
believe they actually filed charges and tried her."

Susan nodded. "She was charged with promoting
prostitution, and convicted by a jury. Although I can't
imagine any twelve people in that kind of town being
her peers. Whatever it was *really* all about, well, your
guess is as good as mine, but she went to prison for
two years."

"Heidi Fleiss revisited."

"Except Heidi Fleiss was a Hollywood madam
catering to celebrities. Our gal was strictly small-
time back then. *Now* she's got a clientele Heidi Fleiss
would die for."

"And that's the catch," Claudia said under her
breath. "People *are* dying. The question is—" She hesitated. Susan was aware of Ryan Turner's death and
Heather Lloyd's, but she didn't know about Shellee
Jones, and Jessica McAllister was an unknown quan-
tity. "You don't think she's running an escort service
now, do you? Everything I've seen looks legit."

"My search didn't uncover any other legal problems or I wouldn't have kept working for her. As far as I can tell, everything she's doing is on the up-and-up. Except for ignoring my advice."

The portobello mushroom was good and juicy. Claudia laid down her fork and dabbed her lips with her napkin. "She told me there was a disgruntled former employee who made trouble for her. I bet that's how the DA got the scoop on her operation."

"You're probably right about that. I think it's so unfair. She may be a little crazy, or, shall we say . . . eccentric? But I've always liked her." Susan's cheeks were flushed and her words were heating up, too. "It's outrageous. If someone wants to pay for sex it ought to be their choice."

Before she could get any more wound up, Claudia interrupted the flow. "What do you think of Dr. McAllister?"

"Yummy. But a little too OCD for my taste."

"That's not what I meant, Susan, and you know it. Did you ever wonder whether he could be involved in what happened to Heather and Ryan?"

Susan's brows rose in surprise. "Ian McAllister involved? In what way?"

"Never mind; forget I asked."

"If anybody's got me wondering, it's that Donna Pollard. There's something peculiar about that woman."

Claudia pushed away her plate. "I know what you mean. When I met her, the first thing she did was try to get me to tell her my deep, dark secrets."

"You, too? She is so nosy."

"What do you think is the problem with her?"

"Not sure, but I got a funny feeling about her as soon as we met. Methinks she's hiding something under that überdefensive attitude." Susan gave her a pointed look. "Lots of secrets in this group."

"Yes, and that brings up another question."

"What's that?"

"You told me you were the one who suggested Grusha call me. Why did you do that? I know you didn't want to go back to work for her after your illness, but was there anything else to it than that? I mean, why me?"

Susan made a show of folding her napkin and neatly placing it on the table. "Do you want dessert? No?" She sounded disappointed when Claudia declined. "Okay, here's the god's honest truth. When I read the newspaper story about that girl's death, I thought it was a damned shame. But when I read about the young doctor—Turner, I think was his name—it started to really bug me. So I phoned Grusha and asked what the hell was going on. She acted like she didn't know what I was talking about; kept insisting that it had nothing to do with her or the dating service. It was just coincidence. Okay, fine. I could accept coincidence.

"But it was pretty clear to me that there was something she wasn't telling me. I got the impression that she wanted to talk, but couldn't make herself get the words out. I thought maybe she was in some kind of trouble, but couldn't go to the cops because of her criminal record. She needed help. And that idiot she'd been using—Andy Nicholson—he's worse than useless. So, when I saw you on *Hard Evidence* that morning, I got this wild hair that Grusha ought to contact *you*. You've been involved in high-profile cases, so I thought you could help her."

"Well, thanks so much," Claudia said. "You might have warned me what I was getting into."

"I did try to give you a clue that day at breakfast."

"Don't you think that was a little late?"

"I was trying to help. The thing is, I don't even know if there really *is* a problem."

Oh, but there is, thought Claudia. *Four young people are dead.*

"I'd like to know where my handwriting reports are," Susan added. "Why aren't they in the files you looked at?"

"My guess is Grusha replaced the ones that didn't suit her with Andy's, which don't say anything of any consequence. That way she's got deniability. You didn't put anything terribly negative in writing, so she can say she never knew there were problems."

Claudia grabbed the bill and flagged down their server. "Thank you for letting me see that handwriting, Susan, and for telling me all this. I've gotta run. Lunch is on me."

The Theater District was located in Manhattan North, NYPD's Eighteenth Precinct. The dating club deaths had all taken place in different geographic areas. Since Claudia knew nothing about New York police jurisdictions, she Googled Manhattan precincts and found thirty-four listed. Manhattan North was the one closest to her hotel, so she made that her starting point.

The weather had brightened and a weak sun shone through the crammed-together buildings as the taxi dropped her off at 306 West Fifty-fourth Street. The old station house was bathed with a shell pink aura in the early afternoon light, the effect somewhat spoiled by the grimy stains mottling the walls from rain that had pooled on dirty windowsills and spilled over.

Passing a row of police vehicles parked in front of

the station house, Claudia ascended the three granite steps and entered through the Eighteenth Precinct's heavy green metal entry doors. In the reception area, a row of seats was occupied by an unhappy woman trying to corral a toddler, an obese man in a sweat-stained shirt who looked and smelled like he needed a shower, and a sullen teenager, staring at his shoes.

Claudia approached the front desk, where a tele-phone operator–receptionist was on the phone. She was trying to explain to someone on the other end of the line that officers would be out to talk to them later in the afternoon. The caller must have been giving her grief, as her voice quickly developed an attitude.

The desk officer came over, a trim African Ameri-can man in a uniform that looked as if it had just been pressed and taken off the hanger. "Ma'am, how can I help you?" he asked.

"Could I talk to a detective, please?"

"What's the issue?"

"I need to talk to someone about a possible crime."

"What kind of crime, ma'am?"

"It's rather a long story. Is there someone I could talk to from homicide?"

"Homicide?" He sized her up, probably deciding whether she was delusional. "I'll check if someone's available." The officer turned away, picked up the phone on the desk and punched in a number. He spoke to whoever answered in a low voice, then hung up and jerked his head at the row of chairs. "Ma'am, you can wait over there. Someone will be down to talk to you."

Claudia thanked him and moved over to the plas-tic chairs. Too restless to sit, she roamed the room, avoiding eye contact with the other occupants. She read the Wanted posters on clipboards attached to the wall. Bench warrants for failure to appear. Robbery with a deadly weapon. Missing persons. Violation of probation. Grand theft. Money laundering. Uttering a forged instrument. The kinds of announcements one would expect to find in a police station. A depressing reminder of the amount of crime that was perpetrated in the city on a daily basis. Crimes that were far too close for comfort, Claudia thought with an uneasy frisson. Criminals were not always caught.

"How can I help you, ma'am?"

Claudia swung around to face a tired-looking man about her own height. His receding hairline, pudgy face, and a nose that had been broken at least once reminded her of Grumpy of the Seven Dwarfs. The faint outline of a scar at eyebrow level stood out against coffee-colored skin. He wore an inexpensive button-down shirt with the sleeves rolled up, a darker blue tie. Claudia noticed that, unlike the spit-shined desk officer, his shoes were worn and scuffed. Probably too busy fighting crime to think about polishing them.

She became aware of the interested looks they were getting from the other people in the reception area. "Is there somewhere we can talk privately?" she asked.

The detective gave her the once-over the way the desk officer had. Her business suit and briefcase apparently satisfied him that she wasn't just some street crazy here to waste his time. He said, "Okay, ma'am, come this way."

He led her through a door to a long hallway. A couple of men and one miserable-looking woman were handcuffed to benches, waiting to be booked. They glowered at Claudia and the detective, who had introduced himself as Isadore Perez, calling out profanities as they passed.

Perez guided her past interview rooms with meshed windows set in the doors. Claudia had seen rooms like these before and she knew what the inside would be like. A metal table bolted to the floor to prevent an offender from turning it into a weapon. A couple of chairs. A video camera mounted high. Walls covered with yellowing acoustic tile. The pungent smell of desperation, fear. Scuzzy, like the man in the reception area who needed a bath.

They rode an elevator to the second floor and went along another short corridor. Perez didn't make small talk and neither did Claudia. He took her to the squad room, a large, open area with eight or ten desks, some of which were currently occupied by detectives doing paperwork or talking on the phone.

The lieutenant's office was half wall, half glass, allowing the commanding officer to look out at his squad of detectives as they worked at their desks. For now, it was empty. In a holding cell, Claudia could see a mean-looking detainee in a dirty jacket with a Jets logo emblazoned across it, and baggy pants.

She took the chair next to Perez' desk, filled with a sudden compulsion to get up and run out the door. She knew what it was like for someone else to have the upper hand. The thought of being handcuffed to a table, not allowed to leave, made her feel sick. And as panic started rising in her, she knew that coming here had been a mistake.

Focus on something else: the four eight-by-ten framed glossies hanging on the wall; police commissioners, spit-shined in dress blues.

Inhale slowly through the nose, exhale slowly through the mouth. Just like when you testify in court. That's it. Relax. You're free to get up and walk out the door anytime you want to.

Forcing herself to remember that she *could* leave at will gave her a sense of control and relief that was nearly overwhelming. The squeezing sensation in her chest that made it painful to breathe began slowly to subside and her heart rate gradually returned to normal.

Detective Perez was speaking to her. "So, Ms. . . . ?"

"Rose."

"What's your last name, Rose?"

"That *is* my last name."

"Okay, Ms. Rose. What can I do for you?"

Claudia cleared her throat, not sure where to start, now that she was here. "I'm in New York for a few days, visiting. I've come across some information that—well, I think it's possible that a crime has been committed."

"Uh-huh." He picked up a pen and asked what crime she wanted to report. He shuffled through some of the many papers on his desk until he found a form printed on only one side, flipped it over and prepared to make notes. "Tell me about this crime."

Claudia had a feeling that if he had been interested in what she had to report, he would probably be taking down her information on a reporter's pad like the one Jovanic used.

"I should have said crimes, plural," she amended. "If I'm right, several murders have been committed."

Detective Perez had begun doodling a series of boxes stacked one on top of the other. Closed boxes, she noted. A need for closure. He gave her a sharp glance. "Murders, you say? *Several* of them?"

"I think it may have to do with revenge. It's the only motive I can come up with."

"And you're here visiting? Where do you live, ma'am?"

When she said Los Angeles, his expression confirmed her fears. He had already passed judgment: *Oh, L.A., land of fruits and nuts.* But to his credit, he had ceased doodling and asked her to tell him what she knew. She outlined the basis of her suspicions and Detective Perez began to listen more closely.

Claudia laid out the facts as she knew them, taking care to avoid any show of emotion. It was important for him to know that she was compos mentis and reasonable. Even so, when she was done, he didn't try to hide his skepticism.

"So, tell me again, Ms. Rose. What makes you think these individuals are *homicide* victims?"

"They were all young, all members of the same dating service, they died within a short time of each other—a few weeks, really. Don't you think it's a little strange?"

He chuckled without amusement. "Lady, I see strange every day of my life. Strange is a naked guy playing a guitar in Times Square. Strange is a dead woman in the morgue who's still breathing. Strange is—"

"Okay, fine. I get the point." She had failed to convince him, and she didn't know what else she could say to make him take her seriously.

Perez said, "You don't even know where the girl's suicide occurred. You got one deceased in the Bahamas, one in Vermont. It's all very interesting, but those are way out of this jurisdiction. Maybe if you talk to the cops in—"

"I've already talked to the detective who investigated Heather Lloyd's death in Vermont. He was more open to what I'm suggesting than you are."

"Yeah, well, Stowe's not exactly a hotbed of criminal activity. He probably wouldn't mind seeing a little bit of action up there. So, you feed him this story, he jumps on it."

"Shellee Jones died in Manhattan."

"Anaphylactic shock—you said so yourself. Peanuts."

She just looked back at him until he said, "Fine, I'll look up the aided card on her."

"A what?"

"Someone called the paramedics, so a patrol car would've rolled out, too. They'd have taken down her name and address, the name of the person who contacted them. Information about who aided her. Like that. You know: fell ill while eating at so-and-so restaurant; name of witnesses. She would have been taken to Roosevelt Hospital. Everything about the incident goes on the aided card."

Claudia got the feeling that he was throwing her a few crumbs to get her off his back, but she decided that she might as well push her luck.

"While you're checking on that, would you please take a look at Dr. Ian McAllister? See if anything comes up on him? He's one person who's connected to all these people who have died. He told me that his wife left him when their daughter was just a little kid. Maybe you could find out whether the wife was ever seen again. And last night he had all those clients' files in his car."

"Had their files in his car? Now, *that's* incriminating for a doctor who saw them in his office."

"You don't have to be sarcastic."

Perez gave her the squint eye and it made him look tough. "Do you have something personal against this doctor, ma'am? Were you dating him and he dumped you?"

"I told you, I just met the man."

"So what makes you think he's guilty of a crime?"

Claudia's frustration was growing. "I've just told you why I think he *could* be guilty. I don't know for sure. That's for you to check out. But you think I'm all wet, don't you?"

"I'm still sitting here listening, aren't I?"

"You may be sitting here, but you look—hell, why do I feel like *I'm* the suspect?"

"I don't know, Ms. Rose. Why *do* you feel that way?"

Well, Detective, I've been under a lot of pressure lately and not long ago, I came close to being murdered myself . . . Yeah, that'd do it.

She hadn't wanted to use the connection, but she laid out her ace. "Detective Perez, my boyfriend is a detective with LAPD. You can call him if you like. He'll tell you I'm not prone to making things up and I don't have a vivid imagination, as you seem to think."

Perez' gaze sharpened. At last, he took out his reporter's pad. "Okay, gimme your boyfriend's info. His name? Where's he work out of? And give me that doc's name again. We'll probably have to go through the AMA or one of the medical boards, but I'll run him through our databases, see what comes up."

"McAllister. Dr. Ian McAllister. His daughter was Jessica." She gave him the names of all the dead clients, which he dutifully wrote into the notebook, and Jovanic's information.

"There are also a couple of other dating club clients that you could check out," she added, thinking of the red flags she'd found in the handwritings of John Shaw, whom she had not yet met, as well as those of Marcus Bernard and Avram Cohen.

Perez looked unhappy, but he added the three

names to his list. "So now we got four suspects? What makes you think—"

"Detective, I've worked in the legal system as an expert witness for more than ten years. I do have some credibility where I come from. Maybe you could withhold judgment until you check me out, too."

"That so? And what do you expert witness about, Ms. Rose?"

"I'm a handwriting expert. I mostly testify in cases of handwriting authentication, but in this case, I was brought here to analyze all these people's handwriting for personality traits."

She thought she would see him mentally rolling his eyes, but the doubt on his face actually eased somewhat.

"Okay, Ms. Rose. You sit tight. I'll be back in a few minutes. Get you some coffee?"

"No, thanks. Please just hurry. I have an appointment." It was a white lie, but the lack of sleep was catching up with her. Not all the hours of the night had been devoted to thinking about Grusha and her situation, or Ian and his foul temper. She had also been going over her final conversation with Jovanic.

In her heart, she wanted to believe that he was right when he said she should trust him. But everything in her past had taught her that trusting was the fastest road to more pain. That was the most brutal demon she'd fought with while she tossed and turned.

You're letting your doubts ravage the best relationship you've ever had, an insistent voice had whispered in her head until she'd sat up in bed and dialed his phone number. The call went straight to voice mail and Claudia told the voice to shut the hell up.

*   *   *

She was checking her watch for the fifteenth time when Detective Perez finally reappeared.

"Okay," he said, plunking down in his chair. "Your boyfriend wasn't available at his station or his mobile number. I left messages. I ran this Dr. McAllister through our database, made a couple of phone calls. His record is clear and he's well respected in the medical community. Hasn't so much as written an illegal prescription that I can find."

"What about the others?"

"No criminal records on any of 'em. Marcus Bernard has had some lawsuits filed against his construction company, but they're civil and either he won or they got dismissed. I gotta tell ya, Ms. Rose, this 'evidence' you've given me—I think you're making a mountain out of an anthill. There's not a thing we can do from here. Nothing you've given me indicates that these deaths are anything more than what the various MEs' reports have stated, not homicides. Hey, look, I understand where you're coming from and you can pat yourself on the back. You've done your civic duty. It was the right thing to do. Now you can relax and let it go."

Claudia rose from the chair and slung her purse over her shoulder. His patronizing attitude irritated her, but he was right. She'd done what she had to do and at least the results would make Grusha happy. "Thanks *so* much for your time, Detective."

"You are *so* welcome. You can go home to California and rest assured, we'll be taking care of things here. And Ms. Rose . . ."

She had started toward the door. She stopped and looked back over her shoulder. "Yes, Detective Perez?"

"You *will* leave the investigating to us, won't you?"

Claudia had no answer for that. She wasn't about to make a promise she had no intention of keeping. She gave the detective a faintly damning smile. "I just hope nobody else in this dating club happens to cash in their chips a little early."

Detective Perez nodded. "Well, you be sure to let us know if they do it in Manhattan North. We'll get right on it."

Chapter 21

When she walked out of the station house, Claudia discovered that iron gray clouds had gathered over the city and a bone-chilling damp had settled in. Since the day had started out pleasant, she hadn't brought her coat. The light jacket she wore wasn't much use against the stiff breeze that swept stray bits of trash along the street ahead of her.

Damn!

The hotel was less than a half-mile walk away, not worth trying for a cab. Staying close to the buildings she passed, she hurried along Eighth Avenue to Forty-eighth Street, asking herself whether there was anything more she could have done to convince Detective Perez. She was comforted by the unlikely thought that despite his lukewarm attitude, maybe once he'd talked to Jovanic, the detective's interest would be piqued enough to do some further looking.

By the time Claudia reached her hotel she was shivering and convinced that she would never be warm again. Rushing through the front doors, she could have wept in gratitude for the blast of warm air that met her inside the brightly lit foyer. She made a beeline for the elevator, thinking that the owners must have spent all the design money on the entry-way, since they certainly hadn't spent it on guest rooms. But right now, she would be thankful to get into that dreary little room and soak up the warmth of a hot shower.

She moved quickly through the lobby, hurrying past mirrored columns and fancy armchairs. She had almost made it to the concierge desk when she heard someone behind her call her name.

In a blink, all thoughts of getting upstairs and out of her damp clothing deserted her. She swung around, trying to make sense of it. She couldn't have heard what she thought she'd heard.

Jovanic?

But there he was, filling the hotel lobby with his presence, overnight bag in hand. Freshly trimmed salt-and-pepper hair, gray eyes filled with concern. The lips she wanted to kiss were compressed in a tight line; an endearing dusting of five o'clock shadow stubbled his chin.

"Why didn't you return my calls?" he demanded.

"I did. Last night. You didn't answer. What are you doing here?"

"I've been calling you for two days. What's the story, Claudia?"

"What are you doing here?" she said again, the thrill of seeing him mixed with a confusing array of feelings. But what rose above the battle was something she couldn't deny: She was incredibly happy that he was there.

As if he couldn't wait until they were alone, Jovanic grabbed her in his arms, burying his face in her hair. "We can't talk here," he said, as hotel guests pushed past them.

"Let's go up to my room."

Between the two of them and the three other passengers squashed into the postage stamp–sized elevator, the ride was cramped and silent. Claudia's mind was racing with questions about his unexpected arrival, but she held on to the solidity of his presence as if he might evaporate as abruptly as he had materialized. As they stepped out at the tenth floor and the doors closed behind them, she released the breath she had been holding.

She felt compelled to make conversation, chattering as they walked along the corridor to her room. "It's not the best hotel room I've ever had, very plain-Jane. Don't expect anything much." Now that they were nearing her room, the atmosphere between them was uncomfortable, stilted, as if they were strangers who had only just met. Not as if they had been partners in a relationship for more than a year.

"At least you got a good retainer," Jovanic said, as she fiddled with the card key. His sudden proximity had raised all her fears to the surface, demanding that she face them. Her hand was trembling a little and he gently took the card from her and stuck it into the slot. The lock clicked, the green light came on, and Claudia pushed open the door.

He followed her into the room, which seemed even more cramped and less appealing than it had previously. Jovanic closed and locked the door behind him, set his overnight bag on the floor. Claudia put her briefcase and purse beside the armchair in the corner. Before she had a chance to say anything, he took her by the arms and turned her toward him. His expression was exasperated and tender as he cupped her face in his hands. "Why do I love you?" he murmured. "You drive me crazy."

Without warning, she found her eyes brimming and she couldn't speak. The urge to let go and allow the tears to flow, to allow herself to be vulnerable, was intense, but the habit of many years made her fight it. She had convinced herself long ago that to cry was weakness, even though something was whispering to her that her instincts were off.

"It's okay," Jovanic said, the cold leather of his bomber jacket pressing against her cheek as he held her close. "I'm not going to leave you. I love you."

Why did hearing him say the words hurt her ears, as if he had yelled them at the top of his lungs? He had said them before, but something was different. She let him tilt her face up and a shudder of happiness went through her when they kissed. He was a tough cop; he had seen more horrible things in his years on the force than any one person should have to. But at this moment in time, he was the man who was giving her his heart and, god help her, she trusted him with hers.

He was treating her as if she were breakable. She didn't want it that way. She let him know with her own urgency. They fumbled with each other's buttons and zippers, shed their clothing in record time, and stripped back the ugly bedspread.

Hours later, after they had slept for a while and then made love again, Claudia curled against him, holding onto his arm around her, feeling safer than she had felt—maybe ever. Something had changed between them. She knew with certainty that whatever it was they had, had risen to a new level. And without his saying a word, she understood that she did not have to worry about Alex, or anyone else.

"I want to tell you something," Claudia said in a voice that was almost a whisper. She hesitated, gathering her courage to share something that she had been avoiding thinking about for a very long time. "I want you to know why sometimes I get so cold."

Jovanic gave a chuckle and held her against him. "Baby, cold is something you could never be. Afraid of being close, maybe, but cold, never."

She thought about that, musing on his perception of her and how accurate it was. "Yes, afraid of getting close, for sure. But there's a pretty good reason for it, and I—" Now that the time had come, it was more difficult than she had expected. The shameful secret that she hated had been with her for so long it had become part of her, like a vestigial organ. She had told no one, not even Kelly or Zebediah.

Jovanic didn't press her, just let her ready herself in her own time, but she could sense him steeling himself, too, for what he was about to hear.

"When I was nine," Claudia began, "something happened. My mother was working that summer and my brother was in nursery school. My parents said I was old enough to stay home alone. It was supposed to be different back then in the sixties. And my dad's best friend, Jack . . ." She paused. Could she do this? Realizing that she was breathing too rapidly, she forced herself to slow down. "He lived next door and he offered to watch out for me." It was getting easier, as if once she had started, the flow of words could not be stemmed.

"He wasn't married, didn't have any kids of his own. He was kind of like an uncle to me, and I adored him. He had this baby blue '57 T-Bird convertible that impressed all the neighborhood kids, but I was the only one who got to ride in it. He used to drive me around with him when he went on errands. He'd buy me ice cream, take me to the zoo. I thought he was the greatest. Then one afternoon I went over to his house to watch TV. I remember it so well. No one was home at my house and it was so quiet. I was bored, didn't feel like doing anything.

"So I went next door. The front door was open and he called out to me to come in. He was in the bedroom. He was lying in bed." She tried to keep her voice nonchalant—old habit—don't show your vulnerability. "He pulled me on top of him and started French kissing me." The memory of how his tongue had tasted as it probed her mouth still had the power to repel her.

He had kissed her that way, sucking on her lips until they were rimmed with blue. An hour later, when he'd let her go at last, she'd run home and put her face close to the bathroom mirror, rubbing and rubbing at her mouth, hoping to get her lips back to their normal color before her mother came home from work. The rest of her would never be normal again.

At the time, it had seemed to happen all at once; yet as an adult looking back at the memory, Claudia recognized now that Jack had been grooming her over a long period of time for what had happened.

"I could feel his erection under the covers, but I didn't know what it meant," she said in a murmur. "I just knew something was horribly wrong. I tried to get off him, but he wouldn't let me go."

"Did he—" Jovanic struggled, but he couldn't seem to say it.

"Yes, he raped me, and—" She took a ragged breath. At last those words had come out of her, and she realized with a sense of amazement that the sky hadn't fallen in. "I couldn't tell anyone what had happened. He said he would kill my cat Tommy if I told, and I believed him."

Jovanic buried his face in her hair, kissed the top of her head. The way he held her close made her feel safe.

"My god, Claudia, I'm so, so sorry, baby. I guessed it had to be something like that, but you never said . . ."

"You did? And you're okay with it? I mean, with, well, you know, 'damaged goods' and all that." She wanted to look at him, but the sense of shame had been burned for too long into her brain, even after she was old enough to know, logically, that the blame had not been her burden to bear.

His arms tightened around her. "*Okay* with it? I'd like to shoot the motherfucker's balls off."

"He died a couple of years later," Claudia said. "Pancreatic cancer, I think. For a long time I felt guilty that I was happy about it. That was hard. My parents were devastated by his death. He was one of their closest friends."

"So they didn't know what he did to you?"

"I've never told them. That wasn't the only time it happened. He'd come to the front door when my parents weren't home and I would run and hide in the closet. I'd scrunch up in there and make myself as small as I could until he stopped knocking. But there were times when they left me in his care, not knowing . . ." Claudia swallowed convulsively. "And that's why I have so much trouble trusting."

She rolled over to face Jovanic. His eyes were squeezed shut and she could see tears between the lashes. She brushed them away with gentle fingers and laid her head against his chest, feeling strangely light. As if unburdening herself had moved a fifty-pound weight off her heart and allowed her to breathe freely for the first time in months.

*   *   *

They ordered room service and sat cross-legged in bed, eating burgers and fries, drinking Sam Adams. She didn't have to ask about Alex; he volunteered the story, and explained everything.

"That photo Annabelle took. It happened exactly the way I told you."

"I know. I'm sorry I let myself believe otherwise. We had gotten so close, it scared me. I think I was unconsciously looking for an excuse to put some distance between us."

"Well, since we're making confessions—"

Claudia gave him an apprehensive glance, not wanting to spoil the evening. "You don't have to—"

"Just hear me out," he said. "You weren't totally wrong about Alex. No, wait a second—" He put his fingertips over her mouth as she started to protest. "She's been coming on to me pretty heavily for a couple of months. I haven't encouraged it, I swear to you, but it hasn't made any difference. She's done everything she can to get me in the sack."

"I knew it." Claudia's anger with Alex collided with a feeling of triumph that her antenna had been twanging in the right direction. "If you were trying to discourage her, taking her to your apartment while you were in the shower wasn't exactly a smart thing to do."

He gave a sheepish shrug. "I know. I figured that out afterward, when you wouldn't talk to me. Hey, I'm a guy—we're stupid."

"Lower than pond scum," Claudia agreed with mock severity. "Lower than—"

"Okay, enough already. Just believe me when I tell you that Alex means nothing to me. She's my partner, that's it."

"Why don't you report her for sexual harassment?"

"And get laughed out of the division? No, thanks, babe. I'll handle it myself."

"Just make sure you do." Claudia swallowed the last bite of her burger and washed it down with a swig of beer. "On another subject, I heard that Grusha spent some time in prison."

Jovanic gave her a look of admiration. "Grapholady, you always were a good detective."

They were in the shower. Claudia stretched her arms overhead and leaned against the wall. Rubbing as much lather as he could squeeze from the puny hotel soap, Jovanic began to massage her neck, moving slowly down, over both scapulae and along her spine. He spent extra time on the glutes, then moved down to her thighs.

"How long are you staying?" Her voice was low and husky as he found all the places that he knew would quicken her breathing. "I've missed this." She felt his lips on her neck and arched against him.

"I have to leave in the morning."

"No way!" She twisted around to look at him in astonishment, the shower drenching her hair and running in rivulets down her face. "You flew all the way out here just to turn around and go right back a few hours later?"

"M'hm." He kissed her again, deep and hot. "You're worth it, babe. I needed to see you for myself."

Jovanic shut off the faucet and drew back the shower curtain. He unfolded two bath towels from the rack, draped one around Claudia's shoulders and hunkered down, drying her legs with the other.

"By the way," he said, pressing a kiss against her belly. "There's one other thing you might not know about your baroness."

"Do I care about Grusha right now?" she asked in a dreamy voice.

"You might be interested in this. She did her time in a minimum security men's facility."

Claudia's eyes flew open. She looked at him, confused. "What?"

"Ha! Looks like you missed something in your investigations."

"What are you talking about, men's prison? Why would they—"

"It seems she was a he, undergoing 'gender reassignment.' "

Chapter 22

By the time Claudia awakened on Friday morning, Jovanic was already gone. He'd left her a note that put a silly grin on her face. On the desk in his familiar block printing was a page from his notebook—he never went anywhere without it.

God, you're hot! Don't analyze my handwriting. J.

In the hours they had spent in each other's arms, there had been no thought of discussing the information that Claudia had gleaned about Grusha's clients. It might have been fun to hash through all the facts together, but she wouldn't have given up a nanosecond of his brief visit to talk about work. And she hadn't brought up the incident with Ian McAllister and his explosive behavior over his beloved car the night before. She hadn't looked on it as a date, but Jovanic might have, and she couldn't bear to have anything else come between them.

Wriggling into a pair of jeans and slipping a teal turtleneck sweater over her head, she smiled, hardly daring to believe how far they had come in their relationship over those few hours. Then she thought about the surprising scoop on Grusha.

Following his news about her sex-change surgery,

Jovanic had said that Grusha, whose birth name had been Georg Orlov, had started to undergo some of the processes necessary for her sex change, but still had a penis. Glancing at his own sexual apparatus with a shudder, he said, "She—well, still officially *he*, at that time—was taking the female hormones and had developed breasts, but there was no choice. You go to the facility that matches the parts you've got right now."

"God, that must have been awful for her."

He shrugged, but not without sympathy. "In the facility where she was in custody, it's mostly drug offenders, so it probably wasn't as bad as it might have been. Yeah, it *was* prison, but it would have been much worse if she'd been placed in a population of violent offenders."

Claudia continued to mull over the information as she took a cab on the way to the Elite Introductions offices. Whatever might have happened to Grusha while she was an inmate, she had risen above the ordeal and made a success of her life. At least, she had been a success until someone started intruding. Now Claudia could understand Grusha's need to uncover what was going on in her dating club before she involved the police. After spending time in prison, she would hardly look on them as her friends.

The vibrating cell phone in her jeans pocket jolted her. She checked the number on the display, thinking it looked familiar, but not enough to place it. Answering, she recognized the Boston accent right away.

"Ms. Rose, it's Detective Jim Gray, Stowe, Vermont. I've got a video I'd like to send over for you to take a look at."

"A video?"

"Yeah. I've been going over the surveillance tapes

from the ski lodge on the day before Heather Lloyd died and I've pulled out a clip of a woman who might be her. She's got a male companion with her. It's not the greatest quality, but I'd like to e-mail it to you and ask you to see if you can ID either one of 'em."

"That's great," Claudia said as the cab arrived outside her destination. "I'm going to see the owner of the dating club right now. She knew Heather personally, of course, so she'd be much better able to make an accurate identification than I could. I'll ask her to look at it with me."

"All right, sounds good. What's your e-mail address?"

Claudia gave it to him with a tingle of anticipation. Maybe this would be the breakthrough that she'd been waiting for.

When she got up to the Elite Introductions offices, Claudia was in such a good mood that she took a moment to admire the arrangement of tropical flowers on the entry table: orchids, proteas, tuberoses. A stately bird-of-paradise rose out of the center, looking as though it were ready to fly away. For the first time in a long time, she felt happy. The Latin beat music playing in the background matched her upbeat mood and she felt like dropping her briefcase and dancing a samba right then and there.

Sonya seemed subdued as she escorted her through the loft to Grusha's private office. It became apparent that her mood was a reflection of her employer's. As they entered, the matchmaker was standing at the display case, gazing at her collection of fake Fabergé eggs, her back to the door.

"Good morning, Grusha, I have some news . . ." Claudia broke off, struck by the violet smudges under the matchmaker's eyes as Grusha turned slowly to greet her. Where had this sad figure come from?

The normally boisterous presence seemed to have diminished overnight, replaced by a doppelganger, a shadow of herself. Her shoulders sagged in the wide-necked dolman-sleeved silk top she wore over narrow black pants. She looked exhausted and beaten, like someone who had given up.

"Please, sit down," Grusha said in a voice drained of energy. Even her hands drooped as she indicated the seating area of the office. She sank onto the sofa. "Sonya vill bring us coffee."

Claudia's good mood took a dive. She already missed the larger-than-life personality of the Baroness Grusha Olinetsky she had come to know.

Now that she was aware of Grusha's secret, Claudia saw her through different eyes, suddenly noticing how much larger her hands and feet were than the average woman's. That was not something that could be surgically changed along with her sexual organs.

She had spent an hour that morning researching gender reassignment surgery. The Internet had offered more explicit information than she would have dreamed was available. She'd read about vaginoplasty, orchiectomy, phalloplasty, astounded by what modern medicine was able to do for the patient who believed he or she was occupying the wrong gender body.

Hormone replacement, hair removal, even facial surgery to femininize the male-to-female patient. Close-up photos of genitalia bore warnings: not for the squeamish. Yet these were people motivated by years of unhappiness to endure months of surgical procedures and therapy. Once the transition had been made, visually, you couldn't tell the difference.

"What did the police say?" Grusha's voice quavered with anxiety. Despite the high-heeled shoes that put her over six feet, she seemed to have shrunk.

"You won't need to worry about the police," Claudia said right away, feeling compelled to reassure her. "They weren't interested in what I had to tell them. Too many jurisdictions involved. Mostly, they just didn't take it seriously."

Grusha squealed and practically jumped out of her seat. "Oh, thank god! If I were to lose my business again—"

"Even if the police aren't interested, we've still got to find out what's going on. I know I've kept saying I'm not a private eye, and I'm not, but I don't believe these deaths are coincidences and I know you don't, either. I'd still like to help you if I can. Cops or no cops, if there's anything we can do to prevent it, I'd like to make sure no one else dies. So, here's the good news. We might actually have an ally in Vermont."

Claudia told her about Detective Gray's phone call and the video he was going to send.

"I know nothing of computers," Grusha said apprehensively. "You vill use Sonya's machine. I vill look and I vill tell you if the young voman in the video is Heather, that silly girl. But I tell you one thing. I did not send Heather skiing vit anyone and she did not tell me who she was going vit. This is strictly against the rules of the club."

"You didn't tell me that before," Claudia said. "Are you saying that whenever the members go out with someone, they have to report it to you?"

"Of course. I must know what my clients are doing vit each other. Otherwise, how vill I know who is available for a match?"

Claudia considered this new piece of information

as they went out to the main office part of the loft together and found Sonya brewing their coffee. Grusha
told Claudia to explain what she needed, and Sonya
showed them to her computer.

Tapping a few keys to open a browser, Claudia
launched her Web mail account, signed in with her
password, and clicked on the in-box. Quickly scanning the twenty-three new e-mails that appeared, at
the end of the list of familiar addresses she spotted
the latest e-mail to arrive: j-gray@townofstowevt.org.
A paper clip icon on the detective's e-mail led her to
a large attachment with an .avi file extension, indicating an AV file.

Once the file had finished downloading, she clicked
on the play arrow and they all fixed their attention on
the monitor, waiting to see Heather Lloyd and, perhaps more importantly, her companion. With Grusha
craning over one shoulder and Sonya squeezing in on
the other side, Claudia felt like a sandwich filling, but
her buoyant mood had returned. Nothing was going
to prick that happy balloon this time.

There were a few seconds of silent black-and-white
static before the video clip began to play. The first
frame was filled with a bank of plate glass windows
and a glass door that opened onto a snowy parking
lot. A split second before the front doors slid open, a
couple could be seen approaching the ski lodge.

Tall and willowy, the woman wore what appeared
to be a white fleece jacket and ski pants with a furry
hat. Recalling that Heather Lloyd had been a model,
Claudia was unsurprised to see that she moved with
the grace of one accustomed to cruising along a run-
way. As they approached the entrance to the lodge,
she pulled off the hat and shook out her short, dark
hair.

Claudia, Grusha, and Sonya stared at the screen in silence, collectively holding their breath as they tried to see the woman's face. "It's like a mirror," Sonya cried, pointing to the bright sunshine reflecting off the snow and the white clothing. "It's like her face is a blank."

The man in the scene wore a duckbill visored hat with earflaps, pulled low on his forehead. His head was bent and he was looking down as he listened to something she said. The couple strolled through the door together and disappeared from view. The entire clip had lasted less than ten seconds.

"*Eto ploho*," Grusha murmured.

"What does that mean?" asked Claudia.

"What? Oh, it means is bad."

"You can't see much of *his* face at all," Sonya said, not trying to conceal her disappointment.

"You were right, Claudia," Grusha said with some satisfaction. She walked away from the screen, the scent of Clive Christian wafting behind her, and began pouring herself a mug of coffee. "Looks like Ian to me. Did you see his beard? Outside, before they come in and he look down."

Claudia was less certain. "Do you really think so?" She reran the clip, focusing on the man. "Sonya's right, you can't see his features. His build seems too broad to be Ian."

"That down jacket, it adds bulk."

"But you do think the woman is Heather?"

"Yes, the poor girl. It is her—the vay she valk. Is terrible video, though. Hard to see anything clearly."

"Detective Gray admitted it wasn't very good quality. He wasn't joking. It's the lack of contrast that's the problem. The sun on the snow washes out the image. Makes the security camera pretty worthless, doesn't it?" Claudia frowned. "I think the man was deliberately avoiding the camera."

"I think you may be right. But he looks to me like Ian."

Claudia clicked the mouse and ran the clip a third time, stopping when the man came into the scene, zooming in as close as she could on his face. "It really is crappy quality, but I think he looks more like Marcus, except for the beard. But then, Marcus had a beard in his file photo. Do you know how long ago that photo was taken?"

Grusha blinked at her. "Marcus? You think he looks like Marcus?"

"You gave me Marcus' folder with the others. Remember, I told you his handwriting had some red flags. That puts him in the suspect range, don't you think?"

"I suppose it . . . No. Oh, please, Claudia, not Marcus." Grusha's voice had squeaked up an octave and she looked ready to cry.

Claudia met her eyes. "What's the problem, Grusha? What is it about Marcus that you haven't told me?"

"Nothing, nothing. I just—I like him a lot. I should not have given you his file. I gave you John Shaw's, too, but you have not said much about him."

"Shaw? That's the photographer who went to Iraq? We talked about him having a head injury. He's the only one of the men whose files you gave me that I haven't met. Why are you trying to distract me from Marcus?"

"I am not. I am just reconsidering—"

"Grusha, his handwriting has red flags. Just because you like him, it doesn't mean you should ignore the danger signs."

The scrap of Grusha's handwriting Susan had shared with her made more sense now. She remembered the covering strokes, which meant that information was literally being covered up, hidden from sight. As long as Grusha continued to conceal important details, Claudia's hands were tied. She had to find some way to break through Grusha's barriers that would allow her to be of effective help.

"Handwriting always tells the truth, Grusha. And Marcus, like the other two men, is problematic."

The other woman set her chin in a stubborn line. "I do not vant to talk about it anymore."

When she continued to refuse to discuss the subject any further, Claudia finally gave up the argument and typed up an e-mail to send Jim Gray, telling him what they'd concluded. They headed back to Grusha's office, Sonya following with the coffee carafe and a plate of morning pastries.

For about ten minutes they kicked around ideas that steered clear of Marcus; then Sonya returned and stuck her head around the door. "Baroness Olinetsky, Avram Cohen is here for his appointment."

"Oh, yes, I forgot he was coming. Vould you ask him to vait for just a moment more." Grusha shuffled through some papers on her desk. "Claudia, I have a new match to show him. I vant to know what you think of her handwriting."

"You're matching him up after I told you he has the potential for violence?"

Grusha gave her a dark look and shoved a piece of paper at her. "Please just look at the handwriting."

"Why bother to ask my opinion if you're just going to ignore it?" Claudia said, looking at the sample. "How old is she?"

"Twenty-two. Some of my clients vant a schoolgirl.

This is as close as I vill come to supplying one. And don't bother to feel sorry for her. These girls are looking for someone rich; that I can tell you. Some of them are also looking for a father."

"Like Jessica McAllister, you mean?"

Grusha huffed. "Not that one. It was her own father who insisted that I find an older man for her. Then he refused to be happy vit every one of the men I brought her. It did not matter what little Jessica thought."

The handwriting Grusha had passed across to Claudia was neat and precise, small and simplified, with clear spacing throughout. The large, showy signature with its flourished capital letters was an incongruence that revealed something important about the writer.

"She's pretty well organized and has good self-control. But she's got a temper—see those sharp little tics on the beginnings and endings of some strokes? There's also the disparity between the signature and the text. It tells me that she has two different personalities. I don't mean like a multiple personality," she hurried to say when she saw alarm spreading over Grusha's face. "I mean she feels one way about herself on the inside, but what she projects on the outside is something different. Her true self is more retiring than she appears. The handwriting looks foreign. Where did she learn to write?"

Grusha grinned as broadly as the Cheshire cat. "You are absolutely correct. Her name is Aisha Negasi. She is model from Ethiopia. Just uses her first name, Aisha." She passed Claudia an eight-by-ten glossy magazine cover that displayed a remarkably beautiful woman with glowing bronze skin. A strategically draped scrap of multicolored silky fabric showed off

a derriere so round and high that Claudia wondered
if it had been airbrushed. Raven-colored hair, brushed
back from a high forehead, curled almost to Aisha's
waist. Bee-stung lips, glossed to look wet, parted se-
ductively. Her eyes sparked with defiance: *Come and
get me, if you dare.*

"So this is who you have in mind for Avram." Claudia chewed thoughtfully on her lower lip as she ran
through her mental database. She recalled his Hebrew
and English scripts and mentally compared them to
what she had before her. "She has the self-confidence
to stand up to him, *and* the independence not to rely
on him to fulfill her every need. I'm more concerned
about the temper tics. Considering how short his own
fuse is, they could have some monumental fights."

"Fighting is okay," Grusha said. "Good sex afterward."

"That's all well and good, as long as there's no violence, but I'm not convinced of that in Avram's case.
And remember, I told you he's sexually frustrated
and may be impotent."

"Yes, I remember, and I cannot believe it. You must
have made a mistake on that one. I must not keep
him vaiting any longer. Claudia, dear, vould you
please vait outside for me. Ve have more to talk about
later."

Chapter 23

Although he was the one with the appointment, Avram apologized charmingly to Claudia for interrupting her meeting. He was sporting a navy blue blazer today, no tie; black hair curled from the open neck of his shirt. As soon as he'd closed the door to Grusha's office, Sonya sent Claudia a fluttery look and breathed, "Isn't he gorgeous?"

Claudia grinned back at her. "Oh, sure. If you like the dark, rugged type, and apparently you do."

"He was telling me about being in the army in Israel. He was a fighter pilot. That's so *macho*!"

"He knows you think so, too." Claudia sat down to wait for Grusha to finish with Avram, flipping through the *People* magazine that Sonya offered her. The magazine wasn't her standard fare, but she told herself that a bit of mind candy would be good for her. She was engrossed in an article about Jennifer Aniston and her latest travails when she heard a loud beep come from Sonya's desk—the short tones that on her own cell phone indicated a voice mail or text message.

Sonya grabbed the phone and looked at the screen. She darted a mischievous look at Claudia. "It's Avram's. He put it here when we were talking. He must have forgotten it. Someone sent him a video. I wonder if I—"

"No, let it go," Claudia advised. "He'll get it himself later."

Sonya ignored her and began pressing buttons. She gave a sharp inhale, then, "Oh my *god*!" With an expression of revulsion, she dropped the phone back on the desk. She couldn't have looked more stunned if the thing had grown teeth and bitten her. "I can't believe he would be into that."

"What is it?" Claudia sprang up from her chair and hurried over. Picking up the phone, she looked at the screen, where the assistant had clicked on the play button. She saw the flash of a knife; a trickle of blood where it was held to the throat of a young girl.

A while back, she had been connected to a case involving sadomasochism. What she had been exposed to then was nursery school compared to this brutal gang bang of a victim who was surely underage. What was Avram Cohen doing with this nauseating trash?

"Somebody must have sent this to the wrong phone number," Claudia said, trying to keep her voice calm. "It's easy to do. I've done it myself." *Though not with anything like this.*

Sonya had a stricken look. "Did you see that girl's face? She was scared to death. I don't think she was acting."

"I don't know," Claudia said. "It's pretty sick, either way."

"I just can't believe he would be into something like that." Sonya shuddered. "It's so messed up!"

At that moment, Grusha's office door opened and Claudia slipped the phone behind her, back on the desk. "Don't say anything," she murmured. "I'll talk to Grusha privately."

Sonya busied herself at her computer and didn't

look up when Avram came over. "Did I leave my BlackBerry here? I can't—oh, here it is."

The screen display had gone dark, so he didn't know they had been looking at it. He gave Sonya an odd look when she kept her head down and didn't flirt with him the way she usually did. "Well, okay then. Good-bye, Sonya, Claudia."

Claudia just nodded at him, not trusting herself to speak.

When she heard about the video, Grusha's face drained of color. "My god, I'll get sued! This is horrible!"

"I told you he's a high-risk client," Claudia agreed. "He might or might not act out violently himself. It's possible he could sublimate those tendencies into watching other people commit violent acts on video. It still doesn't make for a healthy relationship."

"But I have arranged for him to meet Aisha tomorrow at the party. What am I going to do? I cannot let her know, and I cannot afford to offend him, either. What's the matter vit Donna Pollard? She should have seen this in him! Why do I have a psychologist on the payroll if—" Grusha was breathing heavily, her voice growing shrill.

"Grusha, stop," Claudia protested. "This isn't productive. You'll have to figure out what you're going to do about Avram, but right now, there's a more pressing problem. People are dying. That's why I'm here, to help you figure out the culprit."

Grusha took a deep breath and caught hold of herself. "You are right. Yes. Ve must stay focused."

Claudia had thought of something else. "The members whose handwriting you gave me are all male—the ones who are alive. But what about the female club members? Could any of them have a motive? We have to consider everyone."

People were motivated by all sorts of needs—power, revenge, security, love, money. The type who would go to the extreme of attempting to destroy Grusha's business would have to suffer from a serious personality disorder, and if that were the case, indications of that personality disorder would appear in their handwriting.

She wondered whether Grusha's belief that a client was attempting to sabotage her business was even valid. If it wasn't, she was at least a little paranoid. Such a despicable act as sabotage would take some serious motivation.

Grusha's voice snapped her back. "I have thought and thought about everyone who might vant to hurt me. I vill think more. But Claudia, something else. It occurs to me that you do not have to vait for tomorrow to meet John Shaw. You can go this afternoon to his gallery."

"He has a gallery?"

"Right now, he is displaying his own vork. At other times, other photographers and artists show their vork there if they impress him. Just go and have a look. You can have my car drop you off and take a cab back to your hotel afterward. The gallery is only a few blocks. It won't be busy on a Friday afternoon. Most of the business comes at night."

Chapter 24

The Lower East Side of Manhattan had, for most of its history, been a neighborhood of working-class immigrants. Its reputation as a drug- and crime-infested slum had made an about-face early in the twenty-first century, when gentrification of the old neighborhood began to take hold and spread. Soon, the Lower East Side had turned trendy with a capital T. Upscale restaurants, boutiques, and bars replaced most of the old tenement buildings. New art galleries popped up everywhere. Shaw's was one of them. According to Grusha, he had renovated a convenience store. His name was emblazoned on the plate glass window in six-inch-high letters.

With street noise ringing in her ears, Claudia entered silence. Dark wood floors, polished to a high sheen. With the exception of a small round table in the corner and a glass stand bearing an arrangement of dried flowers, there was no furniture.

The empty space put the focus on a series of floor-to-ceiling photographs hung on whitewashed walls, lit by spotlights: New York skylines. A blue filter made the landmarks appear unicolored, seen as through smoke; misshapen, but recognizable.

At the far end of the gallery, a doorway revealed a series of rooms laid out like boxcars, one flowing into the next. Each room had a unique theme. Each was a little smaller than the preceding one, the lighting subtly dimmer.

In the second room, the photographs were of inner city scenes and people. In every shot, the subjects were faced away from the camera, their attitude revealed in body language: defiance, desperation, despair.

The third room featured nudes in black and white—like the buildings in the first room, they had been shot slightly out of focus. The photographs had a haunted quality that raised a feeling of unease in Claudia, but she couldn't quite identify why.

The last room was the smallest and the darkest, in lighting and in tone—a study of pain and suffering. The photographs, all scenes from desert warfare, were larger than life-sized, hung one to a wall.

In the first three rooms, the photos were deliberately out of focus, or were black and white. In this series, the browns were muted, the reds enhanced in gory brilliance.

The first was a close-up portrait of an African American soldier gazing at something or someone off camera, his face wet with tears. The depths of his sadness permeated the little room and penetrated to the core of Claudia's being. The emotion was uncomfortable, and she quickly moved on, but it got worse.

A dead soldier, prone in the sand, both limbs missing from the left side of his ragged body.

An Arab mother cradling her child in her arms. The viewer knew there could be no hope for the seared flesh and the black hole burned into the child's back by mortar fire.

The next image had been taken in a prison cell. A group of laughing soldiers surrounding a cowering prisoner, naked but for a black hood that covered him to his shoulders. One of the soldiers held aloft a vile trophy of war for the camera: a severed finger.

The pictures in this darkroom of abominations repelled her, made her want to run away. Yet there was also something so compelling about them that Claudia found herself continuing to stand there and soak up the ghastly scenes.

The last photograph was of a young marine, hardly more than a boy, really. His bloody mouth was fixed in an endless rictus of agony as his platoon mates looked on, helpless, bearing severe injuries themselves. The photographer had managed to capture the utter degradation of human spirit.

"My god, he's too young to shave." Claudia had spoken aloud without intending to.

Haunted. The word kept echoing in her head and she realized that every one of the images she had viewed since arriving at John Shaw's gallery was haunted in some way. All at once the eeriness that saturated the room swelled when she felt a presence behind her.

A man's voice said, "Stand still, I want to shoot you."

Claudia swung around, ready to defend herself, saw a flash of light and realized that he had a camera pointed at her. "Stop it!" she demanded as the strobes continued to light up the room.

He stopped at once, lowered the camera, letting it dangle from a strap around his neck. "I'm sorry. I didn't mean to scare you. I was observing you observing my pictures. You were so rapt, I wanted to capture what you were feeling."

He was six-four with copper-colored hair standing up in a tuft above his forehead, making him look even taller. A square face with a brownish red moustache and beard trimmed short. Startling blue eyes; a dusting of freckles across the nose and cheeks. He looked like Thor, the red-bearded god. He might have been at home wearing a kilt and tossing a caber.

He matched the file photo of John Shaw.

"Will you allow me to photograph you?" he asked.

Claudia met his probing gaze. "I don't think so. The moment has passed. But I have to say, there's something really disturbing in these photos."

His pale skin flushed with pride. "That's a true compliment." He extended the great paw that was his hand and enfolded hers in it. "I'm John Shaw. This is my gallery." His handshake was warm and firm.

"My name is Claudia Rose," she said. "Isn't it unusual for a gallery owner to also be the artist?"

Shaw smiled. "I welcome the unusual, but I do show other artists, too. You've happened to visit at a time when my own work is on display."

Claudia smiled back. "Grusha Olinetsky suggested I come."

He blinked. "Grusha?"

"I'm the new handwriting analyst for Elite Introductions."

"Ah, I see. Well, nice to meet you, Ms. Rose. My handwriting was analyzed a while back when I joined the club, so I doubt Grusha would expect me to do it again. But I'm glad you took her up on the suggestion."

Claudia tilted her head at the nearest photograph. "I can understand why she thought I should see your work. These photos are—well, you're an amazing artist."

"Thank you." Shaw glanced around the gallery, his eyes lighting briefly on each picture. "This has been an amazing journey."

Grusha had said he'd sustained a head injury in Iraq, Claudia remembered. She flashed on his handwriting sample and the dented upper loops that might reflect such an injury. The results of certain types of head injuries were not always seen on the outside, but they could permanently alter behavior.

As one of Grusha's suspects, John Shaw had to be viewed with suspicion. Claudia didn't think he looked like the man in the video with Heather Lloyd, except maybe for the beard. But she was only going by his size, and the bulky ski clothing might have distorted that. Heather had been a tall woman.

"Your 'journey,'" Claudia said. "Is it something you can talk about?"

Shaw bowed his head so she could no longer see what he was thinking. "Yes, I can talk about it. Talking about it is penance for me. I need to talk about it a lot."

"Penance? For what?"

"I killed them," he said, and a cold chill went up Claudia's spine.

"What does that mean?"

His gaze went to the photographs, resting on each one before he spoke again, his voice rough with emotion. "We were riding in a jeep outside of Baghdad, the four of us. Jerry, Pat, Vince, and me. They were just kids, you know? Just kids. I told them I wanted them to stop so I could take a leak." His eyes came back to Claudia and she could see the depths of the guilt he carried with him. "They said it wasn't safe. If I hadn't insisted on stopping, they would still be alive. They were waiting for me and the jeep was hit by an RPG." His shoulders sagged as if the weight of the soldiers' deaths sat on them. "I lived with those kids for six weeks. I nearly died with them. I should have."

Claudia looked back at the photo of the young marine. Her heart ached as much for the man who was making this confession as for the dead boy. "I'm so sorry. That must be a terrible thing for you to bear."

"They talk to me," he said, as if it were the most natural thing in the world.

"What?"

"Their spirits; they talk to me in the night." His face twisted in pain. "It doesn't matter if I'm asleep or awake. They're always there with me."

"Have you seen anyone for help with post-traumatic stress?" Claudia knew a little about reactions to traumatic events, and John Shaw's behavior seemed to her like someone suffering from post-traumatic stress disorder. His handwriting had displayed signs of his thought patterns being off-kilter.

"I don't need help." He glared at her, letting her know that she had breached an area that was off-limits. "I don't deserve help."

"Were you injured, John?"

He shrugged as if the question were of no consequence. "The concussion from the RPG left me pretty deaf for a couple of days. They dug some shrapnel out of my legs. My head got dinged up a bit." He paused. "I can still smell the disinfectant at the hospital, y' know? They used it to clean the blood off the floors. But what happened to me was nothing. Jerry and Pat and Vince are dead. I'm still here."

"You must be still here for a reason," Claudia said to fill the awkward pause that followed his words. "The universe must have something for you to do." *Not killing Grusha's clients, I hope.*

"You know, you're very photogenic," Shaw said. "Have you ever been photographed professionally?"

The non sequitur left her feeling as though she'd tumbled down a rabbit hole and landed at the Mad Hatter's tea party. "Not since wedding photos, and I've been divorced for a while now."

"Would you consider posing for me?"

She thought of the nudes in the other room. "I might, if I get to keep my clothes on."

"Where's the fun in that?" he said with a wink. "Say, how about a glass of wine? I'll show you my portfolio."

"If that's like showing me your etchings, I'll pass, thank you."

Shaw laughed, flashing a set of large, even, white teeth. "I like you, Claudia Rose." He took a key from his pocket and opened a door at the back of the room. "This is my office. Why don't you wait for me in here. I'll join you in a minute."

Curious, she followed his direction to the office and sat in one of the two sling-back chairs. The walls were windowless and painted black, which made it resemble a darkroom—apropos for a photographer. John Shaw's desk was piled carelessly with photographic contact sheets, a couple of high-powered camera lenses, and a mountain of paperwork.

When he returned, Shaw had a large photo album tucked under his arm. He handed Claudia a glass of Chardonnay. "I thought if I showed you some of my portrait work you might be more inclined to trust me."

"I'd love to see it."

After he'd handed her a glass, he dragged the other chair closer so they were sitting side by side. He opened the album and handed it to her. Even if she had not seen the gallery photographs, the album showed that the man behind the camera had a remarkable gift. These were not standard head shots. Each portrait had been manipulated in a unique way to bring out what Claudia thought of as the subject's soul.

She thumbed through the pages and found that John Shaw's work in this book focused on a single theme: women, women, and more women. An Asian ballerina, light as air, floating above the stage with the grace of a butterfly. The picture had been overexposed to imbue the dancer with a ghostly delicacy.

A figure in a black burka, the traditional Muslim woman's garment. The one who wore it was covered entirely except for her eyes, which were full of mischief, but also wary of the photographer who wanted to bare her essence.

A very young woman whose nude body had been painted in luminescent colors. Her breasts were ringed in shocking pink and turquoise, the colors repeated on her navel and pubic area. She lay stretched out on a couch that was covered by a sheet, staring into the camera with such a pained face that it made Claudia think that she had qualms about being turned into a canvas. The very next photo was of the same model, but an extreme close-up of her face. There was something familiar about her.

"She doesn't look very happy," Claudia remarked.

Shaw paused, his glass halfway to his lips, and glanced over to see what she was referring to. "Oh, Jess," he said offhandedly. "She drove me crazy, begging to pose, but later, she wasn't so sure about it."

Jess? The coincidence was too great. "You don't by any chance mean Jessica McAllister, do you?"

John Shaw frowned. "What do you know about

Jess? I thought you said you were new at Elite Introductions."

"I am new, but I've met her father. I know who she is. Was. Don't you think she was a little young to be doing this sort of modeling?"

"She *wanted* to do it," he repeated, going on the offensive. "She didn't need permission; she was old enough to decide for herself."

Disturbed, Claudia took one last long look at Jessica's face and wondered just how much she really had wanted to do it, and how much was at John Shaw's insistence. Slowly, she turned to the next page. The picture made her catch her breath. Shellee Jones' pretty face scowled angrily back at her. It was easy to identify the woman from Grusha's client folder, but this picture had caught her in the act of some sort of protest, not so unlike Jessica McAllister.

Claudia glanced over at John Shaw, who was eyeing Shellee's picture with an unfathomable expression. "Are you specializing in pictures of dead girls?" she asked before she had a chance to filter the words that had formed in her brain and stop them from pouring out of her mouth.

Shaw snatched the photograph album from her hands and slammed it shut. "So nice meeting you, Ms. Rose," he said. "It's time for you to go now."

Chapter 25

After eating a light meal in the hotel restaurant, Claudia checked in with her brother.

Pete informed her that Annabelle and Monica had gone out to see a movie with a group of their friends. The thought of Annabelle on the loose with her niece gave Claudia a mild anxiety attack, but Pete assured her that he had taken the girls right to the AMC Loews in the Marina and would be picking them up outside the theater promptly at 9:55, when the movie ended.

Then Jovanic phoned and whispered erotic promises about all the ways they would make up for lost time when she returned home. When the sex talk had run down, she brought him up to date on her activities over the four days she had been in New York—what they hadn't had time to discuss while he was there.

"I can't believe you're smack in the middle of a crazy situation again," Jovanic said, exasperated.

"Yeah, I know. I didn't mean to; I just keep landing in these messes. And now I *am* involved, so I want to help Grusha if I can."

"Do you have a special magnet for wacko clients?"

"It's beginning to feel like it. Ever since I met you, in fact. So maybe *you're* the magnet."

Jovanic snorted. "Cute. It's all my fault." Then he said, "Hey, I spoke with your pal, Izzy Perez."

"*Izzy?*"

"A cop can't go around being called Isadore, okay?"

"Well, did you tell him I was legit?"

"Yeah, I vouched for you. But you just can't get involved in this shit. Leave the investigations up to NYPD, okay?"

"I tried to, remember? He wasn't interested."

"Okay, so then, just let it go," Jovanic argued. "If Perez thought it was serious he would have pursued it. You and Olinetsky are turning something that's probably a coincidence into serial homicide."

"Make up your mind, Columbo. You just implied there was something to investigate, and now you're saying it's coincidence? Which is it?"

"I don't give a shit which it is; I want you out of it. But I know you well enough. Once you get a wild hair, nothing's going to stop you, is it?" He was right. She was like a dog with a bone; couldn't let go.

"How about you helping me?" she said. "I'm not convinced Perez actually did check out any of those names I gave him. You could check."

"Let me get this straight. You want me to help you go behind NYPD in an investigation you shouldn't be involved in? Honey, even if you found something, it could take months to break open the case. You gonna move to New York?"

He had a good point. Claudia gave it a moment's thought. "Okay, tell you what. You run a background on the people I've told you about, and I'll make a reservation and come home on Monday."

"You want to cut a deal, is that it?" Jovanic said, giving up the argument.

Claudia could feel his grin. "Yeah, cut me a deal. I'll go to Grusha's party tomorrow night. That'll give me a chance to see all the players at the same time. I'll wrap up on Sunday, and from Monday forward, I promise to limit my involvement with Grusha to analyzing handwritings she sends in the mail. How does that sound?"

"Fine. Call the airlines, make a reservation, and come home." His tone softened. "I want you here, babe. Where I can keep an eye on you."

After they ended their conversation, Claudia was unable to get to sleep. She mixed a Jack and Coke from the tiny bottles in the minibar, threw herself on the bed and used the remote to switch on the TV. With old movies playing in the background, she ran all the complications of the Grusha assignment through her head again and again until she dozed off. The last thing she was conscious of before falling asleep in the early hours was a dinner party scene in *The Thin Man*. As her eyelids drooped, Nick Charles was announcing to the assembled guests, "The murderer is right here, sitting at this table."

The cell phone was ringing, invading her dreams. At first, she wasn't certain what the sound was. The noise had penetrated her sleep and in her groggy state she thought it must be the dinner bell in the movie. She didn't know what time it was now, but one thing she knew for sure—she had not had enough sleep.

Except for the sliver of gray light penetrating the crack between the blackout drapes, the hotel room was as dark as pitch. Claudia groaned and felt around the nightstand for the phone. As she found it she noted that the clock radio read 7:19. *Too early.*

"Hello?" Her voice sounded dry and croaky. Holding the phone to her ear with one hand, she sat up and took a swig from the bottle of water that she kept by the bed, trying to wake herself up.

"I'm going to kill him!" Grusha Olinetsky's voice screamed through the phone. "*Chjort! Chjort!* I—vill—*kill*—him!"

Fully awake now, Claudia moved the instrument a couple of inches away from her ear. "What happened? Who are you talking about?"

Grusha's voice rose to a hysterical shriek, switching to Russian. Hyperventilating.

Claudia raised her voice above the clamor. "Grusha, stop! I don't understand what you're saying. You've got to calm down!"

The matchmaker switched back to English, but the words came out as short gasps. "How could he do this to me? I cannot believe it. I am going to—"

In the background was another voice. Sonya. The assistant came on the line, speaking urgently. "Put on the TV, channel seven, quick." Sonya sounded upset, but not in the out-of-control, panicky way of her boss.

"Hang on, I have to find the remote." Claudia set the phone down and switched on the bedside lamp. Sometime during the night, the remote control had found its way under the covers and ended up at the foot of the bed. Digging it out, she turned on the TV and navigated the channels with a sense of foreboding, as if she already knew what would be waiting for her when she got to channel seven.

"Oh, *shit*." The program to which Sonya had directed her was *Hard Evidence*, and the guest was Andrew Nicholson. She boosted the volume, her heart sinking.

A tall, slender blond, Nicholson was dressed in

an expensive-looking dark suit with a red power tie. He looked ready to testify in court. Worse, he *looked* credible, and for the viewing audience, that was often enough.

"... and you wouldn't believe some of the members she allows in," Andy was saying in a gossipy tone. A dozen expressions animated his face as he spoke, using his hands for emphasis. "If they have money—and plenty of it—she'll take *anyone*. And I mean *anyone*. And the handwriting analyst she's using now, well ... can you say 'hired gun'?"

The camera panned to the studio audience, who were watching with avid attention. The camera moved to the show's host. She looked directly into the lens, her mouth parted in counterfeit amazement. "Oh, my! This is just fascinating. We have to go to commercial now, but when we come back, handwriting expert Andy Nicholson will reveal more secrets about your handwriting and the dating service he once worked for. I'm Megan Jackson. Stay tuned; *Hard Evidence* will be right back."

A commercial began to play and Grusha's voice came back on the line, only marginally calmer. "I'll kill that little *drecksack*. How dare he do this to me!"

Claudia wanted to remind her that Susan Rowan had warned her of Nicholson's lack of ethics, but she doubted that *I told you so* would go over very well right now. And Jovanic had been right; Andy was gunning for her. Maybe not literally, but in a way that could be damaging to her career. Not only had Andy practically stolen the *Hard Evidence* gig right out from under her; he was now using the interview to get back at both her and Grusha. Narcissist that he was, it probably hadn't occurred to him that his words might be grounds for a lawsuit.

"Can you call the TV station and threaten to file suit for slander?" asked Claudia.

"Sonya is calling my lawyer right now. Oh my god, what vill I do? What else vill he say? I vill have to cancel the party tonight. I cannot face my clients after this."

"You can't do that. Most of them aren't going to see the show, and even if they do, you have to show them that he's a lying piece of—" Claudia broke off, reminding herself that she was talking to her client. That meant she needed to maintain some semblance of professionalism, even though she'd only had a couple of hours' sleep. She said, "If you cancel, he wins. You can't let him win."

"But how can I face them?"

"You are the *baroness*. After all you've been through, you can do anything."

There was a long pause; then Grusha spoke in a stronger voice. "You are right. I vill not let that filthy swine destroy me."

The commercials ended and the show came back on with a wide shot of the *Hard Evidence* set, Andy Nicholson relaxing in one armchair, Megan Jackson in the other, chatting and smiling. The camera panned across the applauding studio audience, zooming in on a close-up of the host.

After reintroducing Andy as the country's foremost handwriting expert, which made Claudia want to puke, Jackson leaned in. Her expression was as hungry as a coyote chasing a rabbit as she urged him to continue "revealing the truth" about Elite Introductions.

But during the break, Andy must have thought better of what he had been saying. He began to backtrack. "I don't want to bad-mouth a colleague, so I'm not going to name names," he said, raising his eyebrows in a way that suggested there was plenty to say, and he would love to spill his guts but was just too ethical. "You just have to be *very careful* how you choose a handwriting analyst. Especially if you're an employer. Or in this case, a dating service."

"The dating service you're talking about is called Elite Introductions, isn't it?" Megan Jackson prompted. She looked at the camera. "The owner of Elite Introductions is *Baroness* Grusha Olinetsky, the flamboyant Russian who sometimes appears as a guest judge on the popular dating show *Your Perfect Match.*"

"Clients pay obscene fees to get matched up," Andy said, the camera flattering him. "But when I saw some of those handwritings—the people she asked me to analyze—well, I couldn't in good conscience continue to work for her."

"He is lying!" Grusha shouted, getting worked up again. "Sonya, what are you doing? Is my lawyer on the phone yet?" There was a pause while Sonya said something. "I don't care how early it is! Claudia, what are ve going to do? He is hurting you, too."

"Thanks, Grusha, I did hear that." Claudia's brain was spinning. "I'll contact my attorney as soon as I get back to L.A."

"What is that devil saying now? Oh my *god!*"

". . . and she asked me to help her improve her handwriting," Andy said, blowing any last pretense of client confidentiality. "She wanted to make it look more feminine, so I showed her how to add some embellishments—you know, twists and curlicues—to make it more girly."

Megan Jackson, who had been sipping coffee, lowered her mug. "More *girly*? Why would she need to do that?"

Claudia held her breath. At the other end of her phone there was only the sound of Grusha's quick breaths.

Nicholson gave Jackson an arch grin. "Well, that's a long story, Megan."

"And unfortunately, we're just about out of time for this segment, but Andrew Nicholson, I hope you'll come back soon and tell us the rest of this tale. It sounds fascinating. And now, after the break, our next guest . . ."

Claudia released a long sigh. At least Andy hadn't totally outed Grusha. Somehow, he must know her secret. And he must have guessed that she would eventually learn of his appearance on *Hard Evidence.* What did he hope to gain?

Knowing Andy Nicholson, he might have done it purely out of spite. What a miserable piece of work he was. She thought of all the times they had crossed swords in the courtroom. If she were to waste energy hating someone, Andrew Nicholson would be at the top of her list.

Chapter 26

Cocktails on a Manhattan rooftop under twinkling lights. Or stars if you happened to look up. Potted ferns that belonged to warmer climes, somehow flourishing under space heaters that made the late-winter evening tolerable. Live jazzy music to chat by. A waist-high wall offered a view of other roofs—a city of roofs—from fourteen stories up. Romantic allure. What could be a better backdrop for an introduction to a potential love match than the roof of the building that housed Elite Introductions?

Two bouncers at the door looked like sumo wrestlers in T-shirts, their muscles bulging, shaved heads shiny under the lights.

Claudia had dressed for the occasion in black silk palazzo pants and a long beaded jacket over a gold shell. The outfit had been Annabelle's suggestion. "You gotta take something fancy, just in case," the girl had insisted. Having recovered from her pique over what she perceived as Claudia's defection, she'd decided that it might actually be fun to stay with Monica for a few days. So Claudia and the girls had gone shopping, and now, seeing the results in the mirror, Claudia was glad she had listened to their advice.

The woman who called herself baroness smiled and floated graciously from one guest to another.

Throwing her head back to laugh at something with a man who looked like Benicio del Toro. Dancing a few steps with someone she towered over in her six-inch heels. Excusing herself and hurrying forward to greet a new arrival.

To look at Grusha Olinetsky—fashionable in a simple black silk cocktail dress and diamond stud earrings, her black hair hanging loose, brushed back to accentuate high, full cheekbones that had probably been enhanced with collagen—no one would have guessed at her histrionics of a little more than twelve hours earlier. Knowing what she knew, Claudia thought she detected a certain brittleness under the coolly elegant facade that the matchmaker presented to her clients that evening.

She thought of the large sums of money these people had poured into Grusha's coffers, all looking for their Mr. or Ms. Right. Every male guest she had met that night was a candidate for stud of the month: good-looking, bright, stylish, including the men over forty. The women were knockouts, too: self-confident, flirty, under thirty-five. Claudia fervently hoped that Grusha would not be introducing any of these Beautiful People to a killer.

Avram Cohen was among the first clients she had spied upon her arrival, but he had assiduously avoided her. She guessed that he was probably conjecturing whether she and Sonya had viewed the brutal video on his cell phone, and that he was embarrassed at the prospect.

He should be more than embarrassed.

He was currently giving the impression of being deeply absorbed in Aisha, the model whose handwriting Grusha had showed Claudia the day before in her office. And by all appearances, Aisha was lapping up his attention, engaged as she was in a great deal of smiling and fluttering of sable eyelashes. The lashes were far too thick and long to be natural, but they did an admirable job of framing the liquid amber eyes.

Dr. Ian McAllister moved among the guests, well-groomed and expensively tasteful in a dark suit. Claudia had refused his offer to pick her up for the party when he'd phoned midmorning, and his cold tone told her that he saw right through the lame excuse she'd made. Now he treated her to a sardonic smile, a reminder that he was on to her, before turning away to speak to a pair of identical twins in short dresses. Luckily, Claudia and Ian were both at the party to mingle, and from what she could see, he was mingling with great charm. So far, it had been easy to avoid being alone with him.

Donna Pollard sidled over to where she stood, watching the crowd. "Did you see who just arrived? Michele Frayer! Did you see her in *Somewhere, Everywhere*? She was absolutely amazing."

"Didn't she win an Oscar last year?" Claudia asked, admiring the elfin features and slim body of the award-winning actress. Michele Frayer was a top box-office draw. What was she doing attending an introduction party when she could crook her little finger and have any man in town slavering over her?

As if she had already verbalized the question, the psychologist leaned close and stage-whispered, "She doesn't trust any of the men she dates, so she wants Grusha to find her the perfect soul mate. I interviewed her last week. I was so nervous! *Me*, interviewing the most famous actress on the planet. But you know, I think I might be able to talk her into therapy."

They watched the actress slip her velvet bolero jacket from her shoulders and hand it to a uniformed attendant who had materialized at her side. Under the jacket, she wore a pewter-colored brocade mini-dress, the strapless back showing off birdlike shoulder blades.

"She's gorgeous," said Claudia, finding Pollard's behavior more than a little odd. Then her nose picked up a whiff of alcohol and she put the woman's slightly slurred speech down to some preparty tippling.

Pollard, whose burnt orange jersey halter-neck dress did nothing to flatter her dumpy shape, grimaced. "She's so tiny. Makes me feel like I weigh a thousand pounds."

Claudia smiled. "I know what you mean. By the way, how's your head? Any lasting effects from the concussion?"

"Let's not talk about that here," Pollard muttered, looking around nervously as if she were afraid they might be overheard. "I'm fine. That was just a random thing. Let's drop it."

Before Claudia could express her skepticism about the randomness of the break-in, Grusha advanced on them, bringing her famous guest with her.

"Michele, darling, Dr. Pollard you have already met, but I vant you to meet our new handwriting expert, Claudia Rose. She is visiting us from California. You may have seen her on TV before. And Claudia, I'm sure you recognize this beautiful young lady."

Frayer might be a major-league movie star, but her manner was unaffected and sweet. She held out her hand and squeezed Claudia's as warmly as if they were old friends. "I can hardly *wait* to have you analyze my handwriting," she said, practically bouncing on her toes. "I had it done once before, a long time ago. It was amazing!"

Claudia returned her smile. "I'm looking forward to seeing it."

"I already wrote my sample this afternoon. I need to have my assistant run it over to the baroness' office first thing on Monday." Michele slipped her arm through Grusha's. "I'm so pumped about all this. Do you have any idea how hard it is to meet the right person in this business?"

Claudia had to grin at her excitement. "Relationships are hard in *any* business, but yeah, for someone in your position, it's gotta be especially important for you to know the other person's motivations."

"You're so right about that."

"As long as you have the right tools, you'll be fine. Grusha will make sure of it."

Michele, who had to be close to thirty, had the eagerness of a teenager. She said, "I'm dying to see who the baroness matches me up with."

I wish she hadn't said "dying."

Grusha gave her guest a gentle tug. "Come along, then, dahling. Let me introduce you to some of the other guests, especially the men! I know their tongues are hanging out to meet *you*. Donna, why don't you go and talk to Mindy Jarrett; she is looking a little vallflowerish over there. Claudia, I vant you to meet *everyone*. Please introduce yourself around. They vill all be thrilled to hear who you are."

And of course, they'll expect me to analyze their handwritings on the spot.

Browsing the glittering crowd while she decided whom to approach first, Claudia stiffened as an arm slipped around her shoulders. "Hey, sexy," said Marcus Bernard, leaning down to speak directly into her ear. "You look fantastic."

She gave Marcus a glance cool enough to make him drop his arm. "Thanks. I didn't see you arrive."

"You were too busy stargazing," he said, teasing her. "Damn, Michele Frayer is a hottie. Who do you think Grusha has in mind for that tasty little piece of—"

"I wouldn't know," Claudia snapped, cutting him off. "I've only seen a couple of male members—" She broke off, blushing as she realized her gaffe.

Marcus threw back his head and laughed without restraint. "I'll be more than happy to show you mine."

"Thanks, but no thanks. You know what I meant."

Ian McAllister sauntered over and joined them, moving to stand close to Claudia's side. He looked down at her, his eyebrows arched. "Have I missed the hilarity?"

"Ah, the good doctor." At her other side, Marcus edged a little closer, as if he were staking a claim on her. Not to be outdone, McAllister favored her with his version of a smile.

"You look especially fetching tonight, Claudia. But I see Marcus has left you empty-handed. May I get you a drink?"

Marcus cleared his throat loudly and gave Ian a nasty smile. "In case you hadn't noticed, Doc, we were talking, not dancing. That means you don't get to cut in."

McAllister, who was a couple of inches taller than the construction mogul, gave him a condescending look down his nose. "Isn't the baroness looking for you, Marcus? I'd be willing to bet she has a lovely young lady for you to meet. That's why you're here, isn't it? To connect with a lovely *young* lady? I'll be more than happy to take care of Ms. Rose."

"Look, Doc, *you're* here to make people comfortable, aren't you? Well, you're not making *me* comfortable. There's plenty of gorgeous women here without your trying to horn in on Claudia."

Beginning to feel cornered and not liking the sensation, Claudia interrupted. "This is all very flattering, but I don't currently have a need to feel like a bone between two dogs. I'll see you boys later." She walked away, leaving them snarling at each other, and hurried downstairs to the powder room.

Standing in front of the mirror, she almost laughed. Almost any other woman would be flattered to pieces by being pursued, not by just one, but *two* personable, wealthy men. But then, other women weren't trying to determine whether one of those men was a vile killer.

She touched up her lipstick and blush, tipped the attendant, and headed back up to the party. She wished Jovanic were with her. Everything was more fun with him there. She headed for the bar with every intention of fortifying herself with a glass of wine. Someone had already poured several glasses and set them out on the bar top for self-service. Claudia started to take one.

"Wait!" The command came from Ian McAllister. "Don't drink that!"

Claudia's hand arrested midreach. Dammit, she thought she'd shaken him. "Did you and Marcus kiss and make up?" she said.

Ian damned her with a faint smile and ignored the jibe. "I've got something extraspecial for you," he said. "Show me you've forgiven my bad behavior of last night; just give me a few minutes. Please?" He asked so nicely that she thought it would be churlish to refuse.

He led her to a table secluded behind a Chinese fan palm and with a formal little bow drew out a chair for her. On the table were a rocks glass half filled with a clear liquid and two crystal goblets, about two ounces of something green in each. Claudia took in the arrangement with more than a little misgiving. "What's this?"

"The clear one is water," he promised. "Watch."

Like a magician pulling a rabbit from a hat, Ian produced a plastic bag from his pocket. From the bag he removed a silver slotted spoon that resembled a small cake server. After he had thoroughly cleaned the spoon with a handkerchief, he took a sugar cube from the bag and placed it on the spoon, which he laid over one of the goblets. Next, he drizzled water from the rocks glass over the cube.

"Is this some sort of drug?" Claudia asked suspiciously.

"Of course it's not a drug. It's an absinthe drip."

"I thought absinthe was a hallucinogen. Isn't it outlawed?"

"Not to worry, Claudia dear. It's perfectly legal these days."

"But it's made from wormwood, isn't it?"

"Wormwood isn't the problem," Ian explained patiently. "It's an ingredient called thujone that was thought to bring on hallucinations. There's only a tiny amount of thujone in the modern drink, so you have nothing to worry about. It does have a very high alcohol content." He offered her the goblet with a smile. "Here, sniff. It's flavored with anise. Do you like black licorice?"

"Yes, I like licorice, but I'm not sure—"

"Surely you don't think I would harm you? Oh, come on, Claudia, you must allow me to make up for the other night. You'll love it. It's called the Green Fairy."

"*I've* heard it's called the Green *Devil*."

She took the goblet and put it to her nose. It didn't smell much like licorice to her. She took a tentative sip, half expecting to keel over in a dead faint or have some other exotic reaction, but nothing untoward happened. Ian was looking at her expectantly, waiting for her to enthuse over his concoction. She gave an apologetic shrug. "I'm sorry, but it tastes like medicine to me."

He abruptly snatched the glass away, the liquid splashing over the side and onto her hand. "Forget it," he said, turning his back on her and muttering something that Claudia thought might have been "Philistine."

What's wrong with the men in this club? she asked herself, blotting absinthe off her hand with a tissue that she dug out of her evening bag. The three whom Grusha had identified as suspects all seemed to have serious personality problems. How in the world had Andy Nicholson let them get by? How had Grusha?

She was still sitting at the table, wondering how soon she could respectably leave, when she became aware of a commotion just a few feet away, near the roof entrance. She got up and moved around the palm, which was blocking her view.

What she saw made her wonder whether she had fallen asleep and walked into a bad dream.

Chapter 27

Andy Nicholson was hugging Michele Frayer as if she were his long-lost cousin. Frayer shrieked in delight as several other guests took in her performance with questioning glances.

Across the rooftop, Grusha looked stricken. Even at this distance, Claudia could see the emotions chasing across her face. Hurrying over to the matchmaker, she took her arm, offering her support. "Don't say anything," Claudia said. "Just breathe."

"What—is—he—doing—here?" Grusha whispered. Her hand was at her throat as though she were choking. Her chest heaved under the black silk of her dress. "I cannot—get—enough air."

Claudia took in her pale face with alarm. "Should I call an ambulance?"

"*Nyet*. No." Grusha stumbled backward, leaning against the wall. "What is he *doing* here?"

"Probably rubbing your face in what he did this morning on TV. It's the kind of thing he would do."

"Who does he think he is dealing with? To come to my party and—"

From the corner of her eye, Claudia became aware of someone approaching them. Turning, she saw Sonya hurrying over. The assistant pulled Grusha aside, but her voice carried enough for Claudia to hear. "Did you see who's here?"

Grusha whirled on her in a tightly controlled fury. "Do you think I am blind? Of course I see. How did he get in? He had no invitation."

"Michele Frayer invited him," said Sonya. "They know each other. What do you want me to do about it?"

"Michele invited him?" She spat a few words in Russian. Then, back to English, "My god, it's a nightmare!"

Sonya glanced over her shoulder at Michele, who had begun introducing Andy to some of the other guests. "Should I have the bouncers throw him out?"

"*Nyet*, you stupid girl. You just said Michele invited him. I cannot offend a client of her stature. Even if it kills me, Nicholson vill not see what he has done to me."

Grusha sucked in a deep breath. She made a show of marshaling her strength and put a tight grip on Claudia's arm. "Come with me, Claudia. Smile at the bastard. Maybe together ve can kill him vit our poisonous thoughts."

Andy and Michele had strolled over to the bar together and were having a conversation. Michele took a glass of wine, laughing at something he'd said. As Claudia and Grusha moved closer, Andy pivoted as if he had an invisible antenna that sensed their approach. His stare was as cold as a shark's and just as empty of kindness.

"Grusha, sweetheart!" He leaned forward and plastered a big, sloppy kiss on each of the matchmaker's cheeks. "Wonderful to see you. It's been ages." Only Claudia was close enough to see that he was digging hard enough into her biceps to make the skin whiten under his fingers. Grusha pulled away, her body stiff with tension. She forced a smile. "Andy. I did not expect you."

"I hope you don't mind, but I invited him," Michele Frayer said. "He's the one I told you about who analyzed my handwriting years ago. I couldn't believe all the wonderful things he said."

Even Andy must get it right sometimes, Claudia thought uncharitably. "Saw you on TV this morning, Andy," she said, earning a sharp dig from Grusha's elbow.

Andy turned his head to sneer at her. "Well, well, if it isn't the famous Claudia Rose. I hear you're my replacement at Elite Introductions. Will wonders never cease?" His tone was light, but the daggers behind the words had been honed to a fine edge.

With her best phony smile matching his, Claudia said, "Word travels fast. Do you have a mole in the club?" Without waiting for him to respond, she spoke to Michele. "So, is there any chemistry happening yet? Has Grusha introduced you to your soul mate?"

"Is a little too soon for chemistry," Grusha interrupted. "But Michele, you can have a sneaky peek at someone special I have in mind for you. See if you like his looks. You may visit vit Mr. Nicholson later. Come."

Claudia could see that Michele had caught on that something was up, but the actress went without protest, leaving Claudia with Andrew Nicholson.

When they were alone, she dropped the smile. "Why'd you come here, Andy?"

"Why do you think?" He tossed back red wine and took a second glass, leaving the empty on the bar. "Because I can."

"Why don't you leave Grusha alone? It's not her fault you just phoned it in on the analyses she hired you to do. She doesn't deserve what you did on *Hard Evidence* this morning. She's not a bad person."

"You have no idea what *she* is."

"I know more than you think I do. You waltzed in, did a half-assed job, and left a mess behind for her to clean up. And I saw some of the reports you wrote. They completely ignored the red flags in the handwritings."

The veins in his neck popped out; a dull flush crept over his cheeks. "You don't know what the fuck you're talking about. She *made* me take out anything that didn't look good."

"You told her about the danger signs?"

"Damn right, I told her." He gulped wine, then stuck out a finger and jabbed it against her collarbone. "You're not the only graphologist in the world, Miss Prissy."

Claudia shoved away his hand, wondering whether he was aware of the deaths of Grusha's clients and the suspects' handwritings she had been brought in to analyze.

"You let her change your reports," she accused. Chances were he was lying about it, but she couldn't resist digging at him anyway.

"Hey, she was paying the freight. She was a pretty good cash cow for a while."

"Is that all you care about, the money?"

"I was looking out for number one. Nobody else is gonna do it. Let's see how you handle it when she changes *your* reports."

"What about the people who were affected because you didn't tell the whole truth?"

He shot her a look of contempt. "Fuck you, Claudia Rose. Nobody fires me!" He spun on his heel and melted into the crowd.

Claudia didn't bother to watch him go, disgusted by his rude arrogance. He was a narcissist, only seeing what affected him. Then she groaned as she sensed someone approaching. *Marcus.*

"Has anyone said anything to you about me?" he asked, looking worried.

"What are you talking about?"

"People are talking trash about me, I can tell. They think they know something about me. They're laughing behind my back."

"How much have you had to drink? Why would anyone be laughing at you?"

"Someone's been talking. None of the women are speaking to me. Someone's been telling tales."

"Tales about *what*? You sound a little paranoid, Marcus. What on earth could you have done that women don't want to speak to you?"

"Never mind. Forget it. Hey, was that Andy Nicholson I saw talking to you just now?"

"Yes, he crashed the party."

"Where is that weasel? I'll bet he's the one with the big mouth."

He strode off, leaving Claudia mystified. She stayed where she was for a while, trying not to think about Marcus or Ian or Avram; just watching everyone else enjoying themselves. Most of the fifty-odd guests seemed engaged in a juggling act with a glass in one hand, a plate filled with hors d'oeuvres in the other.

One of the twins who had been talking with Ian earlier danced by, twirling in circles and chanting something unintelligible. She had no partner and she was apparently hearing her own music, as the quartet had taken a break and was preparing for their next set. Other people were just starting to partner up, getting ready to dance. This one was ahead of the curve.

It wasn't more than five or six minutes later that the woman Grusha had sent Donna Pollard to talk to appeared in Claudia's line of vision. What was her name? Grusha had referred to her as a wallflower. Mindy—Jarrett, that was it. Mindy was by herself, standing in a corner, lips parted in a happy smile. Wide-eyed, staring around as if there were something only she could see. Suddenly, her expression changed. She balled her hands into claws, scratching at nothing, fighting off some invisible foe.

The girl needed a doctor and there was one here, somewhere. Claudia glanced around the rooftop. She spotted Ian McAllister sitting at a table with John Shaw, the photographer. Considering the size of the man, it was surprising she'd missed his arrival. *Terrific.* The two men she had managed to piss off most in the last twenty-four hours or so, and they were together.

She hurried over to their table and both men immediately rose. Acknowledging Shaw with a nod, she said, "Excuse me for interrupting. Ian, I need to speak with you privately. It's urgent."

Despite his earlier annoyance with her, the physician allowed her to draw him to the side, where there was less noise.

"Did you give Mindy Jarrett absinthe?" Claudia asked.

"Why would I?"

She thought his look of confusion gave her the answer she wanted, but she pressed him anyway. "That doesn't answer the question. Did you?"

"Absolutely not. What's this about?"

"I think she's hallucinating. Oh jeez, look at her."

Most of the rooftop was carpeted in fake turf, but Mindy Jarrett was sitting on cold concrete in a corner, her knees bent, her short cocktail dress hiked up to her hips. She'd buried her head in her arms and was rocking back and forth. Either no one else had noticed, or they were deliberately choosing to avoid her.

"Good lord," Ian said.

Claudia followed him over there. He hunkered down beside Mindy and put a hand on her shoulder. She flinched, but didn't look up. "Mindy," Ian said gently. "What have you taken?" He took her chin in his hand and tipped her face toward the nearest light, looking into wide blue eyes that stared into space. "Mindy, what drug did you take? Did someone give you something to take?" The second time he used a more forceful tone.

Mindy Jarrett kept shaking her head from side to side. "Don't take drugs," she mumbled over and over. "Drugs are bad."

Ian looked over at Claudia, who was crouched on Mindy's other side. "Her pupils are dilated. She's sweating." He wrapped a hand around her wrist. "Rapid pulse. If she is hallucinating, which is what it looks like, there's no treatment for it. We've got to get her somewhere calmer, quieter. Help me take her down to Grusha's office, Claudia. Whatever it is will wear off in time. That's the best we can do."

With Claudia holding one arm and Ian the other, they got Mindy to her feet and led her toward the stairwell as inconspicuously as possible in a crowd of that size. Any onlookers would think the woman between them had been taken ill and they were helping her.

As they moved through couples swaying to a slow number, Claudia caught sight of the girl who had danced past her just a few minutes earlier. She was still singing and moving from side to side, arms in the air. All she needed was a long, filmy scarf to waft after her and she could have been a latter-day Isadora Duncan. A few heads swivelled her way, but no one paid much attention.

"Someone is handing out drugs," Claudia said to Ian as they arrived at the short flight of steps that led down to the elevator.

He scowled at her. "Well, it wasn't me, and I'll thank you not to suggest to anyone that it was."

"Is getting wasted SOP at these things?"

He looked even more offended. "It most certainly is *not*. Being drug-free is one of the strictest require-ments for membership in the club."

"Well, someone's broken the rule. We've got to let Grusha know."

"You can talk to Grusha later. The first order of business is to get Ms. Jarrett out of here. Help me get her down the stairs."

Mindy wasn't a large woman, but even though Ian took more of the burden, getting her down the steps was like hauling dead weight. At the bottom of the staircase, they leaned her against the wall while they caught their breath.

Claudia said, "Wait here with her. I'll find Sonya and see if she's got a key to the office. Keep your fin-gers crossed."

She ran back upstairs. The music was starting to crank up and the voices were in competition. Stand-ing there, watching the swirling colors on the handful of clients dancing under the sparkle of lights strung above and in the trees, the music pounding in her ears, Claudia felt as if she herself had been drugged. But she knew she hadn't ingested anything since her arrival, except for one glass of wine and the sip of absinthe.

Spotting Sonya, she drew her aside and explained the situation. Luckily, Sonya said she had her office key on her. They agreed that she would help Ian get Mindy down to the Elite Introductions office, then stay with her while he came back up to the party to check on the dancing woman.

If clients were not permitted to use recreational drugs, what was happening? Claudia had no doubt that at least two of them had consumed *something* that had an effect on their behavior. Or someone had spiked the drinks. Then suddenly, there was a third: Aisha Negasi.

"What is this?" Claudia heard the Ethiopian model cry out. She swung around to see Aisha staring into space. "What are these colors? What is happening? Am I *trippin'*? Oooh, it tingles." All at once, her attitude was one of wonder. "Ohhhhh, it's beautiful. It's so—so beautiful." Her voluptuous body began to writhe in ecstasy. Some of the nearby guests who had heard her were staring, whispering to one another. Avram Cohen gawked, bewildered.

Grusha was watching, too, anger tightening her jaw. "Who is drugging my clients?" she demanded of Claudia as if she had the answer. "When this gets out, they vill all sue for their money back. Nobody vill come to me. I am ruined, finished. He has won, whoever he is."

"We'll deal with it," said Claudia, taking charge. "Have Avram get Aisha down to the office and stay with her. Ian's down there now with Mindy Jarrett. He'll be back in a moment to help with the other girl."

Grusha gave an unamused laugh. "Ve might as well put a bulletin on the evening news. I am sure it vill end up there anyway. My god, how could it get any vorse? I cannot—"

Her words were interrupted by Michele Frayer's shrill scream: "Grab him! Quick!"

Beside her, Claudia heard Grusha's sharp intake of breath.

Andy Nicholson, poised atop the low retaining wall, his arms outstretched. John Shaw reaching out to grab him, catching the hem of Andy's jacket. The jacket coming off.

"Look at me," Andy shouted, his feet rocking perilously close to the edge. "I'm Superman. I can fly."

Then he stretched out his arms and he flew.

Chapter 28

Someone—Claudia never found out who—called 911, and then everything was chaos. She had long despised Andy Nicholson and all that he stood for, but if she had been told that she would watch him take the shortcut from the penthouse roof to the street that night, she would have done anything she could to save him.

The police arrived within ten minutes, closing the sidewalk and cordoning off the area with yellow crime-scene tape. Cordoning off the entire block. She knew that because she made herself look over the wall. Not a lot to see from fourteen stories up. People crowding the tape. Andy's body a dark shadow on the sidewalk, a darker shadow spreading around his head.

Maybe now they'll listen.

"I heard he bounced off a couple of awnings on the way down."

"Holy cow! Too bad it didn't break his fall."

"Nah, just broke his head. Big splat."

And, "Lucky he didn't hit anyone."

"He was the handwriting guy, wasn't he?"

"Used to be. They've got another one now. Didn't you meet her? She was here tonight."

The buzz went on and on until the boys in blue

came up to the roof and said that nobody was to leave. First, the patrolmen tried to segregate all the guests so they couldn't swap stories, but there were too many of them and eventually they were all asked to wait in line to be interviewed. They weeded out the actual witnesses from those who said they had merely heard something. The remaining guests were asked for their names and contact information and were then allowed to leave.

Later came the squad commander—the official-looking one in the smart uniform with lieutenant's braids—along with a couple of detectives. Claudia overheard him saying something about this being a "forty-nine," but she could only guess what that meant.

She knew that the big shots liked to be present for the cameras and to make sure the department looked good. If NYPD was anything like LAPD, the brass nearly always rolled out to an incident when big names were involved. Not names like Andrew Nicholson or Claudia Rose, but names with star power, like Michele Frayer—whose pale face wore a look of stunned disbelief as the squad commander gently took her arm and escorted her down to the Elite Introductions office for her interview.

Claudia saw a detective with Grusha. The matchmaker's eyes glittered with a strange light that Claudia, in a mood to see demons everywhere, thought just might be vengeful pleasure. If Grusha was going down in flames, at least one enemy had gone down before her and she wasn't going to pretend she was sad about it. *She's in shock*, Claudia thought. *We all are.*

The young patrolman getting witnesses organized wasn't interested in listening when Claudia said that she had some information that might help their investigation. Busy being officious and in charge, he scarcely looked at her when she approached him.

"Where were you when the incident occurred?"

"I was over there, but—"

"We're talking to direct witnesses first. Please just wait over there, ma'am. We'll get to you as soon as we can."

"But I think it's important for—"

"Ma'am, I said we'll get to you as soon as we can. Now go and wait over there." He turned away and started speaking to someone else.

An hour later when they got around to Claudia, the first thing she was asked was whether she knew Mr. Nicholson and she admitted that she did. She learned that someone had seen *Hard Evidence* and told the cops about it, so they already knew that Andy had been slandering her and Grusha that morning. That left her uneasy.

A detective named Judy Campbell interviewed her about an hour later. She was an attractive blonde with piercing blue eyes that missed little, and the world-weary look of one who had been on the job long enough to have left any illusions behind. Claudia had seen that look on many experienced detectives.

They were sitting at the desk where Avram had provided his handwriting sample on the first day of Claudia's assignment. Detective Campbell sat back and crossed her knees, the jacket of her navy pantsuit falling open to reveal a crisp white blouse. "So, you don't think he intended to commit suicide when he jumped?"

"No, he didn't commit suicide. He was hallucinating. He thought he was Superman."

"Did you know the victim to take drugs regularly?"

"I don't know whether he took drugs at all. I didn't know him that well, just professionally. We're in the same business; we're both handwriting analysts." *Were* in the same business, she realized with a shock. Andy would never face her in the witness box, lying about her, ever again. "Some of the other guests were acting strangely, too. I'm pretty sure someone spiked the drinks or the food with something hallucinogenic."

"Nothing unusual about people getting high at a party," Detective Campbell observed. She threw it out there, then waited for a response.

"Drugs are forbidden, not just at these parties, but club members can't be users, period," Claudia said, repeating what Ian McAllister had told her.

"Forbidden, huh?" Campbell sounded skeptical. "You sure about that?"

"The baroness doesn't need that kind of trouble. She screens her members very carefully."

"Not carefully enough if someone spiked the drinks. Who else was hallucinating?"

Claudia counted in her head. "Besides Andy, there were three that I saw, all women. I don't know any of them personally. One was a model named Aisha. A girl named Mindy Jarrett. The other one I hadn't been introduced to and I didn't get her name. I just saw her behaving oddly."

"Okay. So, you got any idea who might have planted a hallucinogen?"

Claudia hesitated, thinking of the absinthe. Finally, she said, "No."

"You mentioned you knew the victim professionally, Ms. Rose. We have information that he was trashing you and Ms. Olinetsky earlier today on TV. Can you tell me what that's about?"

There it was, out in the open. The *Hard Evidence* tape was probably on YouTube by now. It would be easy enough for the police to see exactly what Andy Nicholson had said about her and Grusha.

"He didn't mention me by name, but he did say some, er, unpleasant things, yes."

"Musta made you and Ms. Olinetsky pretty mad," Detective Campbell said, doing her best to look sympathetic, but failing.

"Yes, it did make us mad, but not mad enough to drug a bunch of her clients—that only makes Grusha look bad, which was probably the objective of the person who did do it. And no one could have predicted that Andy would do what he did."

The detective took a phone call, then returned her gaze to Claudia. "You think maybe somebody thought it would be funny to spike the punch?"

"There wasn't any punch. If the drug was put into a drink, it had to be the glasses of wine that had been poured and left on the bar."

"Did you see anyone hanging around by the bar who looked like they might be up to something like that?"

Claudia shook her head. "I'm sorry, Detective. I was invited to help with the guests. I wasn't watching for suspicious behavior. But I did talk to Andy— the victim—over at the bar, and he was drinking the wine." She paused, still trying to assimilate what had happened. A thought suddenly struck her that should have occurred much sooner. "I went to your precinct a couple of days ago and spoke with Detective Perez. Could I speak to him, please?"

Detective Campbell's head snapped up from her notebook, where she had been making notes. "Mind if I ask what you were doing at the station house?"

Grusha's going to freak.

"I wanted to talk to someone about my suspicions that Elite Introductions clients were being murdered."

Detective Izzy Perez showed up and asked Claudia to come with him to the station house and make a formal statement. Grusha was already on her way over there with Detective Campbell.

Thinking of what she'd heard the lieutenant say earlier, Claudia asked him what "forty-nine" meant.

"It's what we call an unusual report, something out of the ordinary. You know—when there's gonna be something on the eleven o'clock news or in the papers tomorrow—we call it a forty-nine. If it was a regular report, like a complaint, it'd be a sixty-one."

"Oh."

If the amount of media they'd had to fight their way through to get to Perez' car was an indicator, this story was definitely a forty-nine.

Back at his desk in the squad room, Claudia sat in the same hard wooden chair she'd sat in on her last visit to the precinct, and they went over the whole thing again. Everything she'd told him on Thursday, plus the evening's events.

"Your friend the baroness has had quite a string of bad luck," Perez said. "Wouldn't wanna be one of her clients."

"Andy Nicholson wasn't a client."

"No," he said thoughtfully. "But he sure pissed her off." His desk phone rang and he excused himself to answer it, listened with an impassive face. Said, "Figures," then rang off and gave Claudia a look. "Looks like the lady's lawyered up."

"Grusha?"

"She's refused to answer any questions. Wants to talk to her lawyer."

"Are you going to hold her?"

"Not at this point. So far, it's just a witness inquiry."

Seconds later, a door slammed and Grusha came steaming past the squad room without looking left or right. Ian McAllister was in tow, Detective Campbell bringing up the rear. Campbell looked over at Perez and shrugged, then went and sat at her own desk.

Ian's doing double duty tonight, Claudia thought. Grusha could probably use some hand-holding.

Chapter 29

Claudia got a cab back to the hotel and climbed into bed. Not having Grusha's home phone or cell number, she left a voice mail at the office, asking her to call. Then she left a message for Jovanic and propped herself against the headboard with the covers pulled up to her neck, feeling empty and alone.

She considered calling Kelly or Zebediah, just to have someone to talk to about Andy, but what could she say? Impossible to absorb the fact of his appalling death, and impossible to comprehend that she had witnessed his free fall into eternity.

Whoever had drugged the drinks could not have known that the evening would end with Andy Nicholson's death, but it was clear that the malefactor was upping the ante when it came to embarrassing Grusha. *Who could have drugged the drinks?*

Any of the men whose handwritings had red flags—Avram, Marcus, John. Ian, too.

All of them had opportunity, but what about means and motive? Claudia had suspicions about Ian McAllister having a revenge motive because of his daughter, but she was unaware of any motive for Marcus Bernard or Avram Cohen, although their handwriting did show potential for bad behavior. But potential isn't the same as acting.

What about John Shaw, with his PTSD? A head injury might cause him to act violently without a rational motive. Many serial killers had suffered head injuries before they started on that irrevocable path to violence.

She switched off the light and scooted under the covers, but one question kept her mind spinning: *Who drugged the drinks?*

After two a.m., still lying awake in the dark room. Distant traffic sounds drifting up from the street making white noise. *The city that never sleeps.* Whoever coined that phrase got it right. Claudia rearranged her pillows again and rolled onto her back. She did some relaxation breathing and started counting backward from one hundred. She had reached fifty-nine when she heard a tentative knocking at the door. Before forming a conscious thought she was bolt upright in bed, heart slamming against her chest.

What the—

Shrugging into her robe, Claudia dashed across the room. Through the peep she could see a short woman in a winter coat standing in the hallway. Even with the lower part of her face covered by a scarf, the cotton candy hair and anxious expression gave her away. Donna Pollard lifted a gloved hand and knocked again, louder.

Flipping back the locks and switching on the entry light, Claudia blinked as her eyes adjusted. She opened the door wide enough for the psychologist to enter. "What are you doing here, Donna?"

"I'm sorry. I'm sorry for waking you up. I'm sorry for everything. I couldn't wait until morning to talk to you. I hope you'll forgive me."

"I wasn't asleep. How did you get my room number?"

"Sonya."

"Has something happened? Is Grusha—"

"I haven't talked to her. I've tried calling, but there was no answer. I guess she doesn't feel like talking right now, poor darling."

"I saw Ian with her at the police station. It looked like he might be taking her home. Maybe they're still talking." Claudia cleared the chair of her purse and coat and offered it to Pollard. She took up her earlier position on the bed, sitting against the headboard.

Pollard loosened her scarf and coat, glanced around at the room. "She could have done better than this for you," she said. "I hope you're not too uncomfortable."

"It's okay, it's fine. I'm hoping not to have many more nights here. Maybe now the police are finally involved, this thing will get cleared up."

Donna Pollard sighed, a soughing whisper of sadness that seemed to come from the depths of her soul. "Yes, I expect that's what will happen. That's why I'm here. I had some last things to tell you."

"Last things? That sounds pretty final, Donna. What does that mean?"

A soft smile. "It means this is the last time I'm going to be telling you anything about this situation. I've given it a lot of thought, and something has occurred to me that I believe might be important, and I want you to know about it. First, though, I want you to know why I didn't call the police when my office was broken into."

Claudia nodded. "Okay, I'm listening."

Donna Pollard spoke slowly, as if parting with

the words required a great deal of effort. "I'd lost my license to practice psychology, you see. Not in New York—in Idaho. I appealed, but the licensing board ruled against me. They said I didn't have my clients' best interests at heart." Her voice thickened with emotion. "Claudia, helping people is my *life*. I can't not help when there's a need. To be thrown out of a profession that has given me a chance to nurture and help my clients was like a living death for me."

"What did you do to put your license at stake?"

"I was working with a mother and daughter in therapy. The mother was a real ogre, I can tell you that. A *smother mother,* that's what I call the type. She wouldn't let the girl have any identity of her own. The daughter was fifteen, crying out for help." Donna turned pleading eyes to Claudia, silently begging for understanding. "The daughter used to phone me at all times of the day and night. She really *needed* me. After a few months of therapy and not seeing any progress, I couldn't stand it any longer. I let the daughter move in with me."

Claudia remembered when she'd read the notes about Jessica McAllister, how she'd thought it would be hard for the psychologist to keep an appropriate distance. The crowded words meant that being able to get close to people, to get really involved in their lives, was what made her feel good about herself. But it wasn't a good trait for a therapist. "Was the mother abusing her?" she asked.

"Not physically, but in some ways she was a lot like Ian McAllister with Jessie. Constantly on the daughter's back, wanting to know everything she was doing. She was a crazymaker. She constantly put the daughter in a double bind."

"Like what, for example?"

"Oh, she might pile a plate high with food and put it in front of the daughter and nag her to eat every bite. Then, when the plate was empty, she'd berate the girl and call her a fat pig. A double bind. There was no way she could win."

"But if the mother was psychologically abusive and you felt it was bad enough that the girl needed to be taken out of the home, wouldn't it have been more appropriate to put her in care somewhere?"

Pollard wrung her hands, getting upset. "That's what *they* said, but I couldn't do it. You know what those foster care places can be like, don't you?"

"So, the mother reported you?"

She gave a bitter laugh. "Only after the money ran out. She was okay with me taking her daughter, as long as I paid for her silence."

"She *blackmailed* you?"

Dr. Pollard nodded. "She insisted on cash so there was no money trail, except on my end with the withdrawals, and I couldn't prove I'd given the money to her. I told her I couldn't do it any longer and she called my bluff. She reported me. I lost my license and the daughter ended up in foster care anyway. God knows what happened to her after that; they wouldn't give me any information. So I changed my name and moved here to the East Coast, I met Grusha, and the rest—well, here we are."

"Does Grusha know you've been practicing without a license?"

"Of course, but she's been flying under the radar herself, so we figured we would watch each other's backs."

"I don't understand why you're telling me all this," said Claudia.

"Partly because I believe that's why my office was broken into. I think the intruder might have been looking for proof of my past so he could use it against me and embarrass Grusha. I did a pretty good job of covering my tracks, but my files could be taken to the New York State Licensing Board. I could go to jail." Her voice caught and she sobbed on a breath. "Like I said, I've been doing a lot of thinking, and . . . well, I may have let my involvement with Jessie McAllister affect my judgment in allowing you to see her file."

Claudia got off the bed and handed her a manila folder that was lying on the desk. "Here are your notes. I was going to mail them back to you on Monday."

"It doesn't matter now. It's just that, well, I think I may have been looking in the wrong direction when I pointed you there. It's true Ian was overbearing and controlling of Jessica, but there's something else that you should know, seeing as you've gotten yourself so deep into this mess of Grusha's." Another long pause. "When Marcus Bernard joined the club, he and Grusha were strongly attracted to one another. In fact, they started dating and Grusha fell in love with him. Or something approximating love."

Claudia sat back on the bed, thinking of the matchmaker's ambivalence toward Marcus, first giving her his file to analyze his handwriting, then protesting when she had agreed that he could be a suspect.

"But he's now a client. What happened—they fell out of love?"

"I'm not sure how much you know about Grusha . . ."

"I know."

Another deep sigh. "Well, of course, Marcus *didn't* know. The relationship got hot and heavy pretty fast.

She wanted him to give her some time so he could get to know her better before she told him about her past. But he wanted sex right away—he got very insistent. She told me that he talked her out of her clothes, but as they were about to do the deed, she stopped him. She told him that she'd had the operation. It had only been a few months since she'd had it, and she was still working through the changes. But she thought telling him was the right thing to do.

"Marcus totally lost it. Seemed to think that her having had a sex change was a personal assault on his manhood. He went ballistic, frightened her with threats. But he didn't actually do anything; he just stormed out. He refused to have anything to do with her at all for a while after that. Then he showed up at Elite Introductions a few months ago, demanding that Grusha find him his soul mate—said she owed it to him. He knew how much it would hurt her to have to introduce him to someone else. Even now, she's still half in love with him."

The pieces of the puzzle clicked neatly into place. Marcus' paranoia at the party, thinking people were talking about him. The vengefulness that Donna Pollard was describing. He had dated Jessica McAllister, Shellee Jones, *and* Heather Lloyd. Hell, everyone knew he was with Shellee when she died. And Claudia had thought it could be him in the video with Heather. She just wasn't sure where Ryan Turner fit into the picture.

"After Andy jumped last night, I spoke to a homicide detective," Claudia said. "His name's Perez. I'd already talked to him a couple of days before and gave him the whole story then. He didn't believe it the first time, but now he's taking it more seriously. He's working on the investigation."

"Well, that's it then," Donna Pollard said. "Now I've given you the finishing touches."

"You should call Detective Perez tomorrow and tell him what you just told me. Or better yet, get Grusha to tell him so it's not just hearsay."

"She wouldn't do that. It's so humiliating for her, and she still doesn't want to believe Marcus could be the one who is behind all the things that have happened. This is really just my conjecture, but I wanted you to know."

Claudia reached over to her briefcase and brought out Marcus' file, turned to the handwriting sample. *Charming con artist,* that's what she'd thought when she first saw it. But a killer? Could Marcus have planned it all to get revenge on Grusha, destroying her credibility, little by little? It all seemed so farfetched.

Then it occurred to her that men had killed for far less than their manhood.

After Donna Pollard left, Claudia booted up the laptop and instant messaged her brother, who was an accomplished computer hacker, and asked him if he could find any information on Marcus Bernard that she had not uncovered in her original search.

Pete got back to her ten minutes later. He'd discovered several lawsuits that had been filed against Marcus' company. Detective Perez had told her in their first interview that Marcus had been sued more than once and won, but he hadn't given her any details. Now she learned the reasons for the suits: shoddy construction.

In one filing, the buyer complained about leaky roofs and decks in a luxury condominium built by Marcus' company. The leaks had allowed deadly mold spores to grow and sicken the entire family.

They'd had to move out for several months while the problem was rectified. In the end, after years of litigation, the case was dismissed for lack of proof that the builder had been negligent. In a second case, the foundation of an office building had not been properly bolted in place, but the blame had been shifted away from the builder. There were other claims similar in nature, but none of them had stuck. Marcus Bernard always walked away clean, even from allegations of witness intimidation.

He's rich enough to buy his way out. And arrogant enough to believe he's above the law.

By three thirty, Claudia was dizzy with exhaustion. She powered down the computer, turned off the lights, and went back to bed.

Ninety minutes later, someone was again knocking on her door.

Chapter 30

Detective Izzy Perez. Standing outside her hotel room at five in the morning, looking grim.

What the hell is he doing here?

For the second time that night, Claudia undid the locks and opened the door.

"I'm sorry to disturb you, Ms. Rose. May I come in? I need to talk to you."

She stepped back, pulling her robe tighter around her, disoriented from being awakened. "What's going on?"

Detective Perez walked in and flicked a glance around the room, not answering her question. "I suppose you are acquainted with Dr. Donna Pollard, seeing as she was at the party last night?"

Even half asleep, she resented his subtly condescending air. "Yes, of course. You know we're both consultants for Elite Introductions."

"How well do you know her?"

"Not well at all. I met her for the first time last week. We've spoken a couple of times since then."

"When was the last time you saw Dr. Pollard?"

A homicide detective coming to her hotel room before dawn and asking questions was a bad sign. Claudia could feel her heart rate speeding up, preparing for bad news. "She showed up here earlier, a couple of hours ago. Why, has something happened to her?"

"What time did she leave here?"

"I think it was a little after three. What's going on, Detective?"

"The station house got a call from her about an hour ago. She left a message for me to see you. She said she'd given you some information that might have a bearing on the Elite Introductions case."

"And you're here before it's even light to ask me about it? I don't understand. I suggested she call you. Why didn't she just tell you herself?"

"Dr. Pollard has committed suicide."

"What?" That couldn't be right. He couldn't have said what she thought she'd heard. But then his mouth was moving again and words were coming out, and she knew she had not misheard.

"She phoned the precinct and told the dispatcher she'd already taken pills and alcohol, and that by the time we got someone out there it would be too late, so not to hurry. But she asked for me to contact you. Dispatch took it seriously."

I'm really still asleep and this is just a lousy dream.

"She called the police to say she was committing suicide?"

Perez lifted his shoulders in a pragmatic shrug. "Suicidal people do all kinds of strange things when they're feeling up against it. What she told dispatch was she didn't want her body stinking up the apartment for days and someone having to come in and clean up after her, so she wanted to let us to know in advance."

Claudia thought of how Pollard had become enmeshed with Jessica McAllister and the girl over whom she'd lost her license. And she thought of her handwriting. Putting other people's needs ahead of her own was characteristic of Donna Pollard's type. Even in planning how to handle her own suicide, she wanted to cause as little inconvenience as possible to the people who would have to handle her body.

With a sense of unreality Claudia said, "That sounds like what I knew of Donna. Did the dispatcher at least send someone over to try and save her?"

"She was calling from a cell phone," Perez said. "Refused to give an address. By the time dispatch got it pinned down, they sent a bus over, but she was gone."

"A *bus*?"

He gave a slight smile. "Ambulance. Sorry, that's what we call 'em. We send a bus."

It wouldn't sink in. "But she was just here. I don't understand. She never said—"

But she *had* said something. She'd talked about having some last things to say. Without warning, Claudia's legs gave out and she plopped down onto the bed with a groan. "I should have picked up on it. I should have . . ."

Detective Perez went into the bathroom and came back with a glass of water. "I'm sorry," he said, handing it to her, his tough features softening a trace. "I know it's gotta be a shock, especially coming so soon after last night, but have you got any idea why she would do something like this? Did she have any involvement in what's been going on at the dating club? Something she felt guilty about?"

Claudia sipped the water, trying to comprehend what she had just learned. "No, it's not that. When she came here this morning, what she told me was she's been practicing without a license. With everything that's been happening at Elite Introductions, especially after the party, the investigation into Andy Nicholson's death and all, she figured it was going to come out and she would be in big legal trouble. I guess she couldn't face it. Oh my god, I can't believe this." She wiped her hand over her face. "Does Grusha know yet?"

Dark shadows tinted the bags under Perez' eyes. He looked as worn out as Claudia felt. "I've tried all Ms. Olinetsky's numbers, but nobody's answering. Ms. Rose, I need you to tell me everything Dr. Pollard told you last night. What she was referring to in her message."

"Yes, of course. Oh my *god*." Her head was buzzing. She felt as if she'd slammed headlong into a wall.

She told him about everything, including Grusha's sex change, just leaving out her incarceration, which he either knew about if they'd fingerprinted her, or he could discover for himself.

"Dr. Pollard had pointed me toward Dr. McAllister because of his behavior toward his daughter. She'd been seeing her for therapy. Like I told you before, he also scared the crap out of me when I had dinner with him and he acted like a crazy man. And his handwriting had some red flags, but it's impossible to predict that someone is going to act out on potential for violence."

"Okay. And what about the other guy's handwriting, Marcus Bernard?"

She told him what she had seen—the signs of a charming con artist. "I can see him contracting someone to do the dirty work for him, but I don't know whether he would do the killings himself. Except for Shellee Jones. I guess he could somehow have gotten peanuts in her food. But then, Ian was there, too, just a few minutes before she died."

Perez checked his notebook. "Mr. Bernard and Dr.

McAllister were both questioned with everyone last night. So far, there's nothing that ties them—or anyone else—to spiking the drinks. In fact, we have to wait for the tox screen to see what was in the glasses that were recovered. I'll talk with them both today, see if they have alibis for the other deaths. We'll still need some physical evidence that these people didn't die accidentally. Otherwise it's a circumstantial case. Circumstantial cases are hard to make."

"What if I've got it all wrong and it's neither of them? What about John Shaw, the photographer? He's definitely on a different plane than the rest of us. He might find a way to rationalize killing." She gave him a troubled look. "I've even wondered whether Grusha herself might be behind the whole thing. She brought me in, but she's obstructed me at every turn. I've asked myself whether she could be setting someone up. But I can't think of a reason why."

"That's why we do an investigation."

"If it's Marcus, he's good at walking away from things. I looked up the lawsuits against his company."

"A civil lawsuit is one thing. If he's involved in homicide, ma'am, we'll do everything we can to get him; I can promise you that." Perez stifled a yawn. "Don't let it drive you nuts, Ms. Rose."

Claudia managed a weak grin. "Right now, Detective, that would be a short drive."

Chapter 31

Sunday. The day after Andy Nicholson jumped to his death. The day Donna Pollard had killed herself. Claudia had been in Manhattan for nearly a week, and she wanted to go home. Leave Grusha and her problems to the cops. *Their problems now.*

The hotel room seemed like a cell. At nine, she called Susan Rowan.

"Jesus H. Christ, Claudia," Susan exploded through the phone. "What the hell happened? I saw it on the news last night. Were you there?"

"Unfortunately, I was about ten feet away when he went over the edge."

"I can't believe it—Andy Nicholson dead! What happened? Channel seven said he was hallucinating."

"He wasn't the only one. Somebody put acid or something in the drinks."

"Too many coincidences, Claudia. I told you something weird is going on in that company."

"No lie. Well, the police are involved now. They're looking into everything—the deaths you know about and a couple of others, too." She didn't mention Donna Pollard. She just couldn't. "Listen, I need to get hold of Grusha. Do you have a number for her outside the office?"

"Yeah, I have her cell. Hang on, I'll get it for you."

Susan was back in thirty seconds and recited the number for her.

"Thanks, Susan." Claudia gave a short laugh. "I was gonna say I owe you one, but considering it was you who got me into this mess, I think you owe me!"

"Jeez, if I'd known how it was going to turn out . . . Hey, take care of yourself."

Grusha's cell phone went straight to voice mail. Claudia left a message, then phoned the office number. After five rings she got an answering service, where she left an urgent message for the matchmaker to call her.

The last few days had left her edgy and anxious. By ten, she had to get out of the hotel for some fresh air. She changed into jeans and a turtleneck sweater, buttoned herself into her corduroy jacket and boots. A long walk to Central Park would give her time to clear her head. Breakfast wasn't on the agenda. All the death had taken away her appetite.

Out on the street, cold air slapped her in the face, feeling good. Like a tortoise withdrawing into its shell, Claudia pulled her woolen scarf over her nose, shoved her hands into her pockets, and turned left from the hotel. Sunday morning; the streets were teeming. People going in and out of restaurants, people riding bicycles, people filling the sidewalks, walking, Rollerblading.

As she started walking up the block she spotted a black town car that was parked across the street pull away from the curb and merge into traffic, driving slowly. The car pulled ahead of her, then moved to the side of the road. Nobody got out. Maybe the driver was waiting for someone to come out of a building. Maybe he was waiting for her.

Claudia, you're getting paranoid.

Moving quickly past the town car, Claudia darted a look, but the tinted windows blocked her view. She passed a Thai restaurant, hurried to the end of the block and crossed at the light. At the right edge of her vision, she could see that the car was back in traffic, going through the intersection, still with her.

At Seventh Avenue she turned left toward Central Park and started walking faster. The avenue was a one-way street and she was walking against traffic. The black car couldn't turn with her.

She passed the bagel shop where she and Susan had breakfasted a few days earlier. Someone was walking close behind her. Too close for comfort. Stories of muggings filled her head.

Moving close to the wall of the nearest building, she stopped and pretended to look for something in her purse, waiting for whoever it was to pass her by. A gaggle of teenage girls and boys shuffled past, teasing one another, and Claudia laughed at herself for her attack of nerves.

Across the street from Carnegie Hall now, only a block from Central Park. She entered a construction scaffolding shed that covered the sidewalk—there seemed to be construction on every other block in this town. Puddles of water dripped from above the poorly lit shed, and she was glad to come out the other side.

With a jolt of recognition Claudia saw a black town car. It was driving toward her, traveling in the far right lane, on her side of the street. She started to cross the street, but the traffic was heavy and fast.

The town car stopped beside her and a man in a dark Windbreaker jumped out. He wore a baseball cap and reflector sunglasses, but she recognized Marcus Bernard's driver, Mike.

"Ms. Rose!" Mike strode over to her.

"Hey, Mike. What—?"

"Mr. Bernard sent me to pick you up."

Claudia's stomach cramped in fear. "I don't have any appointment with Mr. Bernard this morning."

"He's with the baroness. She wants you—"

"I don't think so, Mike. I'm not going anywhere with you."

He nodded, not at her, but past her.

After that, everything happened fast. Someone coming up from behind. Turning to see . . .

And all at once: a buzz like a bug zapper; the world exploding in a lightning bolt of pain; every muscle in spasm; an involuntary cry.

She dropped to her knees and started to topple. Before her face could hit the ground, she was grabbed by the arms, hoisted up. A man's loud voice said something about a seizure. Powerless, she was aware of being carried a few feet, then shoved without ceremony into the waiting car.

Chapter 32

As her brains gradually unscrambled, Claudia became aware that she was sprawled across the backseat of Marcus Bernard's town car. Mike was driving and another man was in the passenger seat—big, beefy, with a bull neck and a crew cut. Security. The one behind the stun gun.

Owwww.

She must have groaned out loud because Beefy turned and looked at her over his shoulder. "Hey, Mike, look who's back."

"That was quick," Mike said. "I thought she'd be out longer."

Beefy huffed. "Toldya the battery was low."

If that was low battery, a full charge must feel like an elephant stampede.

"How ya doing back there, Ms. Rose?" Mike asked.

"Like . . . beaten . . . baseball . . . bat." Her mouth felt stuffed with cotton and the words were coming out jumbled. She wasn't sure whether the men up front understood what she'd said, but she was pretty certain that neither of them gave a rat's ass how she was doing.

Little by little, the neurological activity that had been interrupted by the stun gun began to return to normal, allowing her brain to regain control of her muscles. One at a time, she stretched her limbs, felt the pain burn along every nerve ending, a massive case of pins and needles.

"Gimme your phone," said Beefy, reaching his hand behind his head and waggling his fingers. When she was slow to respond, he said, "Pull over, Mike. Lemme juice her again."

Claudia dragged herself into a seated position on the leather upholstery and took stock of her situation. There seemed to be no choice but to comply. It took some effort to control her trembling hand as she got the cell phone out of her pocket. "Fuck you," she said, tossing the phone over the seat.

"Tsk, tsk, such a potty mouth," Beefy sneered over the seat back. He leaned down to pick up the phone from where it had landed on the floor and dropped it into a gym bag at his feet, along with her hopes for getting help.

Mike swung the steering wheel and made a left onto Fifty-fourth Street. He glanced over at Beefy. "Call the boss."

Beefy nodded and got out his own phone. He punched in a number, waited about fifteen seconds, said, "It's me—we're good. Yeah. Done." Ringing off, he looked over at the driver, jerked his thick neck. "Back to the office."

Looking out through the darkened windows, Claudia kept a watchful eye on the street signs as they crossed intersections, straining for landmarks, anticipating where they might be headed. Avenue of the Americas, Park Avenue. They were pointed east, traffic crawling now. She thought the Fifty-ninth Street Bridge was coming up a little north of their position. If she was right, it meant they were nearing the East River.

They slowed and came to a stop at a red light. Her chance to jump out and run, if she would be steady enough on her feet.

"Ya can't open the doors from back there," Beefy said over his shoulder, as if he knew she was studying them for a way to escape. Claudia's eyes darted over the blocks they passed, committing to memory the streets they were passing, assessing where she might go for help if she could free herself once they exited the vehicle.

The numbers of the avenues got lower the closer they came to the river, and the town car slowed. They were driving in a mixed-use area. Five-story apartment buildings next to skyscrapers. Business and medical sharing space with condos. Starbucks on one corner, a neighborhood grocery on another. A bank, a liquor store. More of the omnipresent scaffolding.

Mike applied the brakes at a padlocked chain-link fence and jumped out to open the gate. New construction. Sunday; nobody would be working. The building exterior was complete, but heavy equipment still sat in the locked yard. It hit Claudia that the office they were going to was the one where Grusha planned to transfer her headquarters. Pollard and McAllister, too.

Somebody else would be signing Pollard's lease now.

Beefy twisted around and looked at her, his wide face set in a sneer. "Hey, how you doin' back there? Comfy, huh?"

"Fuck you *and* your mother," Claudia retorted, fed up with his sarcasm. Faster than she could blink, he was kneeling on his seat, brandishing the stun gun at her. For a man of his size, he moved like a rocket. Her bravado evaporated. She shrank into the corner, her palms slick with sweat, the blood rushing in her ears.

"Yeah, Ms. Smartass, that's what I thought." The smug satisfaction in his voice was an added insult.

Mike slid back into the car and looked from Claudia to his partner. He gave an irritable shake of his head. "What the fuck you doin', dude? Put that thing away." He put the car in gear and drove into the construction lot, pulling in between a Dumpster and a forklift.

Beefy didn't turn around. He kept staring into the backseat with remorseless eyes, terrifying in their emptiness, until Claudia had the certain feeling that this guy could cut her head off and smile while he did it.

He smirked at her. "Think I oughta hit her again, Mike? A couple more jolts oughta make her shit her pants."

"Shut up, asshole. We gotta get her up there."

Beefy barked a loud laugh and stepped out of the car, slinging the gym bag over his shoulder. He opened the back door and ordered Claudia out, not bothering with any pretensions of courtesy. She pushed herself across the seat, still shaking so badly that she feared she might have trouble standing. Beefy grabbed her arm and dragged her out of the car, and Mike took her other arm. They frog-marched her across the lot and through a revolving door into the building.

The lobby was a repository of carpet rolls and wallpaper, spools of electrical wire and PVC pipe. Mountains of paint cans, stacks of drywall, other construction detritus. A lack of heating made it refrigerator cold.

The men wore soft-soled shoes, but the heels of Claudia's boots echoed between them as they cut across unfinished concrete, past an empty rectangle frame laid out in the middle of the lobby. A reflecting pool, maybe, with narrower rectangles on either side, eventually to serve as planters.

Past a security guard desk waiting for the finish to be applied. If only a guard were there now whom she could signal for help. Into the elevator, where Mike hit the button for the fifth floor. As the elevator car ascended, its glass walls afforded a view of a half-planted atrium that would one day be a lush jungle. But nobody was interested in the view and they rode in silence. Fear and the aftereffects of the stun gun were making it impossible for Claudia to formulate a plan of action. She couldn't think beyond *oh god, oh god, oh god*.

The doors opened and she found herself being borne along a corridor of offices whose doors had not yet been hung. From one of the rooms, a woman's frantic screams broke the silence. Grusha Olinetsky.

Claudia balked, the hair on her arms standing straight up.

Holy shit, what's he doing to her?

Beefy looked down at her with a nasty grin, enjoying her distress. "You're next," he said.

"Give it a rest, wouldja?" said Mike.

"What, all of a sudden you don't have the stomach?" The thick-necked thug gave a coarse laugh and pulled Claudia in the direction of the screams.

She told herself she had to stay calm, think rationally; that she'd been in tough spots before. But her mind was reeling like a drunk in an alley. Beefy had her arm in a steel grip with his left hand. The stun gun was in his right, and the look on his face said he'd love nothing more than an excuse to use it on her again.

Like the Elite Introductions loft, the front of the office suite was a large, open space. A semicircular reception desk with a granite top had been installed opposite the front doors. There was no furniture, no carpeting, and the ceilings opened onto HVAC duct-work, as if the building were a skeleton with bits of its skin peeled away.

Beefy put the stun gun in the gym bag and set it down near a workman's tool chest on wheels. The drawers were closed, but the top was open, revealing an assortment of screwdrivers, a pipe wrench, and a drill. He took Claudia's phone from the bag. "Here's your gear, boss. And here's her phone."

Clean-cut in a banana yellow polo shirt and mole-skin pants, Marcus Bernard didn't look like a multiple murderer. But the dark stain on the back of his hand and the rust-colored splotches on his shirt looked like blood, and there was a woman audibly whimpering in another room of the office suite.

Marcus smiled in greeting as if this were just any Sunday morning and he was enjoying his day of rest. He slipped Claudia's cell phone into the pocket of his pants. "Hey, Claudia. Have the boys been taking good care of you?"

Knowing there was nothing she could say that would improve her present situation, Claudia glared back at him in stony silence. Marcus shrugged indif-ferently and spoke to his thugs. "Get her secured, then take a hike. Go for coffee or something. I'll get on the horn when I'm ready for you."

Mike opened a drawer in the tool chest and pro-duced several plastic cable ties. They were not the thick police plasticuffs she had seen Jovanic carry, but were of the type she'd used before to bundle the elec-trical wires behind her computer. Once it was locked into place, the plastic tie would be virtually impossible to break.

Mike handed a tie to his partner, who wrenched Claudia's hands behind her back and started to wrap the plastic around her wrists. She knew she didn't stand a chance of defending herself that way. Appealing to Marcus for mercy was probably a nonstarter, but it was no act when she cried out, "Hey, that hurts! Do you have to do it like that?"

Marcus' eyes were bright as they stared at her. From where she stood, the pupils looked enormous, and she guessed he was probably flying. He said, "It's all right, Ace. You can do 'em in front. She's not going anywhere."

Beefy, who now had a name, looked disappointed. He ordered Claudia to put her hands together. "Like you're praying," he said, looping the plastic around her wrists. He yanked the tie until it cut into the flesh and she winced. That made him grin.

Marcus watched impassively as Ace shoved her roughly to the floor. With her hands bound she couldn't break the fall and she landed painfully on her shoulder. Mike pulled her boots off and cinched her ankles with another plastic tie. When they were finished with her, she was lying on her side, only her corduroy jacket and Levi's between her and the icy cement floor. She'd lost her scarf somewhere along the way.

"Sit her up over there, against the wall," said Marcus. "The lady and I are gonna have a chat."

When the two men were gone, Marcus crouched on his heels and grabbed Claudia's chin, roughly jerking her face to look at him.

"Okay, Claudia, Grusha's already told me she

talked to you. Didn't take much to get that out of her. I want to know who *you've* talked to about me."

As if to underscore what he'd said, Grusha shrieked again, begging for help.

Claudia tried to keep the fear out of her voice, but she could hear the breathless quaver and she knew Marcus could, too. "What have you done to her?"

"Baby, you don't want to know. Now tell me who you've blabbed to."

She tried to wrench out of his grasp but his fingers dug into her jaw until she cried out. "The cops know you and Grusha were involved. Donna Pollard told me about it and I told the detective."

"Pollard knew, too? See, that's exactly what I mean. Things get out, people know. Next thing, they're laughing at me." He slapped her across the face hard enough to bring tears to her eyes. "Goddamn bunch of gasbags."

"Nobody's laughing, you sonofabitch. Pollard's dead. She killed herself this morning."

Marcus started to laugh. "Well, isn't that fuckin' convenient. She saved me the trouble." Then the laugh fell away and he got deadly serious. "They won't find any evidence pointing at me. Only your big mouth, and that's hearsay."

"So let us go. We can't do you any harm."

"I don't think you understand. I'm not letting that bitch get away with what she did to me."

"She didn't do anything to you except tell you the truth."

"The truth?" His face darkened with loathing. "The truth that's she's really a man."

"Marcus, it's not an affront to your manhood that Grusha had a sex change. It has nothing to do with you."

He was caught up in his revenge fantasy and wasn't listening to her. "Her reputation is gone, and now she's gonna be gone. Poof, disappeared. You've just saved me the trouble of making sure the cops know that too many people are dying at Elite Introductions. I would have done it myself, eventually. But now I have to step up the program. Don't worry, Claudia, my ass is well covered."

His arrogance was beyond belief. She remembered that his handwriting had reminded her of Lyle Menendez'. At the time she hadn't realized how apropos the comparison was. She struggled to remember what else it contained that might help her now. The terrifying truth was that Marcus Bernard was a sociopath. He had no conscience; he had greater personal wealth than some small countries and, so far, had gotten away with multiple murders. That combination didn't bode well for her and Grusha. His sense of self-important grandiosity would make him think that he was above the law.

"Marcus, please, you can stop this now. Hasn't enough damage been done? Too many innocent people are dead."

"Nobody's innocent."

"What did Shellee do to hurt you? Or Heather or Ryan? Maybe even Jessica—she's one of yours, too, isn't she?"

A look of confusion. "Ryan? Who the hell is Ryan?"

"Ryan Turner, the doctor who drowned scuba diving."

"I don't know what you're talking about. Enough—"

"Wait—there's a detective in Stowe who's got video of you and Heather Lloyd at the ski lodge." Stalling for as long as possible; exploring the room with her eyes for something to cut her bindings if he left her alone for a while. She blenched as Grusha sobbed for help again. Her cries were getting weaker.

"You're bluffing," Marcus said, sounding sure of himself. "There's no way I can be identified from any video. I wore a hat and I made sure to look away from the camera. Besides, McAllister prescribed Heather cold medication, which made things easier for me. So you see, Claudia baby, the fingers point at him more than they do me. And like I told you, he was in the restaurant, just before poor Shellee had her allergic reaction. That was a very lucky coincidence. You gotta admit, it's not looking too good for the doc."

"You've been setting him up? What motive would Ian have to kill those women?" But of course, she had already been over that ground in her own head and found a possible motive. It seemed that Marcus had reached the same conclusion as Claudia.

"Easy one. His poor little daughter's suicide deranged him and he's taking it out on the dating club because she was a member."

He spoke so offhandedly that Claudia had a feeling her time was getting short and she hadn't come up with a means of escape. "Was it really suicide, Marcus?" she asked, desperate to stretch things out and buy a little more time. "Did Jessica really kill herself?" As she spoke, her brain suddenly shifted into gear. She remembered that her Bluetooth headset was still in her jeans pocket. Her cell phone was in Marcus', but if she could get to the headset, she could call for help.

"It all works out so well, doesn't it?" Marcus was saying. "At least, for me. The doc looks good for all of it. The cops will see that."

"You can't possibly get away with it, Marcus. Don't make it any worse than it already is."

He laughed. "You don't know me, Claudia. I'm golden. Look how it went at the party last night. Shit, that worked out better than I ever could have imagined. That Nicholson dude looked like a big bird going over the wall. Splat!" A wide grin split his face. "I couldn't have *planned* it so well. And the doc was there, too. See how it goes? It all points to him."

"But what about Grusha and me? You can't pin us on him, too."

"Says who? Think about it, Claudia. If the cops think he looks good for Shellee and Heather, you and that gender-bender in the good doc's examining room aren't gonna be such a stretch. He's gonna have a lot tougher time explaining it all away than I will."

He was either delusional or drug-addled, and it was bad news for Claudia when Marcus straightened. "Okay, enough talk. Get—"

There was movement in the doorway. Claudia looked up, expecting to see Mike and Ace returning early, but it was Ian McAllister who stood framed there, murder in his eyes.

Chapter 33

The hatred that suffused Ian's face made the crease between his brows even more pronounced. "You killed Jessica? *You killed my daughter*?" An animal roar of rage and pain tore from his throat as he charged across the room, tackling Marcus, knocking him to the ground.

Claudia pulled her legs up out of the way as he grabbed Marcus' shoulders and slammed his head against the concrete floor. The impact should have knocked him senseless, but Marcus only grunted and shoved him off. They were matched for size, but Marcus had a slight weight edge.

This was Claudia's chance to go for the Bluetooth. The plastic ties had bit into her wrists and cut off the blood supply, leaving her hands as useless as dead meat. She twisted her arms, grunting against the pain, and dug her fingers into her pocket, hooked onto the little earpiece and pulled it out. She pressed the button and brought the headset to her ear, her mind racing: tool chest, gym bag, stun gun.

"Nine-one-one, what is your emergency?"

"I've been kidnapped." She brought her knees up, scooting on her butt, using the wall to help propel her around to the gym bag. "Please get Detective Perez. Izzy Perez. My name is Claudia Rose, and Grusha Olinetsky is here, too. We're in an office building under construction on Fifty-fourth near the river. I don't know the address. Tell him Marcus Bernard is the one." It all came out in a rush, her voice high-pitched.

"Are you injured, ma'am?"

Claudia could hear the dispatcher typing as she spoke.

"Grusha needs an ambulance. Please, get somebody over here!"

Ian and Marcus were breathing hard, still punching, but beginning to tire. Not like in the movies, when fights lasted several minutes and everyone walked away intact.

Claudia described for the operator what she could remember from the neighborhood, recalling some of the landmarks they'd passed. There were units on the way, the dispatcher assured her; they would have to locate the building.

The dispatcher kept talking and Claudia kept getting close to the tool chest; then she was in reach of the gym bag, awkwardly tugging at the zipper with her bloodless hands. Stuck. Tugged some more. Halfway open.

Both Ian and Marcus were bleeding from the mouth and nose. They were behind her now, struggling. Claudia tensed over the bag, hunching her shoulders, protecting herself. There was the stun gun. Lying on top of a neatly folded sweatshirt, it was the size of an electric razor, with a safety switch on one side, an on-off on the other.

From the corner of her eye, Claudia saw Marcus grab something from the tool box and she tensed, waiting for the blow. But it was Ian who staggered under the impact from the pipe wrench and went down without a sound.

The stun gun was in her hands now, the safety off. Marcus was turning toward her, still holding the wrench, when she reached out and connected with his calf muscle. He let out a loud yell, dropped to the floor. For a couple of seconds he rolled around; then he stopped moving.

Mike had said the weapon wasn't fully charged. The effects on Claudia had lasted maybe five or six minutes. Pushing herself against the wall to a standing position, she scanned the open tool box for a box cutter or utility knife to cut the plastic bindings. She found nothing sharp, but there was a plastic disposable cigarette lighter.

Thank god the top was designed to open one-handed, making lighting it easy enough. Holding the flame steady against the ties that bound her ankles without setting her jeans on fire was harder. A thin stream of smoke appeared quickly and the welcome odor of melting plastic galvanized her. As the tie softened, Claudia pulled her feet apart. The tie stretched, thinned to a thread, snapped.

Marcus' legs began to move. She dropped the lighter and gave him another jolt with the stun gun. "You deserve it, you bastard."

In her ear, the 911 dispatcher was asking what was happening.

"I have to find a knife. Shit, my hands . . . It hurts. . . . Where are the cops?"

"They're in the area; they're looking for the building."

Ian was still unconscious, and Claudia suddenly became aware that Grusha had stopped crying. The hell with getting her hands free. She ran to the doorway at the far end of the office space—the room Marcus had referred to as Ian's examining room. More than thirty feet away from her phone, which was still in Marcus' pocket, she lost the call and the 911 dispatcher.

Grusha lay on the cold examination table, her wrists cruelly cinched above her head with the same plastic ties they had used on Claudia. The ties had been looped and connected to more ties, then connected to drawer handles on the back of the table. Her ankles were lashed to the metal stirrups, the plastic cutting into her swollen skin. Her clothing lay in a heap on the floor.

Blood oozed and dripped from dozens of cuts on the inside of her thighs, her abdomen, her chest, her face. Her eyes were closed against pasty white skin, her lips blue. Shallow breaths. Shivering.

She's going into shock.

On the unfinished sink cabinet was the tool Marcus had used to torture her—a bloody scalpel. Another clue he would have planted to point fingers at Ian, Claudia felt sure as she got it between her hands.

The matchmaker's eyes fluttered open. Her voice was weak. "Help me, Claudia! Get me out of here!"

"I'm going to cut the ties off you; then you can do my hands. You'll have to hold very still."

Grusha flinched as Claudia brought the razor-sharp scalpel near, but it made short work of the plastic. She sat up, gasping in pain. "Where is he? Where are those men?"

"We have to get out of here," Claudia said urgently, rubbing her hands to get the circulation going. Gritting her teeth when it hurt like hell. "The police are coming, but we have to hurry." Grusha was trembling from head to toe, but she did her best to help Claudia get her into her clothes, despite the blood that rapidly striped her shirt and pants.

Marcus was beginning to stir again. Another hit with the stun gun kept him immobilized, but the electrical charge was running down. Ian was still unconscious and the gash on his forehead looked bad. Claudia was worried about his condition, but there was nothing she could do about it now. They had to get out of the office. If Marcus recovered, or his goons returned, she and Grusha and Ian would all be dead.

Grabbing her boots from the corner where Mike had tossed them, she ran back to Marcus, rolled him over and took her phone from his pocket.

Grusha was leaning against the exterior doorway when Claudia hurried over and took her arm. "Let's get out of here."

Chapter 34

Grusha grabbed hold of the metal handrail and leaned over it. "I am going to faint," she gasped.

Claudia helped her to sit down on the concrete step. "No! You've got to hold on. We'll rest for a moment."

Claudia had insisted on using the stairwell because she was afraid of meeting Marcus' goons in the elevator. They caught a break when the door was unlocked, but the stairwell was in pitch darkness and she couldn't find a switch. The lights were more than likely controlled from a main panel in an electrical room. Claudia flipped open her cell phone to add a tiny bit more illumination from the display.

Putting her arm around Grusha, she felt the slick moisture of blood against her hand. "Come on, Grusha, we've got to go. Breathe through your nose, deep breaths. That's it. We can make it; I'll help you."

With excruciating slowness they made their way down the steps. Claudia counted out loud to help them gauge where they were: thirty steps for each flight. They had made it down three flights when Grusha stopped. "I cannot do it," she whispered, her voice only a weak thread as she collapsed in a heap on the step.

Claudia took off her jacket and wrapped it around Grusha's shoulders, immediately beginning to shiver in the frigid temperature. "Can you stay here by your-self for a while? I know it's dark—"

Grusha gave a weak laugh. "After that hell up there, a little darkness is nothing. I am tougher than I look. Go!"

Leaving her with her head bent between her knees, Claudia flew down the last three flights. At the bottom, she cracked open the door marked L.

Halfway across the lobby, she heard a shout from the elevator. Whirling, she saw the doors closing on Ace and Mike. Claudia ran full tilt for the front doors, never so happy in her life to hear the sound of police sirens. Glancing back, she saw the elevator doors opening again, but it didn't matter anymore. The sirens had stopped right outside.

Detective Izzy Perez was professional and detached as he directed operations at the Bernard Building. Sitting in his vehicle wrapped in a blanket, Claudia couldn't stop shivering. She watched them bring Ian out on a stretcher, then Grusha. And she was still shivering when Marcus, Ace, and Mike were brought out in handcuffs—not plasticuffs, the real metal ones—hands locked behind their backs.

She knew they couldn't see her, but thinking about what had just happened and realizing what a close call she'd had brought on a wave of nausea. If she had known what was waiting for her in New York, would she have come? That was a question Claudia had some trouble answering. She was glad she had done the right thing and gotten the police involved, even when Grusha didn't want her to. Without the information she had provided, Marcus might have been successful in framing Ian for his crimes, and Grusha would be dead.

Annabelle's ring tone sounded. Claudia, still wearing the headset, tapped the talk button. "Annabelle, I can't talk to you right now—"

"Claudia." Annabelle's voice was shrill and scared. "You have to come home. Joel got shot."

The world stopped as Claudia tried to make sense of the words. Before she could react, Pete's voice sounded in the background; then he came on the line. "Sis? I'm sorry you had to hear it like that. She called you before I could stop her. She's pretty upset."

"He—Joel—what—"

"He's in surgery right now. The girls and I are at the hospital. Don't worry; we're gonna stay here as long as it takes."

"How bad is it?" The long pause scared her. "Pete, tell me the truth."

"We'll know more when he's out of surgery. He took at least one in the gut."

"I . . ." What could she say? That she'd been busy trying to escape from a killer and his thugs? "I'll be on the first flight I can get."

No time to think about the possibility that Jovanic might not survive. That she wasn't there with him. Grusha would have to take care of things by herself, and the police could wait for her formal statement. She opened the door and climbed out of the car.

Chapter 35

Jovanic was asleep, his lashes a dark fringe across his too-pale face. His hair was standing up in little salt-and-pepper tufts. After an overnight flight back to L.A., Claudia sat next to the bed, smoothing his hair, stroking his hand, careful to avoid the IV that snaked to a drip bag. Swallowing the lump of emotion that threatened to choke her, she thanked whatever guardian angels or spirit guides had been watching over him.

His lips curved into a smile and he half opened his eyes. "Hey, Grapholady . . ." His speech was slurred from the pain medication, but he grabbed her hand and held on.

Claudia leaned down and kissed his forehead. "Hey, Columbo. What are you doing here?"

"Had to get you to come home somehow."

"That's not even funny."

"Don't cry, honey. Wasn't too bad. No major organs."

In fact, the doctor had already reassured her that he would make a full recovery. They had removed his spleen and repaired the damaged abdominal muscles. He would eventually need physical therapy, but she shouldn't worry.

Easy for him to say.

So far, no one had been able to tell her the circumstances of the shooting.

"Are you feeling a lot of pain?"

He gave her a dopey grin. "Morphine. Now I know why they get addicted. It's greaaaat."

Claudia smiled. "I love you, Joel. I'll be here when you wake up."

"Sleepy, babe." He released a long breath and closed his eyes.

Claudia fell asleep holding his hand. When she awoke, Annabelle was peeping around the door. Claudia smiled and stretched her stiff limbs, put a finger to her lips so the girl wouldn't awaken Jovanic. She got up and went into the hallway, where she was instantly mobbed by Annabelle, her niece, Monica, and her brother, Pete.

"He's gonna be okay, isn't he, Claudia?" Annabelle demanded to know when the group hug ended. Monica echoed the question.

"Yes, he'll be fine. He has to take a little time off work and have therapy, but he'll be back to normal and harassing you girls before you know it."

Pete hugged her and said, "We're heading to the cafeteria. How about some coffee?"

"I'll join you in a few minutes," Claudia said. "There's something I have to do first."

Chapter 36

Alexandra Vega was sitting alone in the waiting room. At the moment, she didn't look like a tough police detective; she looked like a woman in pain, snuffling into a waterlogged tissue, her eyes red-rimmed from crying. She glanced up as Claudia approached and jumped out of her seat. "I'm sorry," she said, and burst into tears. "I'm so sorry."

Claudia's gut tightened. "You're sorry?"

"I didn't mean for him to get so badly hurt. I swear, Claudia, I didn't want that."

"What does that mean, Alex? What did you do?"

The young detective dug in her jacket pocket and found a plastic minipack of tissues. She unfolded one and pressed it against her eyes as she tried to get hold of herself.

"What did you do?" Claudia repeated in a cold voice. She had a feeling that whatever was causing Jovanic's partner this level of grief had nothing to do with her attempts to seduce him.

"I should have had his back," Alex said in a strangled sob. "It was my fault. I didn't—" She broke off in a fresh torrent of tears.

"Let me guess," said Claudia. Blood flooded her face and neck, mottling them bright red with anger. "You were pissed because you couldn't lure him into your bed. So when he needed you to cover him, you didn't get his back. And that's why he ended up in *this* bed instead, with two bullets in him."

She knew by Alex Vega's silence that she had pegged it. Her eyes narrowed. "You're lucky he survived, Alex. Otherwise, I . . ." Claudia was shaking so hard, and she was so angry, that she couldn't finish. She turned on her heel and walked away.

That afternoon, as she sat by Jovanic's bedside, Claudia thought about revenge. The revenge of a man whose self-concept was so weak that he had engineered the murders of three innocent women to make himself feel better about his sexuality. The revenge of a woman scorned, which had nearly resulted in the death of her partner. She thought about the utterly useless waste of energy generated by that kind of hatred. And she thought about the revenge that she had, thankfully, never had the opportunity to exact against the man who had stolen her innocence. She would never forgive him, but she had to believe that somehow, wherever he was now, he would have to face his own judgment.

Claudia had almost lost the love of her life because Alex had felt humiliated and wanted to assert her control by allowing him to get hurt. Alex had learned the hard way how powerless and unsatisfied that act had left her. The ancients described revenge as a dish best served cold. It could never change the past, but it could destroy the present and the future. The way Claudia saw it, revenge was a dish better left unserved.

Jovanic stirred, opened his eyes. "Are you really here? I thought I was dreaming."

"Was it a good dream?" Claudia leaned over and laid her cheek against his.

"Mm-hmm. A very good dream. Lie down here with me."

She slipped off her shoes and stretched out on her side next to him. "How's this?"

"I like it. How about we do this forever?"

Epilogue

Claudia spoke with Detective Perez over the phone. As she had expected, he told her she would need to return to New York for Marcus Bernard's trial, but that would be many months down the road.

"You gotta understand my position," he said. "It wasn't that I didn't believe you, but . . ."

"You and I both know you didn't," Claudia said. "But I do understand. I'm just glad you believed me when it counted. Are you sure Marcus' money isn't going to get him out of this one?"

Perez snorted. "Multiple murders? No freakin' way. The judge wouldn't grant bail. Bernard is a major flight risk."

She hoped he was right. "How's Dr. McAllister doing?" The pipe wrench had left him with a serious skull fracture.

"Not so good. He's still in a coma. You might want to say a prayer for him if you're inclined that way."

"I will."

He had told her that Ryan Turner's death had been determined to be a genuine accident, coincidental to the murders of the three women.

Grusha Olinetsky never knew that Claudia had learned her secret. She wrote Claudia a handwritten letter, thanking her for saving her life, and offering her a trip to Europe as a bonus. The handwriting was shaky and she said she was still on a lot of drugs, but she had hired Dr. Pollard's secretary, Dorothy French, who was taking good care of her. She had the best plastic surgeon in New York to repair the cuts to her face, but best of all, the notoriety she had attained in the media as a result of her role in Marcus' drama had brought a flood of requests from new clients. Sonya was scheduling them for after her recovery from surgery.

Claudia couldn't help laughing as she read that line. She had a feeling that no matter the situation, Grusha would always rise to the top.